MACHINIST
OF
MANA

MACHINIST OF MANA

✳ BOOK I ✳

WANDERING AGENT

Podium

Podium

MACHINIST
OF
MANA

✶ BOOK I ✶

CHAPTER 1

FIELD OF NIGHTMARES

The lathe spun and, carefully, bit by bit I removed the material. It was a delicate thing, time consuming, but meditative as I worked the small piece of steel into the exact shape it needed to be. I had notes, of course, and measurements, and the original bit sitting on the bench nearby, all to get this metal the right size.

As I pulled back, I heard a voice shouting, "Making another six-shooter there, Liam?"

I turned and, after confirming my visitor, switched the machine off before removing my earplugs and glasses. The radio buzzed in the background, news playing for some white noise.

"Nah, nephew broke his favorite toy. Just making a replacement part. How's it hanging, Mitch?" I rose to greet him, hugging one of my oldest friends where he stood in the door.

"Good, brother, you? Just came by to see if you wanted to go with Lee and me up to the mountains this weekend. He's found some place he wants to try camping, says the views are great."

"Hate to say it, but I've already got plans," I said as I motioned him toward the house.

We turned from the roll-up door of the shop and to the small home that I'd bought last year. The price had been great for being this close to the city, mostly because it was torn to bits. None of that really mattered to me though. What had mattered was the beautiful outbuilding. The last owner had apparently loved fixing cars in his younger days but had been unable to keep it up as he got older. Cleaning everything had been an absolute pain, but worth it.

"Date?" my friend asked as we entered.

"No, seeing Grandma," I said with a shake of my head. "She's . . . old ya know? Might not get too many more chances."

"Spend time with them while you can," he answered with weight. I'd never known much about his grandparents, but I knew he'd lost one just last year. Then he perked up. "Anything else going on?"

"Not much, if I'm being honest. Work and playing around here," I told him with a shrug.

Mitch didn't stay long, and I hated to see him go. We'd known each other for years and years, but sometimes it felt as if we were drifting apart. Now we had different lives, some separate friends. Perhaps that was the way of things—old friends leaving us, new ones being found—but it still hurt.

I gave my 3D printers a once-over, making sure they were still doing their work without going all screwy on me, before heading back to the shop. It was still early, barely even noon, so I decided to take an extended break. One by one I turned off my tools and lights as I went for the door.

". . . is due to be executed this evening . . ." the radio said as I flipped it off—some report about a psycho doctor or something.

"Now, where to go?" I asked myself. "Need some onions, maybe . . ."

There was a small vegetable stall about a mile away, less if I cut through some old fields. It was quaint, an unmanned thing that always surprised city folk. Many would ask themselves how everything didn't get stolen, but as far as I knew, the people who ran it never had major problems. The owner was a nice old man, sometimes joined by his wife or grandkids. I could pop over there for some produce and be home soon enough. The fresh food would go well with dinner.

With a pep in my step, I went through the backyard, crossing a small patch of woods and into an abandoned field. The trails were well-worn by game and myself, the walk easy. I didn't know what this little vacant area had been—probably either grazing or tobacco some years back—but now it was just an overgrown lot with head-height grass on forty acres total, give or take. Some real-estate developer was sure to buy it up someday and fill it with ugly cookie-cutter houses.

I kept to the trail. There'd be enough chances I'd pick up ticks either way, but less was better. At least, that was my intent. About halfway across, the ground rumbled and I tripped, falling from the path. I picked myself up and turned back around, but the route wasn't there.

For a few moments I searched. Game came through here all the time, so it shouldn't have been difficult to locate where I'd been walking, but it was gone. That was no matter. The meadow wasn't that big, and I knew where the road was, so I turned and started walking.

Things got weirder and weirder. The weeds and grass were all the same, and it looked like every step I took forward made them get taller and taller. It hit me then that there were no bugs—not a cricket or anything. A brief look around on the ground didn't reveal any either. That shouldn't be so. There should be something around; there were always little critters in an area like this, but there were none.

A few more steps and I could barely see the sun through the tops of the surrounding plants. They'd always been tall, but this wasn't right. None of it was right. I tried to turn back, tried to run from wherever I'd stumbled into, but it didn't work. Even when I headed back the way I came, the grass still grew taller, the ground darker, and fear began to mount into panic.

Then the grasses parted, and I found myself in a circle. The ground here was stone, covered in some sort of vine I didn't recognize. In the center of the little clearing there was a glowing pool of water. That was odd, but not the oddest part. The grasses that I'd been running through, which had grown to insane heights, curved up to form a sort of ceiling.

"Who are you? What do you want?!" I asked nobody, pulling a small knife from my pocket, but there was no response.

I spent several minutes trying to work things out while I calmed a bit. I even tried to head back to the grasses, but before I could push through, I was wrought with mind-numbing terror. No matter what I tried I couldn't leave the circle. Even trying to jump into the hedge failed, feeling as if I was almost physically pushed back. I really wanted answers, and only one thing came to mind.

"It's a trap. I'm in a trap," I told myself. "Only questions are whose trap, and is it a live trap or a roach motel?" Other questions flitted through my mind, but until I got out of there, they weren't as important.

Working around the circular opening, I began to examine things. The vines were odd, and when I tried to cut them, that too caused fear. Walking around was fine, but attempts to damage always failed. The symbols on the ground were likewise meaningless to me, though they reminded me of some kind of fantasy gobbledygook.

"Doesn't look alien, unless aliens have a weird sense of style. Fairies or magic maybe?" I said with a shrug.

Eventually I gave up. Time would tell what was going to happen, and at the moment I had little to do but wait. So wait I did, playing a few phone games, then a bit of tic-tac-toe with myself on the ground.

I didn't know what time it was, but it was late when I fell asleep. The next morning was similar, so very similar, except for one thing. There was a flower just beside where I'd slept, opening into a beautiful blossom.

"That looks friendly," I said, "and I hate to, but it's time to find out if this is poison."

Marching to the central pool, I leaned down. There was a chance, and a very good one, that this would kill me—but if it didn't, I'd need the strength for whatever came next. Carefully, I cupped my hand and took some of the liquid, sniffing it first before I drank. It was sweet, cool, and nearly perfect.

"Well, tastes better than the stuff from the spring in town. I drank from that once, tasted like metallic fart," I said to whomever might be listening, hoping to get some reaction. It was true too, there was a mineral spring in the local town that people thought was good for you, and it did in fact taste disgusting.

I spent another day doing little, for there was little to do but look at the big rock I was on. It was an odd sort of thing, the grain strange and almost unnatural, but I didn't really know much about rocks, so who was I to judge?

As I woke up on the third day, there was another new addition. The flower from the day before had turned to fruit. The thing was periwinkle and about the size of a mango. It was also a clear invitation.

"Time to find out if whoever set this up wants me alive or not," I said as I bit down, eating the whole thing. Sure, there were stories telling you not to do this, but I had little to lose at that point, so it became breakfast, washed down with some more of the water.

It was an hour later, and my insides began to burn. It was subtle at first, a bit of water from the pool cooling it, but it got worse and worse by the moment, until no matter how much I drank the burning never stopped. I'd not cried many times since childhood, but it was enough to send tears down both cheeks.

"Ah, ah, I guess roach motel then," I said through gritted teeth. "Didn't have to make it hurt so bad though. AAAHHHHH!" I screamed as another wave of pain washed over me.

As I opened my eyes and looked down, I saw my hands starting to flake and burn. Desperate, I crawled into the pool. The water had cooled the pain before, and any relief would do. More and more I drank, begging for reprieve as bits of me floated off and away.

The pool glowed brighter and brighter until it became an almost physical pushing on all sides. With a final scream, the pain ended and the light overtook me.

The world around me shifted as it pushed me forward, the light fading into only a bit above, where I was going. It was strangling, stifling, and I struggled, but still I was pushed, thrust ever forward.

It all came to a fore in what seemed like only a second—first my head, then the rest of me pulled out and into the air. I felt weird, gross and wet, and confused. I couldn't properly see, everything a blur of colors and shapes. Then somebody smacked my ass.

I tried to yell at whoever had done that. This was all too weird, too strange, but that had seemed intentional, and rude. The noise came out as a high-pitched cry, though, not sounding at all like my voice.

There was shifting and movement as I was turned around again, and with effort, I opened my eyes and saw giant figures all around me. One in particular was looking down at me with a smile, or what I thought was a smile. My vision was still not great.

What the fuck was going on?

CHAPTER 2

✶

BABY LIFE

All right, several weeks in and I had come to a number of conclusions. The first was that this was definitely not where I was from. The styles of clothes were different, vastly different, and the house I was in was frankly massive. It was hard to tell exactly how big things were, and I would admit that I didn't get the best views of everything, but that didn't mean I couldn't see anything at all.

My mother, for she had to be my mother, was far younger than my father was, probably in her twenties. She spent much of her time around me, singing lullabies and generally doting. Not all of her time though; I had a wet nurse as well, who took care of many of the things that must be done with any baby. I felt no need to think too much about things like feeding and changing, but they had to happen. Getting back to the wet nurse, she was decidedly pregnant. Also of note was that if I were any judge of body language, my father was definitely too close to her. None of this ever happened in the presence of my mother, but people didn't really expect a baby to realize what was going on around him.

And I was decidedly a *him*, to my relief. I'd confirmed this by peeing while being changed. Sorry Mrs. Nanny, but I had to know. There'd been days of worrying more and more as I saw all the nonsense my mother and her maids went through to get ready—the layers, the amount of coverage, and lack of movement. It all looked horrible. Added to that, being a woman after being a man would just be weird; I wouldn't have wanted to go through that.

The maids also had actual maid outfits, like black with white frills and all that, like something from an old photo or one of those cafes in Japan. Of all the things so far that had surprised me, that was the biggest. I mean, there were really only so many ways to build a lot of things, but that style? I felt like someone had beaten me to this world and injected a little of my old one, or perhaps it was the reverse. Who could say?

Language was still a struggle. I'd never been particularly good at them, and there was limited context for so many things. People weren't speaking to me very much, more around me most of the time. When they were speaking to me, they were only saying very limited things, like a peek-a-boo type game or songs to keep me happy.

Physically, my parents seemed a bit taller than those around them. Mother had long raven hair in tight rings all the way down her back, whereas my father's slight greying hair showed that it, too, had once been black. Everything around me seemed well made and almost fancy, a big change from Earth, where I'd been a bit of a hick.

I didn't see outside much, and other than my parents, the only people I really met were what had to be my grandparents. Both sets showed up, but one was noticeably older than the other. I was only guessing based on their interactions, but the ones that I thought were the maternal set seemed a bit young, particularly my grandpa, who looked almost younger than my dad.

As he played with me, I noticed something odd. The tips of his ears came to a point. It wasn't much, no longer than any normal man's, but the point was there. Perhaps there were different lineages of people? Maybe even different races? From that point forward, I began to look more closely at those around me and their features.

It took days for me to confirm, but my mother, too, had oddly shaped ears. They weren't as odd as my grandpa's—only a slightly similar shape and mostly hidden under her hair, but the point was there.

I tried to check myself, but with weird pudgy baby arms that wasn't really possible.

My crib was, of course, in my parents' room. Even so, I did try not to be too much of a pain at night. I'd had kid sisters in my previous life and knew well how awful having a baby around could be. Therefore, unless something was quite wrong when I woke up in the middle of the night, I stayed silent, ruminating on the things I'd seen over the day.

During one of these ruminations I saw something which I'd half expected, but had only really been hoping for. Father rose to find the lavatory, but as he did, he didn't take a candle or lamp with him. Instead, he made a small motion with his hand and a tiny glowing orb appeared there. As he returned I called out, not crying, but loud enough to get his attention.

He seemed to hesitate a bit before coming over and leaning over my crib, a small smile on his face as I cooed and reached up toward him, and the light he'd made. With a low laugh he placed his hand within my reach, letting me hold onto his finger as the little globe of light drifted up and split into dozens.

His impromptu mobile hung there, the light fading to barely visible above me in shades of blue and cool reds. While I looked on, he spoke, and though I had no idea what he was saying, my guess was that he was telling me about what would come. My new father had been distant until this moment, aloof or busy with something other than tending to me and my mother, but for a few seconds he was gentle and calm. After a time he left the mobile in place and went back to bed, the glow of the magic eventually fading into nothing.

From that point on, I kept a hard eye out for any sign of magic. There didn't seem to be much, if any, in the house though. Perhaps the lights in some of the main rooms were, but I was seldom taken there and couldn't get a good look. I didn't like the disappointment and tried to get father to repeat his performance, but for some reason he didn't seem to get the message, or just didn't want to. Maybe magic was taboo? I really needed to work out the language so I could ask these things.

CHAPTER 3

TERRIBLE TODDLER

Go!" I said enthusiastically as I was picked up.

"Now, now, Percival, stop giving Mrs. Lutte so much trouble," my mother chided as she carried me.

I let my little legs wiggle, careful not to hit Mother as I worked them. She was the only one in the house who could catch me now, able to move far, far faster than her dresses would imply. To my dismay, I'd never developed the magic that my father displayed.

No, I couldn't throw fireballs or bolts of lightning but, on the other hand, I could run almost as fast as a car. The sensation was something else, wind blowing through my hair, muscles tensing and releasing all at once. I was strong too. It's one of the reasons I was being careful not to strike my mother accidentally.

"Go! Down!" I said as I was passed over to Mrs. Lutte.

"Little bundle of energy recently, aren't you?" my nursemaid asked.

"Please be careful, dear, and let me know if he hits you. We'll get you healed up right away," my mother told her with a caring voice. "Doesn't know his own strength yet; something we'll have to teach him soon."

"My lady, I think the boy knows more than we realize. He's always had care with me after that first time, and while he might be a bit of a handful now and then, he's never been one for fits," she answered with a smile.

She was right, and as I sat in her arms quietly, I wondered if she did indeed know just how much I understood. Over the last two years, I'd all but mastered the local tongue and already knew my way around the house well too. I even knew parts of the grounds, but with my tendency to wander, I was never allowed outdoors without Mother close by, lest I should run off.

The other part of what she said pinged a bit shamefully in me though. When my powers had first activated, I'd been trying to escape from Mrs. Lutte and kicked her in my flight. I'd not thought anything of it at the time, not knowing how hard I could kick. The snapping of one of her ribs had put a quick end to my misconception, and I'd been unbelievably careful around her and everyone else since.

Once more I winced as I remembered the scream she'd let out, and the wincing pain as the butler tried to help, beads of sweat running down his face. He was one of several servants my family employed who had minor magics called "talents," his being a small healing spell he could use once or twice a day.

"Still, be careful. I had to ask around for advice on this, since almost no one manifests at his age. Some of the ladies suggested that I hire someone with a talent for durability, but finding such servants isn't easy," she said with a frown.

"Like Mrs. Lutte," I replied, getting a smile from both women. "Kaylee too." That was met with a slightly more complicated look.

"Percival, you are not to touch Kaylee," my mother told me with a hard look.

"Won't," I replied.

"I mean it, Percival," she repeated, eyes turning to steel.

"Won't, promise," I told her truthfully.

Kaylee was Mrs. Lutte's daughter and, whether Mother knew it or not, my half-sister. I'd been pretty convinced of father's infidelity as a baby, something that had become more and more clear as Mrs. Lutte's pregnancy and conversations with him had gone on. When the child had been born, my beliefs were confirmed—she looked too damn much like my father.

Being that I was so little and Kaylee was still a baby, it was fine that she was kept in the nursery as well. Her mother did need to look after her, and two children weren't too much worse than one. I was satisfied that I got to keep an eye on her, hoping that I might find some way to help her one day. Sadly, I didn't know enough about this world or have enough power to do much yet.

Mother soon left us, and my nanny carried me back to the room I'd spent most of my time in and gave me a gentle smile. "How about I read you a story m'lord?" she asked.

"Okay!" I told her. After all, I still needed to improve my reading skills; knowledge was power, regardless of your world.

For example, I'd learned this world had trains of a sort, though I'd never seen one. I also learned that I was nobility; a title would be passed down from my father to myself one day, as it would from his father. More interesting was that the nobles of this world were newish. A few hundred years ago, things had been shaken up, and while they'd settled back down, we were not some ancient institution.

There were no cars yet, but I had depicted things like guns in a few pictures from some of the books. Those, therefore, must exist in some form somewhere. Overall, I was putting our level of technology somewhere around Earth's 1800s, though with magic involved everything was a bit wonky. For instance, I knew that my father had a number of items that could heat or cool parts of the house, and Mother had something akin to a mirror with brilliantly bright lighting around it, though it seldom saw use.

I'd also come to learn that last year my parents had elected to skip something called the Season, some sort of yearly migration of the nobility to one of the region's capitals. They'd received a number of letters asking if everything was well, and they even had a few visitors. I'd been introduced to some of them as their explanation for skipping the event, since Mother didn't want to travel with me. The year prior to that she'd been pregnant, but I got the impression that she also didn't really like going.

This year, however, there would be no skipping the yearly event. In about a month's time my family, and many of our staff, would be picking up and moving. I wondered where we would be staying as I read along with Mrs. Lutte, making the little choo-choo noises at all the right times.

"Are you excited about tomorrow?" she asked when we finished.

"Why?" I asked, a bit confused.

"You're going to visit your grandparents," she replied. "Didn't anyone tell you?"

They had not.

"Yay, Grandpa!" I told her, not hiding that I loved those trips. Upon seeing her raise an eyebrow, I added, "Yay, Grandma," but I didn't manage the same feeling.

My grandma mostly ignored me, other than the times she was trying to force manners into my skull. Her husband was really my kind of guy, and one of my favorite people. My father's parents were . . . oddly distant, never really seeing us anymore. They lived in one of the region's capitals and didn't travel out our way.

CHAPTER 4

✶

GRANDPARENTS

My grandma and I sat across from each other at the small table, engaged in a game. Upon the table between us there was a small piece of cake, beside it two small forks. The game went thus: first she would take a small bite, only large enough to fit on the fork, and then I would repeat the process. If the piece of cake should be too large and fall, it was lost. If I should display any particularly bad behavior, the whole thing was taken.

She had enough magic to stop me even if I tried to take the whole thing and shove it in my mouth, which I was often tempted to do out of spite. I hated this game. The cake was too sweet, and she always insisted upon this annoying game. I'd even tried pitching a fit to cut the game short a few times, but that just made her go to other, often more frustrating, things. The strange boosted chair was also uncomfortable; it was just one more con in this whole endeavor.

"Mother, he is two," my own mother said as she returned from some business elsewhere in the house. "And far too young to even understand what you want."

"Percival understands plenty, dear. Now come and join us," Grandma insisted, producing another fork from somewhere unseen.

"Seriously, Mother? You didn't even try this with me until I was what, five?" my mother said as she sat down, taking her turn.

"Yet he understands what I want. It's never too early to learn good manners."

Grandma took her turn, and I considered some options. I'd tried to get out of this game many times, and in several ways, all while acting my current age. Perhaps I could take another approach. It wasn't that I didn't like Grandma, though she was frustrating most of the time. It was that this cake really sucked. I liked sweets, but there was nothing but sugar here. It was too much, like eating icing. So I made my gambit.

"No thank you," I announced, leaving the utensil where it lay.

"What?" Grandma asked, stunned.

"No thank you," I repeated.

Grandma looked like I'd smacked her, Mother began to laugh, the local maid, who was about to serve tea, nearly dropped a dish.

"Don't . . . don't you want some though? It's sweet," the older woman prodded.

"No thank you," I told her once more.

"Looks like he learned to turn you down," Mom said between small giggles.

"Oh, I insist, Percival," Grandma tried once more.

"No thank you," I answered once more.

"But . . ."

"Being rude," I told her.

That was the crack in the dam. Grandma was a stickler for manners, an absolute hardcore lover of procedure. I'd turned her own power against her now. Mother began to fully laugh, trying her best to hide her face behind her hand. The maid was biting her lip to try and hold it back, and when Grandma started looking around, she quickly turned away, red creeping up her face.

Grandma set down her fork, looking completely shell-shocked. "Well, that was unexpected," she eventually managed.

"That was the single most adorable thing I've ever seen," Mother said, looking over at me.

"I have never known any child to turn down sweets," the flummoxed old woman admitted.

"And you can't even fault how he did it, can you?" Mom asked, still smiling.

"Gloating is unbecoming," Grandma said with a scowl.

Now it was my turn to try not to laugh. Luckily, before we could continue, the nearest door opened. In strode one of my favorite people in this world. Grandpa Darksky had short hair and a small constant smile. In one hand he held a small cane, which he decidedly didn't need but seemed to keep as an affectation.

"Ah, there you are, Percival!" he declared, enthusiastically.

"He just declined cake," Grandma griped.

"Why, of course he did, dear. Tea and cakes and talking is for women. My grandson is a man of action, of magic and science! Isn't that right, Percival?" he asked, tapping his cane on the floor just a bit harder than was proper to emphasize his point.

"Rightly so!" I replied. One of his favorite sayings.

"Heavens above, now there's two of them," Grandma said with a shake of her head.

"Don't worry, lad, I've come to save you from these two chittering birds," he said, winking at the two in question in a way he seemed to think I wouldn't catch.

"Huzzah."

With that he scooped me up and turned. "I just got the most interesting little machine from the city the other day, my boy. How would you like to see it?"

"Yes, please." Even with him I kept my words short and to the point.

Grandpa carried me through the house and into his small workroom. Unlike my own shop from Earth, this one was fastidiously clean. I didn't think he actually made much in here, but rather just liked his machines. The newest was sitting on a small workbench.

Magic had long been in this world, from what I could gather, but science, real science, was new. It was also all the rage in some circles, with gatherings of men all over the country, trying to prove this or that. There was a ton of work going on in chemistry, medicine—though much of that was just weird beliefs from old codgers—physics, and machining, the latter of which Grandpa favored. The intersections of science and magic were still a bit odd to most, but it was proving fruitful.

"See here, this is an engine, like they use in the locomotives," Grandpa said in almost a whisper.

The machine in question was indeed an engine, though rendered within some kind of glass so the internal structures could be seen. He let me watch as heat was applied to the little boiler, and the whole thing sprang to life. This was a toy here, a display for teaching or amusement, but back on Earth it would have been difficult to make.

Magic supplied a number of materials that were just . . . well, not really reasonably possible on Earth. This glass was able to hold the heat and pressure like a metal would, and might even be lighter. The fuel didn't need to be pollution-spewing coal. They didn't know it yet, but this meant that one day the people of this world would far eclipse those of my previous world. It wasn't there yet, but I could already see the inklings of it coming.

I wasn't allowed to be set down in this room, nor was I allowed to touch things. Grandpa always keeping me in his arms. It was dangerous, so I understood, and I was still two to the outside world. There were things like engines, and lathes, and mechanical mechanisms that could easily crush small hands, so I was kept in his arms the whole time. He did let me press some buttons on things every now and then though.

Even if I couldn't work on them, hearing the exuberance in my grandpa's tone as he talked of this or that was fun. He had the spark of a hobbyist who loved what he loved, and wouldn't let anyone tell him no. He also made sure he understood everything he had and explained it all to me.

So, for hours I listened as he explained every part of the engine and what it did. He also showed me drawings, pointing out the parts in one of the trains and how they matched up with the little one. Together we sat there as he went on and on, the smile never leaving my face.

CHAPTER 5

✱

SETTING OFF

I had once posited that my mother hated the Season, and now I knew that that was not only true, but that I fervently agreed. Everyone had been in an absolute state for the past week—things being packed, things being left, what went where, when, and how. She, as the woman of the house, was bearing the brunt of it and was clearly straining under the pressure. I got a light layout of the itinerary by listening in on conversations. We'd be taking carriages to the local train station, and from there we'd be on a train for a day and a half. The train would take us to a port, where we would then be passing by boat to the island where the local duke resided. This was the gathering point for our part of the country's nobles. The whole thing would take nearly three days, and that was if everything went perfectly.

Things didn't stop, even the evening prior, something which kept me from getting to sleep easily. People were running round the house well after dark, gathering up all the cases, stacking them, labeling them. Even if I had the mind of an adult, my body was still that of a child, and staying up that late wasn't normal at all.

Which didn't improve the next morning, when before dawn even arrived, I was scooped out of my bed by Mrs. Lutte.

"Owah!" I shouted as I found myself going from sleeping in my bed to being hoisted into the air.

"Sorry m'lord, but you have to get up," she told me in a low voice. "We're leaving soon, need to hurry."

It took me a few seconds to get my bearings, as I looked around with bleary eyes. "Where are we going?"

"To get a bath." She seemed to hesitate. "I know you like to run, but please, today we don't have the time, and your mother is very, very busy. If you behave, I've arranged a little surprise for you." It was clear she was desperate that I behave.

"Okay," I agreed. I didn't really want to do much more than sleep right now, so I could easily behave.

"Good, let's go," she said. "Not a moment to waste."

Honestly, the next hour or so was a blur. I was washed, given a quick breakfast, and carried out to the carriage, where I got to doze as boxes were piled aboard. It was a bit chilly, but someone, ostensibly Mrs. Lutte, had put a blanket around me to keep me warm. She was in and out constantly, checking on things.

"All right, we need to go. Anything else can be sent later," Mother loudly proclaimed as she hurried down the front steps. "If we don't get going, we'll be late, and the train won't wait."

"Right behind you, love," Father said as he turned to give some final instructions to the under butler, who was to be in charge of the estate while we were gone. The head butler was of course joining us.

"Percival? Where is Percival?" Mother asked as she looked about outside.

"In the carriage, my lady, sleeping," Mrs. Lutte said. I was just awake enough to give my mother a small wave out the little window. "All his things are packed as well, just finished checking the last of it."

"Oh, you're a wonder. Didn't give you any trouble, did he?" she asked.

"Not a bit, ma'am, not a bit."

There were many, many disadvantages to being as young as I was, but there were also upsides. One of these was that if you were sleepy, nobody cared if you just slept, and they'd oftentimes try to let you continue doing just that. For this reason I napped the whole way to the train station on my mother's lap, hardly even registering what was going on. It wasn't until some hours later on the train that I finally woke up.

"Good morning. Sleep well?" Mother asked as she patted my head, looking down at me.

"Mmm, yes," I told her as I rubbed my eyes.

"Well, I'm told you were a little angel this morning. Your grandpa made you something for today, a present if you were good." That comment got me fully awake, blinking and looking at her. "Oh, I thought you might like that."

She pulled out a little toy train engine. The design was much like those from my old world, though some of the aesthetics were a little more refined, the metal more decorated than most locomotives had been. It had doors and windows that opened and closed with a bit of effort, and the wheels moved, taking the small bars that connected them with them. It was a very impressive toy, particularly for something handmade.

I was struck. The amount of effort he must have put into this, the amount of time. I wasn't even sure how he'd made some of the pieces with the equipment he had. It didn't seem like a huge thing, but to know he'd gone through all that trouble for a gift was truly touching. I'd have to find the right place for it.

"Where's Father?" I asked after thoroughly examining my new possession.

"He went to one of the lounges to smoke," Mother said with a crinkled nose. She didn't smoke around her. As a point of fact, Father never smoked around any women as far as I knew. He had a separate room for it that I'd never been in, where he and his friends sometimes retired after their visits. I wondered if it was some sort of social rule that I'd never known. That wouldn't be too odd, as back on Earth it had been the same for a time. Some of the social conventions had strictly separated men and women during leisure time. As a child, I was still too young to get pulled into any of that, or much social interaction with adults at all, other than the servants. I turned to Mother and began asking questions. I asked about the train, and where we were, and why we were going so far. I knew the answers to most of these already, but I wanted to see if I got any new information. For a long time I didn't, and then I asked the right question.

"What's the duke's island like?" I asked.

"Oh it's big, very, very big. If you got in a carriage, it would take you two days to go from the top to the bottom, and half a day from one side to the other," Mother told me.

"Wow," I said. That was quite the sizable island.

"Yes, and there's a huge city on the south side of it. You see, a long time ago some nobles were very, very bad. They did things they weren't supposed to, not at all, and so the king and the Orders got together and banished them. Their children were all taken away for what they did, and they weren't allowed anymore."

That was a surprise. I knew a bit about the Orders, the moralistic groups that all the priests belonged to. They didn't do much, from what I'd heard, but were the masters of healing magic. To hear that they'd taken such action was very out of character from what I knew of them.

"What did they do?" I asked.

"They stole a bunch of children," she told me, "and hurt some of them. When people learned of it, they were furious, so they were banished. Even then, they had some family and one or two friends who wanted to help them, so they didn't suffer as much as they should have." She sighed. "In time, they began to build new homes and a small city to live out their days in. One by one they got old, and when all of them were gone, well, the city was mostly empty except for the priests that had kept them in their place. So it was given to a duke to own, and to grow."

"The priests stayed?" I asked.

"They'd made homes there, too, Percival, and had families. Over time they and the duke grew the city, and it was passed down through the duke's line as each father left it to his son. Now it's huge and full of people. It's not as big as the capital in Lithere, but it's pretty big."

"Lithere?" I asked.

"Where the king lives. Now, I'm a bit hungry. How about we go to the dining car and see if we can get something to eat?" I didn't miss how she'd changed the subject. Maybe it bothered her for some reason.

CHAPTER 6

✦

ARRIVAL

It had been a long, long trip, but I'd finally managed to get away from my mother and her friends. That didn't mean I was alone, of course. I was now in the care of my omnipresent nanny and her very unhappy daughter. I honestly couldn't blame little Kaylee. This trip had been awful, the boat heaving for the majority of it.

Now though, it was nearly over, the port slowly approaching before us. We had plenty of time, but the city we were going to was just now coming into view. Exion slowly came into view out of the early morning fog, lit by the many lights. It looked packed, and the mist, I was told, was ever-present over the water.

Before I could fully take in the sight, the smell hit me. It was foul, disgusting, like an open sewer.

"Gross! What is that?" I asked loudly.

"I told you we should stay inside, Percival. The city dumps its waste into the river, which of course goes out to sea." She laughed for a moment. "Don't worry, in the nicer districts it's not as bad."

The wind shifted, and I quickly moved to go back into the ship. I had no clue how anyone could live with that stink, nor why anyone hadn't done anything about it. Maybe nobody cared because it was the poor that suffered through the smell, but it couldn't signal anything other than disease and sickness. I only had one or two places I could go inside the ship, the obvious choice being where my mother was. She and her friends had been just shy of insufferable the whole trip, never allowing me a moment of peace.

"Back inside already?" one of them asked.

"Stinks," I informed her.

There was a chorus of giggles. "Oh his little face is so precious, look at his nose."

Mother's friends seemed to think my serious, short responses were adorable, and they were constantly prodding me to try and get more reactions. The fact that I didn't like to talk too much only encouraged them. They would engage in conversation with me, or get their children to, just to see what I would say. My manners were better than most kids my age, something Mother attributed to Grandma being an absolute monster.

All this had kept me from doing the things I wanted to do, like see the innards of the ship. She'd kept an annoyingly close eye on me so that I couldn't sneak away, and between her and her friends, they'd been quite successful. If she wasn't watching me, either they were or Mrs. Lutte was right beside me.

"So, little Lord Shadestone, could I interest you in some tea?" one of the ladies asked, looking at me.

"No thank you, Lady Starshine," I said formally, sending another wave of laughter through the surrounding women. I'd tried to ignore them or be rude once or twice, but Mother had quickly put a stop to that, knowing I knew better.

It struck me as odd that every noble's last name had something to do with darkness, night, or some similar concept. Commoners, on the other hand, had names that were common. Mrs. Lutte's first name was Nancy, and I knew a few other of the servants had similar ones. Perhaps there was something in the past involving darkness that was important. After all, the royals were the Penumbra family.

The ladies' squawks began winding down. Things had to be cleaned up and put away where they belonged, the staff subtly working in the background to keep the mess to a minimum. From the windows, I could see buildings and land rather than the water and chill rain, which had been common during our voyage. The ship even stopped moving, with noise outside letting everyone know we were docking.

Nobody rushed though. These women didn't need to worry at the moment. There were other people cleaning up and getting everyone's things off the boat. There wasn't much more to do until it was time to disembark, a moment heralded by the arrival of a new face.

The captain was an older man who carried himself with an almost physical weight. His back was ramrod straight, and his uniform maintained a state of perfection. Even his short white facial hair was perfectly groomed, not a whisker out of place.

"Good afternoon, ladies," he said, removing his hat in a gesture of politeness. "I've come to inform you that the ship has docked, and we will soon be ready for passengers to disembark. Furthermore, to thank you for joining us. If you should have any further needs, please let one of my staff know." When he left, Lady Starshine looked at Mother. "Well, I'll see you soon, and hopefully you, too, little Percival." I didn't like that sort of a threat, but I smiled. It wouldn't do to be rude. "Have to introduce him to my niece." About an hour later, our carriage was making its way through the fog, wheels clacking over the cobblestones, passing by house after house. At first, many of the homes seemed rather poor, like tenements, but slowly they became nicer and nicer. The difference between the districts was clear, and they were separated with small walled sections.

Walls had never fallen out of favor in this world. Back on Earth they'd gone the way of the dodo when guns had gotten big enough to smash them, but here that wasn't their primary purpose. No, here they were to keep out monsters, or at least contain them to sections, should one area get invaded. Even if I'd not seen cities other than those we'd passed on the way here, I knew that much. There was even a wall around our country estate, though it wasn't manned.

As the carriage rolled to a stop before our three-story city home, our servants brought our luggage. It would all need to be checked and seen to—checking and helping unpack the boxes, and all the other heavy manual labor. It seemed excessive. The house alone was the size of a small school building back on Earth.

The driver opened the carriage door and then the one to the house when we arrived. What greeted our arrival was nearly as stunning as anything I'd seen before in this world. On the right was a line of women, and on the left a matching set of men, twenty in all, waiting there with the butler, and what I assumed must be the housekeeper at their heads. It was around half of what we supposedly had at our other larger house, but still ridiculous for one family of three.

"Welcome home," they all intoned as one.

We had to walk past them all, I suppose so that my parents could look them over. Each and every one of them was in a clean and organized outfit, even those who didn't have a particularly nice one. There was also a clear delineation between those we'd interact with normally and those we wouldn't. The end of the line had a boy who looked like he was sent to fetch things; he had a runner's body and worn shoes on his feet, and there was a girl across from him who was maybe fourteen in a simple dress, whose hands spoke of long work under hot water.

The air was still as our family passed. The head servants had gazes of steel, looking for anything out of place, warning their lesser coworkers against any misbehavior. Father seemed uninterested, but Mother looked at each and every one with a critical gaze. After all, the home was *her* domain, and anyone who didn't meet her approval would be gone before sunset. Honestly, I thought it was all show until we reached the end of the line.

"Mrs. Rider, who's this?" Mother said as she looked at the last girl in the line.

The girl opened her mouth before snapping it shut; she'd not been addressed.

The housekeeper walked over to us and began to speak. "Sinea Leeds, my lady, the new scullery maid, hired last year, as per your instructions."

"Where from?"

"One of the poor houses, ma'am. I know the mistress of the place from long ago, and she assured me Miss Leeds has no history of trouble. Just an orphan and quite willing to work."

"Her work?" Mother asked, still not speaking to the girl who was now white knuckling her hands to keep them steady and trying, and failing, not to tremble under the scrutiny. I couldn't imagine the idea of going back to a poor house was one she wanted to even entertain.

"Exemplary for where she comes from. Took to the training like a fish to water and no problems to speak of." There was a bead of sweat on the housekeeper's brow now. If she'd hired a girl who was unacceptable while the lady of the house was away, there might well be trouble.

"Sinea."

"Yes, ma'am, uh, m'lady," she stumbled. Sinea had a thick accent.

"I'll speak to you later."

"Yes m'lady."

"Speech needs work," Mother commented as we left.

This was a side of my mother I'd never seen—commanding, hard. Around me she'd always seemed stern, but never harsh, never mean. To that girl, though, she'd spoken no kindness. Something which hit harder as I heard Sinea's words from the next room, sensitive ears were another perk of being a super-baby.

"Please help me, ma'am. I can't go back, please," she said through gasping breaths.

"Breathe, girl," the older woman replied. "Breathe, it'll be okay. The missus is hard, but she's not unfair. Everything will be fine, you'll see . . . Now the rest of you lot, don't you have work to do? Get the luggage out and put away, now, all of you, quickly." I could hear the snap as she turned to anyone who might have been looking on at them.

Mrs. Lutte was sent to organize the nursery and my room, while Mother took me with her into the dining room. I was put down in a chair while she began to micromanage where everything was supposed to be, such as which dishes would be used instead of others they had brought, depending on a number of factors I neither understood nor cared about. She also took the time to go over a few days' worth of menus.

I sat there for a while, frankly, completely stunned that I was being ignored. We were in a new place, so I really couldn't believe it. Certainly, you'd think they'd have learned better by now, but I supposed some lessons bore repeating. Not long after that thought passed through my head, I saw a moment when all their backs were turned and quickly made my escape.

CHAPTER 7

WANDER

I had a whole new house and grounds to explore. Oh, the hours of fun. Well, maybe an hour before Mother realized I was missing and sent up an alarm to everyone, but some time to look around at least. It was almost like nobody wanted me wandering about on my own, an idea I could never truly get behind after having been unable to walk for months.

So, I moved through the house; it wasn't hard. I could sense people so much more easily—hear them coming and hide. Nobody really expected me to be able to jump atop banisters and cupboards or know when they'd be there.

My progress was slowed by the many people running around, but not by much. Before long, I had made my way through a serving room and out into the main house, popping my head into room after room. Most of them were variations of sitting or reading rooms, but there was also a library full of books. I'd not managed to learn much of the written language of this world yet, but I knew I'd love to explore this one day. I came upon a room that did indeed make me stop. It looked almost like a training room or gymnasium, with padded floors and a rope divider between the center and the outside. All along the walls were cases filled with trophies and swords. There was even some gear on one side, kept in pristine condition, as if ready to be used at any time.

The blades were all rapier types, long and slender, and looking like they could slice and cut in a flash. I didn't know much about swords myself, other than the passing interest all boys had, but these were clearly dueling blades, not weapons of war.

Then there were the trophies. Dozens of small and large medals and ribbons, along with larger pieces decorated the cases. What surprised me was that each and every one depicted a female fencer. I wondered if Mother had a hobby in her younger days. I'd never seen her so much as pick up a blade, much less fight anyone, but either she or someone else had done so.

Briefly, I considered taking one of the swords out, just to see how it felt in my hand, but that would have been a bit much. Instead, I ruefully let my fingers brush the wood on one of the cases and turned back toward the door. Perhaps if I hurried back, Mother wouldn't even realize I'd left.

I made it all of three steps, fingers running along wooden frames, before I stopped. One of these doors was different, solid instead of filled with glass. The style was the same, but there was just something off about it. As I neared it I felt a breeze and smelled air that tasted different, like old wood, hot water, and polishes.

In a fit of curiosity, I opened the cabinet door and found that it wasn't a cabinet at all. It was a door. Behind it there was a small, dark hallway, undercoated and hidden. I knew that there were a few hidden ways around the country house, back stairs and walkways for the staff to move around. I also knew that I wasn't allowed to explore them, even if I wanted to.

Well, if swords called to every young boy, so did secret passages, so I slipped in. I made my way carefully down the hall to a connector and a stairwell. There was just enough time to hide in a nook in the stairs as I heard the *clack, clack, clack* of hurried heels on wood.

"One day, not even one day, and the mistress' child is already gone! What'll we do, Renton?" came the panicked voice of Mrs. Rider, the housekeeper. Renton was the head butler, a man I'd met more than once.

"Don't worry, Shelly," he replied. "He won't have gone far. The boy likes to wander, as I've told you, but he seldom tries to leave a building. I'll have a footman go to each door while you get the girls to search the house. Make sure they check the closets and cupboards. He's fast, and I've seen the lad jump a man's height."

"If he's half as strong as the missus, what'll we do if he decides he doesn't want to go back to her, hmm? None of my girls can make him, that's for sure," Mrs. Rider quipped.

"In that case, keep him distracted while we get his mother or Lutte. I wouldn't worry about it though. He only hurt someone once, and that was an accident. Boy sat there looking worried the whole time I healed her up," Mr. Renton assured her as they passed my hiding place.

Did Mrs. Rider really think I'd hurt someone? That sort of stung. I'd never try to hurt one of our people. Well, at any rate, if they were looking for me, it might be best to head back. First I was going to find another exit. I really wanted to know where all these hidden passages went.

As I worked my way along, I heard someone approaching from behind. These steps were less rushed, lighter than the housekeeper's or butler's had been. I hid once more in a small cranny in the wall, at least until I saw who was coming.

Sinea, the scullery maid, was making her way down the same hall I was in, one hand carrying a steaming bucket of water. It seemed word hadn't filtered to her yet that I was missing—she seemed determined but in no real hurry. I considered continuing to hide, but instead quickly came up with a plan that might well help her out, if things went well.

"Hello," I said, popping out right after she'd passed.

For a moment Sinea seemed very confused, turning in place and looking around before her eyes lowered and found me. There was a brief look of worry before she bent down to speak to me. That alone put her a few notches up in my book, most people around here liked to tower. Having someone get on my level was nice.

"What're ya doin' back here, little sir?" she asked. "Yer not supposed ta be in the servants' stairs."

"Playing," I answered lightly.

"Well, here's not the place for it. Where's yer mother, do ya know?"

"Dining room." It was good to keep my responses short.

". . . not supposed ta go in there . . . Why don't we go to the servin' room and I'll see if we can find one o' the other maids, shall we?" she said, giving me a worried smile.

"Okay," I told her. She quickly picked me up with one arm, retrieving her bucket with the other. That alone was a bit of a surprise. Sinea wasn't a large girl, and at her age I didn't expect her to do so with such ease. Adding my weight to that of the water didn't seem to bother her in the least though. She carried me, resting on her hip, in a way that spoke of long experience dealing with small children.

We popped out of another hidden door and into the serving room I'd passed through earlier. This time there wasn't even a cabinet, just a section of wall I'd ignored. Of course, I instantly memorized where it was. There was no way I was going to let a massive maze of hidden doors sit there unknown to me. I was going to try to find more when we got back to the country house.

Sinea hadn't even closed the concealed passage when my mother came through the door to the kitchen, hissing at one of the women behind her. "Find him!"

"Hello, Mother," I said, her head snapping around to me.

My angry parent marched up to us, fists settling on her hips as she glared. Then she turned to my escort, her eyes slightly less hard.

"You found my son," she stated.

"H-he was wandering the servants' stairs, my lady," Sinea squeaked out, trying to hide her accent.

"Secret passages!" I enthused in a stage whisper.

"Not for you, young man," Mother uttered as she turned her eyes back to me, taking me from the girl. I had no illusions about just how difficult it would be to slip away for a while, so I just laughed maniacally. She was going to punish me, regardless. No reason not to go for broke.

Now returning her attention to the servant girl, Mother fixed her with an iron look before nodding.

"Good job," she told Sinea, who looked like she was ready to panic again.

As I was carried out, I looked over my mother's shoulder and gave Sinea a wink. As she blinked and tilted her head in confusion, I nearly laughed again. I'd successfully given her a chance, so long as she didn't royally screw up, there was no way Mother would sack her now.

CHAPTER 8

*

SERIOUS TALKS

My mother found me once more in the sword training room, sitting quietly and looking at the many different medals. I'd been coming here when I could over the past month or so, though with how all the staff were keeping an eye on me, that was getting to be a pain.

Of note was that whenever I disappeared, Sinea was sent to check the back corridors and niches. Not where the family was supposed to be because her clothing was generally unacceptable to be presented in public around them. Personally, I found that to be hilarious, and so, if I happened to be back there, I'd let her find me. I'd seen a few of the maids poking fun at her and how she'd "pulled me astray" or some such nonsense. That amused me even more. For goodness sake, I was two.

"Waited until Mrs. Lutte's day off, I see," Mother commented.

"Didn't want to make trouble," I told her.

"How thoughtful," she replied. "What about the other maids that are supposed to be watching when I'm not around?"

"Don't know them," I pointed out.

Mother had never been much for baby talk, and since I understood her just fine most of the time, she had begun to speak to me more like an adult. If nothing else, that was appreciated.

"Percival, in the future, just tell them you want to come here. You're allowed in this room, but not alone." She came to pick me up once more.

"Were you a fighter?" I asked, pointing to the trophies.

"Why ask me?" she asked.

"Those are girls, not boys, and you're a girl," I said as I pointed to one of the little women atop a golden award.

"I am a girl, yes. When I was younger I was a fencer," she answered.

"A fighter?" I'd not before heard the word *fencer* in this life.

"No, fencer. Fencing is a sport, not war. I did it for fun, so did others."

"Will you teach me?" I tried. It might be good to learn, if for no other reason than to protect myself.

"When you're older. Those like us still use it sometimes if we have to fight."

"Like us?" I knew I was different, but maybe I could get her to explain how.

"Strong," she said. "That's our magic. We're strong and tough, and we can see and hear things others can't. Your father has magic too. He can make things happen by thinking them, and some make them happen by singing, and some by believing them to be right. You and me, though, Percival, we're strong and fast."

"Can I learn to be like dad?" I asked.

"No, you can't. We are what we are, my son, and there's nothing wrong with it." There was something more in that statement, some old hurt, but I had the feeling it went deeper than just being strong.

I patted mom's shoulder. It just seemed the right thing to do at the moment. "It's okay."

"It is, but you wandering off isn't, Percival. I've got guests coming in just an hour and can't have you making a mess." I hated guests. I was too young to participate in their dinners, so I was always banished to the upstairs, where I was watched like a hawk.

"Boo!" I said, unhappy about that prospect.

"Tell you what—behave tonight, and I'll take you somewhere fun tomorrow, somewhere you've never been," she offered.

"I agree!" I may have been a troublemaker, and may hold to my own form of right and wrong, but I was also easily bribable, and being two meant that I sometimes wanted an extra nap.

She laughed with a shake of her head and took me upstairs.

The next morning Mrs. Lutte was back in action. I had surprise guests, too, in the form of my paternal grandparents. I saw them so rarely that I hardly recognized them. They decided to join me and my nanny in the nursery while Mother prepped for the day. It seemed some emergency had come up. Of course Mrs. Lutte was there, along with her daughter, who was never far from her side.

"Oh dear," Mrs. Lutte said as a maid came by to ask her something. "Seems they can't find the stroller. What a mess."

"Go and help them, dear. We can watch the children for a moment," Grandmother told her, and when she hesitated my grandmother continued. "Goodness, it won't be my first time, go. You'll be better for it than some cleaner will." And then she shooed her off.

Grandfather was trying to play with me, some game with blocks. He seemed a nice sort, with a kind smile and bushy eyebrows. Not as enthusiastic as my maternal grandfather, but a good guy. While he did so, his wife went over to the crib where Kaylee was sleeping.

"That's Kaylee," I told her.

"I am aware, Percival." She looked conflicted as she stood over the sleeping babe, eyes sad.

She knew. They both knew, and now they were alone with a child who many might consider a stain on their family. I didn't know what this society required, or what it expected. On Earth there had been times and places where such things had gone wrong, terribly wrong. The powerful could often get away with it, and my grandmother was powerful. None of that mattered to me though. That girl was my sister, and no one would hurt her while I was around.

"Mother says don't touch her. Do. Not. Touch. Her." I didn't bother keeping the steel out of my voice, even if it was odd coming from so small a child.

She snapped, head turning to me as a gasp escaped her lips. Her husband seemed completely taken aback. I felt something pulsing, pushing from my body like water boiling to the surface as I locked my eyes with her. There was recognition. She saw my legs, coiled beneath me and ready to spring. If she tried hurting that girl, I'd be on her like white on rice.

"Calm down, boy," the older man said. "Everything's fine." He was moving to try something, too, in case I did act.

Of course it was that moment that Mrs. Lutte decided to come back, appearing in the door.

"Silly thing got put under a bed," she announced, not realizing the tension in the room. It broke a bit at her comment.

"Ah, yes, such things happen." Grandmother gave one more look at the baby, then at me, then at Mrs. Lutte. "Dear," she said with some weight, "if anything should happen, if you ever find yourself in need of help, I want you to come find us. Understand?"

Mrs. Lutte froze for a moment, processing the words and actions. I could see it on her face, the understanding, the pain, the shame. Everyone in the room understood what was being offered, even if I wasn't supposed to get it. I'd wager my grandparents thought I might. She bit her lip, turning her eyes away for just a second before propriety took over.

"Thank you for the offer, my lady. I'll keep that in mind," she finally said, still not looking up.

"Good, why don't you stay here and clean up while we take Percival downstairs. Where was the stroller?"

"In the hallway, my lady," Mrs. Lutte said, her voice slightly hollow, dejected at what had been revealed.

I was picked up and carried by my grandfather as we walked, but I didn't miss grandmother stopping and touching my nanny's shoulder before whispering in her ear, "I don't blame you, dear. It's his fault, not yours, and he knows it."

There was a stifled sound of weeping behind the door when it closed, and my grandfather turned to look down at me, grandmother still a ways behind us.

"I want you to promise me something, Percival," he asked, eyes serious.

"What's that?" I asked, curious as to what he wanted and more than a bit suspicious.

"Grow up to be a man who'll make me as proud of you as I just was." I could see the shining wetness in his eyes as he spoke, his emotions pouring through.

"I'll try my best," I told him solemnly.

"Good lad, good lad."

CHAPTER 9

★

CIRCUS

Come one, come all! See the greatest show in the world! We have beasts from faraway lands, monsters to thrill and terrify, and magics the likes of which you've never seen! Step right up, this way folks, right here for thrills and wonders galore!" the man announced before the series of tents, waving out to the audience.

Apparently, Mother's surprise was a circus that had just come to town. I knew little about the various things they were advertising, but doubted all were as they seemed.

We'd arrived just in time for the main act. Music peaked and the lights fell as the ringmaster made his way to the center of the largest tent, surrounded on all sides by stands. The prime part of his act involved a sort of trained magical beast that would've put a lion to shame. The creature in question was a cat, as well, but was nearly the size of an elephant, mane bristling with silver spikes and teeth gleaming in the spotlight. It was led through a number of tricks with a flaming whip from the ringmaster's hand. It stood atop a small box, jumped through hoops, ran around the ring.

There was a thrilling moment when the beast lunged at the ringmaster, only to be driven back by his fire whip spell. It was surprising, but clearly part of the show, as the man barely flinched. He continued on as if nothing had happened, save for a small smile for the crowd.

Not all of the performers were magical, but many were, and they managed feats that would make the greatest of those on Earth seem like parlor tricks. There was a woman who danced across wires so thin above us that it looked to most people like she was flying. There were men running up posts and using fire as part of their performances that seemed to dance around them like it was alive. A lot of the classics were left out, of course. No strongmen were needed in a world where someone like my mother might be able to bend steel.

After the show my grandfather carried me to some of the other tents. Some of the animals from the show were there, as well as a few others. Most looked rather like Earth's counterparts, but had multicolored glowing feathers or shining metal skin. They were pretty, but seemed rather . . . tame, tired, like they'd been through this a hundred times.

Soon enough, though, we came to a show that hadn't been opened up yet. Before it stood a man in full regalia, his cane twinkling as he spun it to get attention.

"This way, folks, this way! We have a brand new attraction, never before seen in these lands! These monsters hail from an island shrouded in storms, first documented centuries ago by intrepid explorers but lost to the annals of time! We found those records, and through trepidation and the marvels of modern technology brought them here for you!" He slammed the cane he held into the wooden platform as he motioned, the curtain parting to let us enter.

There had to be around two dozen of them, caged and being worked up by one of the staff into a near frenzy. Their green bodies writhed as they were prodded, leaving them screaming and raging behind the bars. They were short, three feet at most, with large ears and red eyes.

"These monstrosities are goblins, good folks. Be not confused; while they may have some small resemblance to men, they are savage and wild, uncontrolled. We've tried and failed several times to teach them even the simplest tricks, but their rabid nature forbids it!" the announcer said, leaning in toward the crowd.

I was flabbergasted, seeing these things. I was also worried, as there'd been a lot of stories about these particular monsters back on Earth. There was slight relief that some were obviously female, meaning that the more concerning stories were likely untrue, but they did seem wild and chaotic.

Well, all but one of them. One of the goblins, who looked to be male, sat in the center of the cage, eyes flicking about, watching, seeming to wait. Most of the others avoided him, and when one who'd just been prodded drew too close I saw why. With what looked like a practiced move he slammed the other green-skinned creature, leaving it sprawling in pain.

His eyes met mine, and for the briefest moment I thought I saw curiosity, interest. Then Grandfather started moving again, and I lost sight of him. It seemed we had other attractions to see today.

"Did you have fun, Percival?" Mother asked as our little group rode home.

"Food was good," I informed her.

That was a fact. Carnival food had been given to me in small amounts. It was fried, roasted, sweet, and mouth-wateringly savory at times. It wasn't the well-made, subtle food that I was fed at home, but rather called to my inner redneck, reminding me of the state fair back home and the goodies they might have there.

"Have to get you a more refined palate," she griped.

"Oh, don't be so crass, dear. All children like such foods," my grandmother said.

Soon enough I found myself back home. Mrs. Lutte had managed to pull herself together and greeted me with the same smile as always, though perhaps a bit less enthusiastically, and before long I was readied and sent off to bed.

It would be wonderful to say that most of the season had been a magnificent adventure, but that would be an outright lie. I had good moments, fun moments, but so very many that also bored me half to death. I was still too young to participate in much, and therefore wasn't allowed to do much. I hated it, my mother hated it, pretty much everyone involved seemed to either be a bore or unhappy to be there.

So, as I fell asleep, I dreamed of what might be one day. I planned to explore my house, to learn more of the science of this world from my grandpa, and to build things of my own. I may not know how yet, but learning could be a joy. Perhaps one day I'd even have a lot more fun on one of these awful yearly trips, who knew.

Until then, though, I could rest.

CHAPTER 10

✶

GOBLIN PHYSICIAN

Dr. Anton Parkov

"Extra, extra, read all about it, circus monsters escape, panic as wild beasts allowed to roam the street!" a boy shouted above me, his voice filtering down through the sewer grate.

Well, that seemed a bit much. Certainly I'd freed myself and some of my fellows, and perhaps I'd allowed one or two of the other creatures from the circus to go as well, as a distraction, but panic on the streets? No, most people seemed to be doing just fine, thank you.

Of course, there were exceptions, I thought to myself as I looked back at the man I was dragging behind me. His eyes were panicked, even as his body refused to move. I longed to speak to him, to tell him that things would be perfectly fine, perfectly fine indeed, but sadly my vocal chords were not really properly made for human speech. That was one of the things I was hoping to fix, but I needed some examples to work on the designs. Without them it was slow going.

This year had been the most interesting since I'd come to this world. I'd finally found humans again, something I'd not seen in nearly a century, stuck as I was on that island. They were even starting to discover science, if some of what I'd heard was right, though I did have to admit that my understanding of their language was still a work in progress.

I mused on my time here as I pulled my captive along behind me. This place, which had killed and saved me, had given me another opportunity to continue my work, had shown me wonders I couldn't have dreamed of. Oh, I loved it here, so very much, even if my current accommodations were a bit less than ideal.

As I made my way into the deepest parts of the sewer system I turned down an unused path, dried up and blocked off years ago. Down here we'd begun constructing the new nest, the place where my people would begin to rebuild our numbers. If I had my way, and I would, it would be so much nicer than those back on the island, so much cleaner and more advanced.

When I'd first arrived, some hundred years ago, I had been born in a cave. It was packed, a horde of goblins, my new people, shoved in and seeking shelter from the constant rain that made the surface dangerous much of the time. There was an organization, of course, with the younglings kept away from most others, but it was still chaos.

That nest had been one of a dozen or so at the time. The females of our species would keep mostly there, as close to the center of it as their social status and the others of their sex allowed, while the males were interspersed similarly. The strongest of the males lived at the center of the nest, mating often as they went in and out to hunt and gather food, while their mates often hid, keeping the young and bearing more.

Goblins were an obscenely fecund species, with a gestation period of around two months and an ability to reach sexual maturity in only six. Full maturity took about a year, though that hardly stopped most of us; and females, unlike those of many species, often did get pregnant while nursing. This was good, because we were also short-lived and violent, with a maximum age of around twenty years and an average of around ten.

Most goblins fell in conflict either with another nest, or with one of the many monsters that had made their way to our island. Those creatures were the primary source of food for the nest, mixed with whatever plants could be gathered, and they were killed by simple human wave tactics. Sure, a seabird the size of a hatchback was capable of eating a goblin in one swallow, but it could hardly fight fifty of them at once, and once it was on the ground everything was all but over.

When I got to the nest proper I saw one of the smaller, younger males on the fringes, digging, trying to form a little sleeping area for himself. Well, I could hardly disapprove of that, but his placement was less than ideal, so I pointed, letting out a series of grunts and screeches that sent him to another section of wall. It wasn't a formal language of any sort, but translated roughly to "wrong, there," the simplest of messages.

The simplest of concepts could be transmitted through the many noises we could make, but it never amounted to anything more than a dog might manage. There weren't even any names. Social dynamics also played a huge role, with expressions and body language being key.

As I came to the central area of our nest, the females and young perked up. There were only three of the former, with the latter soon to increase. They were already doing their part, either pregnant or nursing, growing our little group. These three approached as I entered, screeching hungrily at the human I was pulling along the ground, only backing off as I bared my teeth. They couldn't have my subject until I was done with him.

This place had once been a tank of some sort in the sewer, blocked off, but it was flat and I'd gotten it mostly clean. For now, it would serve as my laboratory while I tried to improve myself further. Some of those improvements were easily visible. I was far older than any other goblin I'd ever heard of. I was also unusually tall and muscled, though I'd hidden these physical attributes from the humans. There were a number of internal changes, as well, things nobody could see unless they cut open my body.

When I'd first come to this world I'd been female, a change from my previous life, but one that had probably kept me alive. Rather than being thrown out into the wilds to gather food, I'd had time to acclimate myself, to grow and learn about these new powers I had. A small minority of our species were born with an affinity for magic, one which I'd gained. I could mold flesh and shape living things to my will, a huge advantage, and one my fellows had celebrated when they'd learned of it.

For a time I'd been a sort of shamaness, revered by my little tribe as one who could heal the injured and ease the birth of new members. I'd even had a few children of my own out of curiosity. Slowly, though, I realized that I had problems, and I went about solving them.

The first issue was lifespan. It didn't take me long to realize that goblins didn't live long, and I didn't want to die. Using what I'd learned about in medical school I began to undertake a series of treatments both on myself and on a few experimental subjects to increase lifespan. Those had been a resounding success, and by elongating telomeres, regenerating organs, and putting in a few extra fail-safes, I was able to keep myself young and healthy.

That took a few decades, though, and around the time I finished that work another problem began to rear its ugly head. The males of my tribe had never liked how few young I was willing to spawn, making their complaints known, but keeping them restrained after a few had died complaining. Sadly, that particular controlled group ran into issues. Another of the tribes arrived, slaughtering our males and taking all of us hostage.

Now I could have held them off, as by that time I was quite skilled at magic, but without a tribe it seemed pointless. Our many members were what had allowed me to continue my work unbothered, and sadly, I'd not realized how many were dying until they were already dead. By the time I was made aware of the intruders, seventy percent of the male goblins in the nest were dead.

Male goblins are odd about females. One might assume that they would be sexually violent based on some of the media in my previous world, but that simply wasn't the case. Much like the difference in chimps and bonobos, the females of our species grouped too much for that. A male might complain, might even make some attempt at restraint, but should he attempt something like rape, he would be set upon by all of the females, something nearly none of them could survive. For that reason, the females of our tribe weren't harmed, but rather taken, kept in the new nest, and shown that there was only one way to increase their social standing, something most took to well.

I didn't like the new tribe, and I didn't like that I'd been brought there against my will. So, I shortly escaped and returned to my old home. It was empty, but that was solvable. I undertook a mission to gather some of the males who were sent out, not for any base usage, but rather to experiment once more.

It took some time, as gender determination in goblins was slightly different than in humans, but with some effort I managed to give myself a new set of organs. I didn't throw away the old ones, of course. Who knew when being a hermaphrodite might come in handy, but I did put them in a kind of cold storage, inactive inside my gut.

As I began to carve into my subject, seeing tissue samples to work with, I wondered briefly if goblins and humans were sexually compatible. I doubted it, but I'd have to find out later. Perhaps some attempt at in vitro? That might be for the best, less trauma. I was a doctor, after all.

The man screamed, just as many of my own kind had screamed when I'd finally reclaimed my normal state as a male. I'd marched into a nearby nest killing every other male goblin with little more than a wave of my hand until I reached the center. The chief of that tribe had stood against me briefly, his own magic protecting him to an extent, but he was so young, so inexperienced with using it, that soon he too fell.

After reestablishing myself as a goblin chief, I'd only had to defend my title a few times. Goblins weren't the smartest of creatures, but even they eventually learned that if you attacked my tribe, I ended yours. That allowed me to continue working in peace, trying to improve myself and our species slowly.

Over the years, I'd increased the lifespan of my progeny from the normal two decades to what I estimated to be five. Their size had also grown slightly, making them a bit bigger. This had led to an increase in intelligence as they were able to learn more over their longer lives. Conversely, their rate of reproduction fell, maturity slowing slightly, as well as birth rate.

This was what I had wanted to do as a human—strengthen my species through hard-won experimentation. Many had to die for it to succeed, but that was a small sacrifice. Even the man I was working on at present wouldn't die in vain; I would learn something. Why had so many failed to understand that? Was the first vaccine not tested on an unknowing child? Was the first attempt at using insulin not an innocent? Not to mention how much we'd learned from those monsters in Germany. I couldn't justify what they'd done en masse, but without it, we'd not know nearly as much about hypothermia. At least goblins didn't have massive hangups about that kind of thing.

When the humans had arrived, I'd decided that I simply had to go with them. It was a risk to be sure, going into one of their traps with a few of my favored mates, but I had to get off that rainy, dismal island and see what was in the world, and keep growing. That had been the only chance I'd had, and I wasn't losing it, and it had worked out so well!

I now had a city, an actual city, full of people with new genetic material I might manage to build off of to improve myself and my race. It should be quite possible now to give myself speech, and more power, and give these things to other goblins as well. I could turn us into something respectable. Oh, how I cheered internally as I began to dream of it, of what I might do.

One day my work would be out there for the whole world to see, the whole world to praise. I might have to break a few eggs making that omelet, but that was a small thing. Soon, so very soon, a new world would see my brilliance. Knowing this made all I had to do so much easier, and I smiled down at my subject. He, too, would help.

CHAPTER 11

SIX YEARS LATER

There was a ringing hiss as steel slid along steel and time seemed to slow. I angled my weapon, turning my hand and trying to close the line of attack as the point of the other weapon pushed forward, ramming into my chest. As the blow landed I felt my own connect, burying itself in the neck of my opponent.

"A tie isn't a win," Mother said, looking down at where we'd struck each other, the foils bent.

"No, but it's better than a loss," I retorted.

It had been eight years since I'd come to this world, and six months since Mother had begun teaching me to fence. At first I'd been bad, terribly, horribly bad, but practice helped. She'd still never had a clean loss to me, but every now and then I managed to tie her like I did today.

Both of us were fast, deadly fast, and strong enough to bend steel now. Even now, I got the feeling that my physical abilities were just a bit higher than hers, but she had skill and reach that I didn't, and that mattered in this game quite a bit. If I continued, then one day I may be able to beat her, but that day certainly wasn't today.

We were also dripping sweat, the hot protective suits soaked in it. They looked much like the fencing gear from back on Earth, or at least as near as I could remember, but hers had a long skirt-like piece that hid her legs and—gasp—ankles from easy view. Almost all of her clothing was like this, covering every inch.

"One more?" I asked.

"That was the third 'one more' Percival, and I think that's enough for the day. We've both got to freshen up before dinner."

"Yes, Mother," I answered.

With a slight frown I shed my mask and went to put our foils away. I enjoyed this time with her. It was active, fast, and one of the few times I could really go all out with my speed without inconveniencing anyone. Too often, in my opinion, I had to hold back, careful not to damage things. Perhaps I could have gone wild in a forest, but such behavior was "unbecoming," a word I'd grown to hate.

The house was much as it had always been. There were a few changes in the rooms, for instance this old fencing room at the country house had been renovated, now that it was to be used again. Most of the same servants were still here, or at least the core ones. There were a few more grey hairs among the staff, a few more wrinkles, but nothing wildly different.

After changing from my fencing attire I returned to my rooms, plural now. Mrs. Lutte was there, fussing around as she always had. She'd graduated from nursemaid to nanny and was often in charge of my day. Perhaps if Mother had another child she'd go to take care of them. Now that I could talk to her normally, we got along fine, but as she looked at me she frowned.

"You'll need a bath, young lord, so don't run off. I'll prepare it for you, but then I need to get your clothes for the evening ready."

"Thank you, Mrs. Lutte," I said. I desperately wanted to ask how Kaylee was doing but couldn't.

I knew if I did she'd probably tell me, but there was an understanding that she was to be ignored, and if someone else heard me, they might well start trouble. The staff would want to know why I cared, not like I hadn't been around the girl until I was almost three, not like I didn't see her now and then around the property, normally a bit far off. I did what I could to check on her now and then, to see that she was well. One day I might be able to do more, but not today.

After I washed and dressed I headed down to dinner. Finally, I could eat with my family, and I was expected to. That wasn't because of good times, no, but because this would be my first year participating in anything during our yearly migration for the Season, and I couldn't embarrass the family. And, dinner wasn't just sitting around and eating, it was a whole *thing*. There were the entries into the hall that had to be just so, paired so that men and women would come together. There was the discussion before and after, only some of which I was privy to, but some I had to join. This wasn't every night, thankfully, but as the Season drew nearer and nearer, the frequency increased, my family determined that it went well.

It also led to guests, though not many. My maternal grandparents were the most common, Grandma still trying to force manners into me like she was pushing the last items into a suitcase—hard, and often with light kicking. Conversation was apparently my weakest point, with me having a terrible time keeping up with subjects that really were just boring, like watching paint dry.

"What is your opinion on the new fashions, Percival?" she asked between the third and fourth courses, looking at me intently.

"I think that the new dyes and colors are lovely, though I do have some concerns about the reports that the lovely green one is causing some health issues. A pretty color it may be, but causing sickness is unacceptable," I answered.

"Congratulations, you managed to turn a conversation about fashion back to science and medicine. I'm impressed," she said, dripping sarcasm.

"Thank you, Grandma," I replied with a perfectly straight face.

I saw my grandpa chuckle into his drink, earning him a venomous glare.

"He was subject adjacent, dear," he said, then turned to me. "Though I believe your grandmother meant more on cuts and styles, Percival."

"Ah, I see. I find the newest cuts of ladies' wear slightly more practical than the older fashions, even if I know you think they're too revealing. Also, someone needs to beat that fool Vunell before he destroys all color and style in men's clothing; and if I get a chance, I'll gladly do just that."

"You'll do no such thing," my mother said, locking eyes with me.

"No, Mother, of course not," I answered, not bothering to hide the smile that crept up my lips. I was absolutely going to knock that man's teeth out if I was ever given a chance. He'd already pulled us from the riot of color we used to have to muted ones, and some of his designs looked a bit too much like suits for my liking. I was already wearing something too close to that hated garment for my taste.

On Earth, violence was seen as a terrible, unacceptable thing, a crime in most cases. Here, though, there was a bit of a different feeling. So long as there was no death, and you were willing to pay a fine and a priest to fix what you'd done, you'd barely get a slap on the wrist. There were exceptions, of course, particularly for those with magic using their power against the powerless, but Vunell was high enough in the social hierarchy that I could duel him with impunity.

Well, the law wouldn't punish me. My mother and grandma, though, were both fixing me with looks that could cut glass. Father was uncaring, as he often was, though Grandpa looked a bit miffed. Perhaps I should behave. Then again, what was the good in having power if you couldn't use it to rid the world of evil?

The rest of my night was spent in an extended verbal spar. It was exhausting how much people wanted to talk, to poke and prod to make sure that I was up to date on potentially any subject that could come up. Would every child be put to this? My first go around, I don't think I'd have managed it. There were just too many things to remember, to think about and have opinions on. That wasn't even counting the things I liked to do for fun.

When it was all over I crawled into bed, thinking about what the future would hold. There were so many things planned for the next couple of weeks that perhaps I could get some time over at my grandparents' place. Maybe one day I'd even get some tools like my grandpa had, so I could make things once more.

CHAPTER 12

FORWARD ONCE MORE

There were some things in this life that I never tired of, and one of those was spending time with Grandpa Darksky. He was endlessly excitable, loved making things, and generally treated me less like a small child. The latter was so important. It was painful as time went on, having to relive education under tutors and teachers who really did view me as a troublesome youth.

"I can't believe it goes that well, Percival my boy, and the design, odd, but inspiring," Grandpa commented as he watched my little toy zoom away.

"It's the wings," I replied. "I told you a rudder shape would be better."

"Indeed you did, indeed you did. Treating the air like a fluid is an interesting theory. Why, I don't even think I've seen any papers on this." He leaned back, hand resting on his cane as he tapped his chin.

Grandpa also loved his papers. From what I gathered, he read all the reports from the local scientific societies and journals, trying to keep ahead of the growing field of research. He was a wizard, a magus that used knowledge to do magic, and one of the few who was keeping up with the scientists.

"Then perhaps you should write one? I'm sure there is much more to go than we have with this kind of thing," I said encouragingly, as we walked out to where my little glider toy had finally fallen.

"Yes, perhaps we could even make proper flying machines one day. There are legends of such things from Elazia, but they were huge constructs, more like balloons than anything else."

"Really?" I asked, surprised. The technology of this world wasn't that advanced yet.

"Oh yes, a legendary king made them, flying fortresses armed with weapons that sound like they're from stories."

The chances of there having been others like me skyrocketed in my mind. If someone had made devices like that, then they'd almost certainly come from somewhere like my world. Not planes, but blimps, and not a bad choice if nobody else could fly.

"What happened to them?" I asked, wondering if I could perhaps see them somewhere.

"Oh, that was thousands and thousands of years ago, Percival. Sadly, all that remains now are stories," he said with a shake of his head, "but perhaps we can make something similar."

Well, that put a damper on my ever meeting another reincarnated person. Shame. Though I also needed to keep my grandpa from making something and killing himself with it right now.

"It'll take time and effort, not something to do quickly if we want to. Also, Grandpa, please let me test it. I'm quite a bit more durable than you." That comment was met with a scoff, until I picked up the toy and showed him where the front had caved in slightly.

"Your mother would skin me alive should something happen to you, Percival, but you are right about one thing. We clearly need to do more tests."

"Rightly so!" I answered, getting a smile from him and causing my grandpa to draw up to his full height, smile blooming upon his face.

"Well then, let's crack at it, my boy, and make our way forward unto a new day!" he said as we rushed back inside to redesign the glider.

Sadly, we were soon pulled away for social engagements. This wasn't a one-day project anyway, but rather something that we'd need to spend years on before a satisfactory result could be had. I'd never made a plane, and he hadn't either, so it would take time, time where others were always pulling us this way or that.

Much of that was taken by the impending coming of the Season once more. We were now only a week or two away, and Mother was once more in a state. This year particularly she seemed stressed, worried that I would do something to ruin the whole endeavor. It was almost like she didn't trust me or something, which was really annoying because I rarely ever caused a scene.

"Percival, I mean it, if you ruin this, I will find a way to punish you. Not sure what would be best, but I assure you that I will," she emphasized one afternoon over tea.

"Mother, please drop it," I griped. "I have no plans of ruining your time. Why would I bother?"

"Because you have a long and storied history of going places you're not supposed to for your own amusement," she said with a pointed finger.

Okay, that was fair. I did indeed like exploring the world around me, even when I wasn't supposed to, but it wasn't that bad, probably. Maybe I'd snuck into the servant areas of the house a few times, or run through the local forest once or twice. Perhaps there had been an incident in the nearby village with me sneaking through under cover of darkness to try and examine the shops. On second thought . . .

"You know, there is a solution that makes us both happy," I began.

"Or the solution that makes *me* happy, as *I* am the parent here," she said tapping the table with one sharpened fingernail.

"This year I'd like to see some of the city that isn't the inside of our home," I said, ignoring her. "Some of the places you almost never let me go. Grandpa even spoke of one of the sections of the Royal Society there where they give lectures. Certainly that would be a good place for a young gentleman to go?"

Narrowed eyes and lips pulled into a thin line met my offer. After a time, though, Mother did speak. "You're not completely wrong, so long as you behave. There are also a few youth fencing tournaments that you should participate in, being that I've already signed you up."

"You what?" I asked. "Why didn't you tell me about that?" I didn't mind going to those, but I did mind my time being taken without my consent.

"It was supposed to be a surprise, but if you're already planning your days, you should know." There wasn't even a hint of regret there. Though she briefly looked behind me as the door opened. I didn't turn, but I could hear steps approaching.

"Please tell me before signing me up in the future," I said, staring her down. Her only response was a huff.

"Now, dear, the boy isn't making an unreasonable request, and he needs a bit more independence, does he not?" my father's voice intruded.

Father and I were distant, very distant, but he seemed to want well for me. We spoke little, shared few interests in earnest, and I still couldn't get over the fact that he'd knocked up a maid. That said, he wasn't abusive or unkind, and he did every now and then make attempts like this.

"Very well," she conceded. "In the future I will tell you about things I plan on signing you up for." That was only half of what I wanted, and I didn't believe a word of it, but it was something.

"I saw that everything is well underway for our trip, love. Thank you for that," Father said as he joined us, and it was true, much of the packing was done. "Still trying to get those solutions mixed just right . . ."

Father worked with a form of alchemy. He made potions and inks, and other compounds used in magic, particularly magical crafting. While that would have normally been something I'd have loved to see, he didn't like discussing it. I didn't know why, but for whatever reason he'd always rebuffed me when I showed interest, the complete opposite of Grandpa. In the end, I'd all but given up trying to reach him.

"Are you ready as well, Father?" I asked. "Certainly we'll be busy."

"Hmm? Oh, yes, Percival, all is well."

CHAPTER 13

★

TRAINS

Family trips were the same here as they had been on Earth. The insanity, the trips back and forth to make sure everything was ready, the final trip to the bathroom my father invariably took once everyone else was in the car, and me, sitting there once I was ready, bored. I was happy to see that this tradition continued in my new world as well.

Now that I was a bit older, I wasn't carried around like I had been as a baby, but I still ended up awoken at an unreasonable hour and forced to ready myself. To aid in making this as painless as possible, I'd taken to preparing everything I could the night before. If I was sleeping but ready, nobody could really complain, nor did they want to, as they had other concerns.

Of course, as soon as we were on the way I was awoken. I wasn't sure what it was exactly, but Mother seemed to have some form of distaste for any man being asleep when she had to be awake and simply wouldn't have it.

"Percival," she said, poking me for what had to be the fifth time. "Get up, we need to look proper when we arrive at the train."

"In an hour and a half Mother," I retorted, not even opening my tired eyes.

"Not the point. What if someone should see you as you slump there? Didn't you go to bed properly last night? Up, now." I felt another finger make its way into my side and very nearly lost my patience.

"Are we meeting Grandma and Grandpa there or on the ship?" I asked, hoping for a change in subject.

"The train, of course, now up."

Fine, she wanted me up, she would get me up. I opened my eyes, looking at her with the thoughts of mischief brewing. Now there was nowhere to go here, no way I could really get out and run. Well, I could totally get out and run, and even keep up with the carriage pretty easily, but that would be rude. No, I needed to lean upon the weapon of young boys in every dimension, incessant chatter.

"I'm actually quite excited, Mother. Do you think Grandpa will be willing to ask to see the engine for us? He's shown me how they work, you know, and I really want to see one up close. Could he ask the conductor? Did you know that the fuel . . ."

An hour and a half later of constant facts and questions, and we finally pulled into the train station. Father looked exhausted, Mother looked frustrated. After all, she'd brought the deluge down upon them. I'm sure if you asked her then and there if she'd ever wake me when I was trying to sleep in such a situation again, she'd swear up and down that she wouldn't, but of course she probably would in the future. It was just her nature.

Luckily, we had little to do at the train station, as from this point the servants took care of everything. Instead, we were shown to our compartments, rented well in advance, and right across from those of my grandparents. As soon as we arrived, my parents spoke almost in unison.

"Well, I'll head off to the smoking cart," Father announced, fleeing.

"Father, Percival is quite excited about the train," my mother said, addressing Grandpa. "Perhaps you two could see if he could get a look at some of the engine parts. Mother and I should head to the dining car to greet the other ladies. Goodbye!" She spoke in nearly a single breath, grabbing Grandma and nearly dragging her from the room in her haste.

"Good heavens, boy, what did you do?" Grandpa asked, looking down at me with suspicion.

"She wouldn't let me sleep, so I told her about every paper I've ever read on thaumic engines. I made sure to go into great detail," I explained with a smile.

He looked divided on how to respond to that answer, but I could tell he both wanted to laugh and scold me.

"Were you at least in good sorts for the trip before sleeping?" he asked.

"Of course," I said, a bit offended. "It would be unsuitable to not have my things together properly."

"Well then, your mother did suggest we try to get a look at the engine. What say you then?" My answer seemed to have mollified any desire he had to tell me off. If my mother was going to be troublesome, then I supposed in his book she could find the trouble she deserved.

As it turned out, the staff on the train was quite happy to show us the engine, or at least tolerant. We were nobles, and therefore, we had a lot of leeway when it came to certain things, a privilege due to the power we could bring to bear. I'd never seen it, but I knew that in wartime one magical soldier could bring down dozens, sometimes hundreds, of non-magical ones. This, added to the fact that there were a lot of jobs nobody else could do, meant that we had to be respected, at least on paper.

"As you can see, sirs, most of the engine itself runs on simple principles of boiling water. Now you could make one of these without magic, but the whole thing would be a mess. The heat loss alone would be astounding, and the sheer quantity of smoke it would spit would pollute all the cars behind. That's where the enchantments come in," one of the junior engineers explained as we watched the machine run; it wasn't even that loud.

"Yes, I'm told that there are constant advancements in heat retention and air purification, yes?" Grandpa led him.

"Right you are, sir. Now over here we have the readouts . . ."

The engine itself was a variant on a steam engine, but all around it were magical devices. Sound was dampened, air cleaned, and most importantly, heat was preserved. I'd not yet gotten a good handle on how magical items worked in this world, but I did know there was a sort of language to it, and the effects were often dramatic. In this case, I could walk up to the boiler and put my hand on it without feeling the warmth, such was the efficiency of the work.

This translated to a much smaller engine, requiring a fraction of the fuel that one from Earth would need. It also meant that there had to be someone somewhere charging the thing up periodically to keep it going, but that was minor in comparison to the volume of fuel saved. It was a true marrying of magic and technology, and a beautiful thing.

The other important bit was that magic could define sizes and make parts to a specification that made the machinist in me want to weep. Things dreamed up by engineers and builders could be made exactly the way they needed to be, even if the dimensions in question would make it near impossible to build with the "modern technology" of my previous world. Parts fit exactly as they needed to fit, with just enough room for lubrication and movement. A true wonder.

Ideas ran through my head as we were shown around, thoughts and potential uses of these things. Sadly, I wasn't an engineer, nor had I been trained in a lot of the intricacies that would allow this to be taken to absurd levels. I could make a lot of machines, sure—but I didn't know well enough the principles of, say, a jet engine to make that a reality.

"Where do you get the magic to power this?" I asked once the tour was over.

"Excellent question. Larger stations along our route have dedicated magic users for charging them. We also try to keep either a talent or weaker magic user on board to handle any unusual situations," the young man explained. "I'm in training for that myself. Though I'm only a talent, the pay for the work is good."

Talents seemed to run a lot of things. Those quasi-magicians had very limited abilities, but with even a whiff of magic you could run an item, at least for a little while. Many of them were lesser children from branches of noble families, removed from the main line but still respectable. Sadly, there were never enough people with magic to go round.

"Well, thank you for the tour, young man, but we really should let you get back to work," Grandpa said, smiling and slipping him a tip with a wink.

As we returned to where we were actually supposed to be, I wondered if all the modes of transport used the same kind of engine. For example, the boat . . . Well, perhaps they, too, would let me take a look, but if not, it wouldn't be the end of the world.

CHAPTER 14

✶

RETURN TO EXION

Grandpa and I sat in one of the many reading rooms aboard the ship, the papers before us held as the vessel swayed gently in the sea. He'd taken a number of notes on the engine here and the one in the train; and though they were not particularly different, there was a difference in size. The ship's engine was so much larger and required so much more magic that it really was limited to shorter journeys. Mostly it went between the continent and Exion, or up and down the shore carrying passengers who could afford such luxury.

"So, do other ships have the same sort of engine?" I asked him as I poured over some of the documents. It really was impressive how precisely magic could make these kinds of parts. Many of these looked like they'd come from a modern machine shop on Earth, not a quasi-Victorian society.

"I'm not entirely sure what's most common, my boy, but I believe that older variants are used. Some of the ones without magic are definitely still running supply trips." He made a move like he was reaching for a pipe that wasn't there and frowned. The smoking areas were pretty limited onboard.

It was frustrating just how restricted my life was. Sure, all of my needs and most of my wants were met, but there was just so little information available to me on some subjects. The nobility lived in an isolated world, unable to truly see what else was out there. It wasn't because we couldn't get the information, but because nobody cared to look, to ask, to seek answers. Without something like the internet and a search engine, it wasn't readily accessible.

Perhaps I could have talked to people in different social groups or professions, but that was easier said than done. From the way I spoke to the way I'd learned to hold myself, I radiated "fancy" in a way that most people would detect. There wasn't even a good way for me to learn the way the poorer classes spoke because my family would refuse to let me near such people. Even if I could, they'd not be truly honest as soon as they realized that I was a noble, lest they bring someone's wrath upon their heads.

"There's so much I don't know," I griped.

Grandpa laughed heartily. "My, what a complaint. Enjoy the feeling, lad, for how boring would the world be if you knew everything? Mysteries are what spice things up. I live just to see what will come next, what new thing will appear. Doesn't it bring you joy?"

After a few seconds of thought I realized he might have a point. "I like the learning, but hate that sometimes it's hard to find what I want."

"That's half the fun. When we get to the city we'll have plenty of time to go to libraries and the society meetings. I'm sure you'll find things there you never expected."

While I'd expected the latter, the former hadn't really occurred to me. I'd come from a time when the good old-fashioned library had fallen from style, replaced by the internet. Would they let me in? Well, if Grandpa was with me, almost certainly so, though there might be a problem.

"Are you sure Mother will let you take me off to look at books?" I asked him.

"Oh, after what you did to her with the trains I think she'll agree," he said, snickering. Mother was still avoiding drawing me into any more discussions in places she couldn't escape.

Before too long we'd arrived at our destination and I was hurried off once more. Here, Grandpa and I had to split, he had to go to his home.

It wasn't far from our city house, or so I was told, so he could visit, but he had things that needed to be set up himself. After wishing him and my grandma well, I headed to our carriage.

"Do we have any plans for tonight?" I asked Mother as we clattered along down the road, passing storefronts and masses of people who were all too eager to get out of our way.

"Unpacking, Percival, though tomorrow you'll get to spend some time with your paternal grandparents," Mother answered without looking up. "You never get to see them."

That was fair enough, and while I didn't really know my father's family well, they seemed nice. Perhaps if we lived in the city I'd know them better, but maybe this would be a good chance. As I was getting older, my parents were finally letting me have more and more exposure to the world. Maybe they'd even come to some of the tournaments or meetings with me, if they were interested at all. If not, perhaps some other thing could be arranged.

We pulled into the house and, as always, the servants were arranged in the entry for inspection. It seemed this was a tradition designed to inspire terror, and if it wasn't, it certainly managed to regardless. The men and women who worked for us were all ramrod straight, dressed in perfectly prepared uniforms or work clothes.

Over the last five years there'd been a few changes, but very few. Good help was hard to come by, and once you had someone you trusted, you hardly wanted them to leave. Plus, working in a noble's house was a fairly good gig, as I understood it, and turnover was sparse. There were a few changes though.

Our old cook had retired. She'd gotten married or something and had been a bit older for her profession, so she'd left us, one of the younger cooks taking her place. This, of course, meant a bit of a shakeup in the kitchen, leading to the girl who'd been terrified of my mother all those years ago taking on the position of baker. Sinea was still young, too, so if she continued, she might one day be our, or someone else's, head cook.

Mother's inspection found a new addition—a boy working as a runner and aide to the staff downstairs. After her normal inspiration of fear into the lad, who was around my age, she continued onward. I, however, stayed back for just a moment.

"Anything good in the oven for tonight, Miss Leeds?" I asked Sinea. A conversation which had become sort of a tradition of its own.

"A couple of new pies, recipes that I got over the last season that I think you'll like, my lord," she replied. She always did try to find something new.

"Excellent, well I'll not keep you any longer then." With that I left, knowing that the staff really couldn't get to work until I did.

Over the years I'd developed a bit of an attachment to some of the staff, and Sinea was only below the top place because Mrs. Lutte had my half-sister at home. I'd gotten to watch Sinea grow from a terrified girl, afraid of being sent back to a work house, to a young woman, competent in her profession. It was gratifying, and while she still had a bit of an accent from her younger days, it was clear she was trying hard to speak properly around the family. That alone would make it heaps easier for her to find a new job should something happen, and even improve her marriage prospects, should she choose that route.

After some basic unpacking, and changing up some of the smaller things around my room, I headed to dinner. It was still a bit formal, with my mother not wasting time with her normal acts of conversation and making sure that I was following all of the rules of etiquette. There was a surprise, though, at the end when the pies were brought out.

Most of them were the usual—sweetened meat pies or fruit pies— but there was this one . . . I'd not seen any pecans in this world, but there were other nuts, and this particular pastry could have fooled any southern grandmother of Earth. My heart sang as I took my first small bite, loving that it reminded me of my former home. Sure, the taste wasn't exactly like pecan pie, but it was close, and that alone was enough to make me love it.

"I take it you like that one?" Mother asked with raised eyebrows.

"Quite so. You should try it," I said, encouragingly. Now if I could only find somewhere to get a decent plate of pulled pork, we'd be in business.

CHAPTER 15

GUNS AND SWORDS

While I liked my paternal grandparents I really just didn't get them. They were both talkative and far less obsessed with propriety than my maternal grandmother seemed to be. I wondered why that was, if there was something I was missing. Overall, I liked Grandmother and Grandfather Shadestone.

These thoughts were going through my mind as I met with them. While they were only around for one season, what I did know was that these two cared for me, and they cared for my little sister, which put them high up in my book.

Today they were joining us for lunch, a rather less formal affair than dinner tended toward, though little food was served.

"What will you be doing for the Season?" I asked Grandfather.

"Nothing special, Percival, a few parties here and there. No hunting right now for reasonable men." That surprised me. I'd never known he was a hunter.

"What do you hunt? There aren't many animals around here." I'd never seen anything like deer on this island. Of course, I'd only seen the city, but I doubted large game was a thing in the countryside.

"Oh, birds mostly," he answered with a smile.

"He uses guns of all things," my grandmother said, rolling her eyes.

"That's interesting," I said in response, thinking back to my old world.

"Oh, they're nothing special, but they make the whole thing sporting. Most nobles can take down flocks if they so choose, but that's hardly fun, or fair for the animals. Giving them a chance, taking only those you choose if you can. It's much better, isn't it, lad?" There was a slight sparkle in his eye as he leaned in.

"Actually, I think guns are interesting," I answered.

There was a *BOOM* as my mother's hand slammed down onto the table with enough force to make the whole thing shake.

"You are too young to have one, Percival, and they are too dangerous. I may let you get away with a lot, but you will not be having one, so get the ideas I can already see spinning around in your head out now." There was a finality in her statement that spoke on how she felt about this.

"I'm not planning on getting one right now, Mother. I just think they're neat." I'd in fact owned, and made, several in my previous life, but I'd not had a chance to see one up close in this world.

"They are dangerous, Percival," Mother said, still looking irritated. She knew me well, and that I tended to get ideas in my head, even if I really didn't intend much now.

"Please calm down, dear," Grandmother Shadestone said, reaching out a hand to Mother.

"This is me being calm. The boy needs to understand that there are things he cannot play with."

Grandfather Shadestone looked thoughtful for a moment before speaking.

"Your mother is right, you're far too young for a firearm, lad," he said, getting my mother to nod. "But if he is interested, we should at least show him how they work, and teach him about safety." His bushy mustache twitched as he looked at me.

"He is—" Mother began.

"—old enough to understand," Grandfather said, cutting her off. "I taught his father the same at about his age, and I'll tan his hide should he act a fool. Teaching him to be safe will be better, Lucille."

"Fine, when you get a day free, then will you handle it?" Mother finally acquiesced, though I could see from her eyes that I'd be getting an earful later.

"Of course," he answered, patting her shoulder.

The next day I found that I had a new outfit. Today would be the first of the tourneys that Mother had entered me in. As I left the dressing room at the small arena, I felt excitement pulsing through me. Around me there were men and women in kit with foils of various sizes and shapes. The youth rounds weren't the only ones happening today, with a number of physical magic users and those without that advantage as well.

The small hall we'd be using was still in use, two adults bouncing around it at speed, pulling off moves that were a mixture of kung fu movie and anime. Physical reality still held some sway, so the more insane things were not really possible, but their speed and the power in the blows was something to behold. Either of these men could have wiped the floor with me easy. Once the match ended, Mother found me, and she wasn't alone. With her was a familiar woman, one of her infrequent visitors, Lady Starshine, or well, one of them—it was a rather large family. This particular woman had in tow what could only be her daughter, who was perhaps a year or two younger than myself.

"Percival, there you are," Mother said. "You remember my friend, yes?"

"Greetings, young man," the woman said, taking quite a bit of the pressure off of my end.

"Lady Starshine, you visited us last year, correct?" I asked with a smile. "But I don't think I recognize your companion."

It was considered rude to address a woman you didn't know publicly without some invitation, one of many rules. I could have said hello to the girl myself, but since we'd never been formally introduced, it would be a major faux pas.

"Oh, you do remember, how lovely. This is my daughter, Rowena," she said, offering a light nod.

I nodded politely, and now we were at an impasse as the girl looked at me and I at her. She had to be the first to speak here, like her mother had. She could, of course, refuse to, and I would then be disallowed from speaking to her. Such were the expectations.

After a few long moments, clearly designed to make me wonder if she would speak, she smiled. "Greetings, sir. I am Rowena Starshine. May I inquire as to your name?"

The line sounded rehearsed, like something she'd been drilled on again and again. Not that surprising really, since my own grandma had done something similar for me.

"Of course, I'm Percival Shadestone. A pleasure to meet you."

"And you as well."

Now that the societally mandated pleasantries were out of the way, our mothers retreated to their seats. They were still in view, and I knew for a fact that mine, at least, could still hear our conversation.

"Do you fence?" I asked Rowena, a bit lost on what to say to a girl this young.

"No, my brother does," she replied. "We're here to watch him. He's participating in this tourney too." There was a brief lull before she spoke again. "Do you mind if I ask a favor of you?"

"What would that be?" I asked without committing.

"Beat him. He's been a bit insufferable lately, and I'd love to see him humbled." I wanted to snort at her request, but there was probably more to it. She sounded coached, almost like she was reading a script, even if the last part did seem a bit ad-libbed.

"Well, I was planning on winning anyway," I answered with a smile.

Behind her I could see our parents smirking. Those two were trying at playing matchmaker. I wanted to yell, tell my mother that I was eight and this girl was maybe seven, but I had other things on my mind, as the announcer had begun to call the participants.

"Ah, I must go, please excuse me."

I got a smile and a little wave. She seemed like a nice kid.

CHAPTER 16

FIGHT

Reflecting back on it later, I found I had been hard on most of my opponents throughout the day. They were children, had trained like children, and fought like children. To most of them this was just another sport, another thing to do, and while some were quite skilled, they lacked the sort of controlled aggression that could really change things. They became flustered easily, angered easily, and didn't know how to focus their aggressions.

In a fight, and these were fights, regardless of what my mother thought, aggression can be the difference between victory and loss. Skill is, of course, also an important part of things, but if you don't apply it correctly, you cannot use it. Beyond that, strength and speed are also needed, the basis by which one applies what they know.

Two strikes had landed on my blade, skidding and bouncing back. Across from me, my opponent had his teeth clenched, nearly snarling as he charged, only to find me closing, turning to throw him off, and nearly taking him off of his feet. I scored a hit on his leg as he tried to reposition, before advancing again, my own dulled blade leading the way.

He'd tried to recover, bringing his weapon back up, only to find it slapped aside and me striking him again. While trying to back off, he tripped, and that was all but it for the match. Unable to rise without me allowing it, and unable to effectively fight back in his position, a bell soon rang, indicating that the round was over.

"That was a good fight," I'd said, holding my hand out to help him to his feet.

"Not good enough." I'd hurt his feelings. He still took my hand, though, and rose beside me.

"Best I've had all day," I offered, and it was true, though I still wasn't even sweating.

"Thanks, care to go again sometime?"

"I'd love to."

Mother had pushed me hard, very hard, and while I'd thought the adult fighters were something, the kids were not. It looked like there was a big gap in skill, which made sense as people got older and grew into their magic. I also realized that I was a lot stronger and faster than my peers, the physical magic in me exceeding what they could manage. I wondered why, or how that strength had developed. Perhaps it was because I had the mind of an adult? Or maybe something with genetics was involved? One day I should ask someone.

The semifinal now over, I found my way to the small side area for some water, and there I saw young Lucas Starshine. The next match would begin soon, so I didn't have time to waste. Rowena's brother was a year or so older than me and looked much like her, but with short hair and laughing eyes. He'd breezed through his matches, blitzing his opponents with speed. Of course it was he who I'd meet in the final match.

Another bell and we walked out to the floor.

"Your sister asked me to beat you," I told him, trying to gauge his reaction.

He chuckled as he put on his mask. "Did she, now? Well, I'll need to have a conversation with her about it later."

"I'd hate to let her down, you see, so I'm afraid I'll have to oblige." I had a feeling this would be real fun.

"You're welcome to try," he said as the bell rang and we both charged forward.

If the previous matches had been boring, this one was anything but. Speed and strength between us were almost perfectly matched, and he was no newbie. With a year or so on me, he'd seen tournaments, fought in them, and knew what to do. While neither of us was able to do the anime-like speed moves the adults could, we could have overpowered the most skilled swordsmen from Earth. Masters could likely have out-skilled us, but even they would have trouble keeping up.

Steel flashed and flashed again, a chorus of rings and the sound of metal scraping metal played like fast music through the arena. Neither of us could get a clean hit, could make our blades or points touch the other, no matter how hard we tried.

I slashed and he blocked, then he turned his blade, trying to plant the point in my stomach. What followed was almost a dance, the edges never separating as we stepped, forward and back. I ducked as he pushed, moving under his arm and sword. Eventually our blades locked and we both leaned in, trying to overpower the other.

"You're good!" Lucas enthused, right before he punched me in the stomach.

Strikes, while uncommon, weren't against the rules, and even if it didn't hurt much, it was enough to throw me back and take my breath for a second. In that second he seized control of the bind, tossing my blade skyward with a flourish.

There was a gasp from the crowd as I lost my sword and, of course, my opponent did the natural thing and tried to thrust forward. Under the eyes and collectively held breath around us, I slid to the side, one hand wrapping around Lucas' wrist while the other went under his arm. Throws weren't illegal either, and I got a good ten feet as he was sent tumbling in the air.

While he flew, I ran, sliding to catch my sword. As I did so, I saw him roll, push off the ground, and spin midair to land on his feet. The bell rang twice. Nobody had scored any points yet, so we were in a sudden death phase, the next strike determining who would win.

Time seemed to stop as we looked upon each other, then we both charged. Once more our blades met before we did, and we both turned our hands, trying to control the line of the other's thrust. The point of Lucas' blade passed my face, not even an inch away, while immediately afterward, mine landed into his chest, right over his heart.

The crowd, while small, gave a hearty cheer as we bowed to one another, and I was presented a small medal for winning. There was a prize, but it was to be donated to charity, and it wasn't much anyway, since this was just a small event. Commoners normally kept their prizes, but as nobles we had expectations on us, and giving it to the poor was one of them.

At the end of it all, I found my way back to my mother and her friend. Lucas, while seeming a bit flustered at losing, took it rather well for a kid, though not great.

"I'll win next time," he said, challenging me.

"You're welcome to try," I answered with a laugh. He guffawed before leaving us to change.

"Thank you for that, Percival," Rowena said when her brother was no longer within hearing distance, smiling at me.

"Well, how could I deny your request? Though he may be even more insufferable until we have a rematch."

"Probably," she said, laughing. "Well, I should hope to see you again soon. If you'd please excuse me."

I gave a small bow as she left, joining her sibling and their mother once more.

That night we received a small envelope, inviting us to join them for a dinner party in a week's time. Briefly I wondered if we would have been invited should I have lost, but with mothers playing their games, it may well have. At any rate, it would be my first real social engagement.

CHAPTER 17

*

ROYAL SOCIETY

The Royal Society was, in a single word, chaos. I was sure that somewhere there were men and women writing papers in stuffy offices, but it certainly wasn't here. The building was occupied by lecture hall after lecture hall, any one of which might be the site of vigorous scientific discussion at any given time.

My favorite part was that nobles seldom frequented this location. Studying science was done by the nobility, but being on the bleeding edge, the researchers, the examiners who brought the data here to correlate and argue, that was for commoners. It meant that many of the social strictures that I had to abide by in my daily life were lifted in favor of the local culture.

There were dozens of rooms to explore, and subjects to look into. The section on biology alone had no less than five lectures going on about current theories revolving around microorganisms and their various forms, one about evolution of all things, and a demonstration of some new techniques to try and isolate various compounds. There were a few areas discussing new discoveries in radiation, though it seemed word had gotten around that playing with it was dangerous, as I could see safety equipment being brought in. Chemists had a hall for "practical demonstrations," which was in a detached building.

There was also an entire section devoted to new machines and their uses.

Grandpa and I headed straight toward the last section. My chaperone was happy to let me lead, this being my first time, and soon I found a room where something painfully simple was being described, which had taken my home world many more years to realize. It was an Archimedes screw, but rather than rotating the screw itself, the cylinder around it was spun. This had been found in living memory back on Earth by an enterprising Mr. Olds in Australia, and I was glad to see that this world's people were just as clever as the ones in my previous world.

"Darksky, is that you?" an older man asked as we approached. "Why, I haven't seen you in years, old friend. Wherever have you been?" He seemed to smile under his bushy beard.

"Oh, pah, it hasn't been that long, come here," Grandpa replied as he moved to give the man a half-hug. Clearly they knew each other. "As for what I've been doing, mostly tottering about, teaching my grandson this and that."

The older man soon looked down at me. "Ah, and that must be you, my boy. Though I'll say your grandfather looks barely old enough to be your papa, doesn't he? Have to admit I'm a bit jealous."

"Percival, this is Longdon, an old friend of mine," Grandpa said, seeming to want to change the subject. I didn't know why, but it seemed a sore point with him.

"Hello Mr. Longdon," I dutifully replied, greeting the older fellow.

"So, anything of note going on today?" Grandpa asked, looking around.

"Certainly, certainly, why I've got a demonstration coming up in just a few minutes. Care to come and watch?" Longdon asked.

My grandfather looked at me and I shrugged. Not knowing all that was going on, it seemed as good a lead as any. Soon we found ourselves in one of the lecture halls, looking over a rather large piece atop a table. It didn't take me long to see what exactly it was, but it was so primitive that I was surprised it worked at all. Longdon reappeared, shepherding people in and bringing up some diagrams.

"As you can see, my dear guests, this engine runs not on steam, but the burning of volatile chemicals—in this case, ethanol. The speed and power that I'm already finding from this device appear to match, or perhaps exceed those of conventional engines. Admittedly, there are some problems, but I'm sure that with time those can be worked out. Now, if you will direct your attention to the pedestal."

He started his device and almost instantly it sounded . . . off. I couldn't place it, but something about the way the engine was running just seemed wrong to me. I wasn't the only one either, as Mr. Longdon began to look over the device with a hard eye, adjusting the control knobs carefully.

"That doesn't sound right . . ." I managed as the engine began to shake. "Oh no."

Longdon tried, and failed, to get things back under control, but soon his work was bouncing up and down at speed, faster and faster until the moorings holding it in place failed, and a couple hundred pounds of metal jumped upward like a pogo stick.

Time slowed as I rushed forward to grab the old man and pull him to safety. That much weight throwing itself around was an impending disaster, and he was too close. Before I could make it, though, I saw something that seldom happened—Grandpa using magic.

In an instant the engine was enveloped by light from his extended hand, and it froze. Not just still, though it was that too, but it began to radiate cold like an arctic wind. I could feel it many feet away, see the ice ripple across the surface and the device shatter as moving parts couldn't, the steel made brittle by the sudden drop in temperature.

Worse than that, though, was the look on Grandpa's face as he held the pieces, finally letting them fall. It wasn't rage or fury. It was ice. It chilled me to my core, just as it had the engine.

It made sense, in a world with monsters you had to know how to fight. Did I wear a face like that when I fenced? No, I was an amateur, too much of a novice, and had never needed to really do battle. Would I in the future though? I didn't know how to feel about that.

Longdon looked up from where I'd pulled him back, also catching the look in his friend's eyes, and I heard him gulp.

"My apologies, I . . . That's never happened before," he managed to say with a nervous voice.

"Such things sometimes happen, but see that it doesn't around my grandson again, yes?" my grandpa said, his eyes not losing their edge until the other man nodded.

"So . . ."

"Well, Percival, what say we go and find another demonstration then?" he asked.

"Ah, that sounds good."

We kind of needed to, since this one was quite thoroughly destroyed. There were a few people making rude comments about the failure, but most were being rather polite about it. Hopefully, Mr. Longdon's reputation wouldn't be damaged too badly by the disaster, since internal combustion really was a good technology.

"Mind if we go to see the chemists next? I'd love to see what they're doing," I asked as I was led out of the room.

"Oh, certainly, though personally, I find that a bit tiresome. The moving parts and bits are much better."

While I personally agreed with my grandpa, many things needed to come together.

CHAPTER 18

BASIC SAFETY

The day after my visit to the Royal Society, I ended up in a heavily fortified building with Grandfather Shadestone. He'd reserved a private room for today's activities at this facility and was waiting when I arrived.

The room itself was perhaps thirty feet wide and around one hundred fifty feet long, with a counter and separated bays. He stood at one of these, with several weapons laid out upon the bay and targets set up in the distance. One of the servants had escorted me here, since everyone else was busy. As far as I knew, he would be taking me back home too.

"Come here, Percival, and take a look," he said as I came in, motioning to the table.

I did as he bade me, looking over the weapons on the table. They looked much like the guns from my previous world, though all appeared to be either muzzle or breach loaders, and all were single shot. While there were some stylistic differences, there weren't many, since really there only were so many ways to comfortably hold a gun. There was also a lack of something like a pistol.

Compared with the rest of the world, this being so primitive was a bit surprising. There were plenty of machines, simple and otherwise, but nobody had added those advancements to weaponry. Perhaps that was due to the newness of mechanization, or maybe the presence of magic was seen as such a tipping point that they just weren't used. I'd not figured that out yet.

"Well, I'm glad to see you didn't touch any of them," Grandfather Shadestone said.

"Of course not, they're weapons," I answered.

"Good answer, Percival, but tell me this—which ones are loaded?" he asked, chortling but continuing to watch me.

"As far as I'm aware, all of them," I replied confidently.

"I was looking for 'I don't know,' but that's not a bad answer either. One can never tell if a gun is loaded or not, Percival, so you should always treat them as such. Sometimes you can't even tell the difference between real and fake ones, so all should be treated as real." I nodded. That was basic gun safety.

"Of course, Grandfather."

"I also want you to think about what's in front of them. Make sure you know where the dangerous end is pointed at all times, and never let it point at anything of value." Once more I nodded agreement.

This fell right in with the basics of gun safety from my old world. Sometimes the order differed or the specific wording, but the general rules were as follows:

Treat every gun like it is always loaded.

Never point a gun at something you're not willing to destroy.

Keep your finger off the trigger until you're ready to shoot.

Know your target and what is behind it.

It was widely observed that as long as those rules were followed, accidents were very unlikely. Normally you had to break more than one for something to truly go wrong.

"Now, let's cover some of the basics."

Before I was allowed to shoot, my grandfather showed me how to clear each of these. Then he showed me how to clean the guns in exacting detail. These were important lessons and gave me an opportunity to get me an even better look at the internal mechanisms, though they weren't very impressive.

We started with the muzzle loaders, something I'd never dealt with in my old life. They were a pain, requiring a slow, multi-step process to clear, ready, and load before they could shoot. You really, really didn't want anything going wrong with these, as your hand might well be in the way while you were putting the powder in. They made me slightly uncomfortable.

Once one was loaded, I was run through the basics of shooting, stance, aim, and the like, and I was also given earmuffs. The sights used in this world were a bit different than I was used to, but it was the same concept. They just used more decorative shapes rather than just raised bars. In retrospect, though, that might have been because these belonged to a nobleman.

After a few shots, Grandfather Shadestone had us take a break.

"Not bad, Percival, not bad at all. Maybe you should come hunting with me next year," he said with a smile.

"Mother would lose her mind," I retorted, earning me a hearty laugh.

"That she would, that she would. Well, let's move on."

The breach-loading weapons were a lot easier. They functioned like a lot of shotguns from back on Earth, though there were a few oddities here and there. The paper cartridges were odd to me, having been something long out of style on Earth before I was born. Sure, the concept was the same, but the care was different, something I was informed of as we worked our way through these. I was quizzed on the rules and methods throughout, each being drilled into me, and I couldn't say I disapproved at all.

After everything was cleaned and put away, we went to look at the results. Grandfather seemed quite pleased, but to me the results were . . . unsatisfactory. I was out of practice, and these items weren't made for someone of my size. Add to that the unfamiliarity, and my shots were nowhere near what they should have been at these ranges. It was a bit disappointing to see how I'd done, even if my grandfather assured me that it was very good for a first-timer.

"That was fun, thank you," I said as we finished.

"Oh-ho? Enjoyed yourself then? We can come back sometime if you want. Be a good idea to go over things more than once anyway," Grandfather Shadestone said.

"Please."

Before I even made it back to our carriage, I was running through all the different things I could do. There were so many tools I'd need, so many specialized bits and bobs if I wanted to make things like I had before. Where would I even start? Making my own weapons would come in time, but which to go with? What would be the best designs and methods to use? With the available technology, could I even reasonably make anything? The last answer was quick to pop into my head. I most definitely could make a lot of things, and things this world had never seen.

That of course led to a moral question. Should I? Was it wrong to introduce things like that? I could follow the whole moral idea of the Prime Directive, but that seemed stupid. If war came, I decidedly wanted my people to win. The best way to ensure a win was be to make sure things were ready to go and laid out.

CHAPTER 19

DINNER PARTY

The day had finally come, and I had a dinner party to attend. This was going to be an interesting affair, riddled with rules and meeting new people. A fresh experience. My mother was stressed, of course. She seemed to always be stressed, but mostly because she meant well.

Most of my afternoon was spent with either Mrs. Lutte or my mother, going over the many rules and regulations for attending such a party. I wouldn't be alone though. There would be a number of chaperones for the youths tonight, both to observe how we did and correct any terribly bad behavior on the spot. For us kids this was almost like a training exercise, preparation for what would come when we were adults.

It was a relief when we finally arrived, mostly because I would no longer have to listen to it all anymore. Even on the way I was getting lectures and reviews from bothered adults.

I followed right behind my parents as they greeted the Starshine couple and introduced me. I'd met the lady of the house, and her husband seemed well disposed, almost chortling when he saw me in my miniature suit before mastering his expression. I was shown to one of the side rooms. As this was practice, things were as close to proper as they could be, but there were still some changes. Normally the adults spent time in the lounge as everyone arrived. Instead, we were in a side room that had been set up to look like one. When the time came for dinner, we'd not be going to the actual dining room, but another sitting room that had been arranged as such.

Rowena and Lucas stood off to one side, and their parents the other, greeting guests and making introductions. They were the first of the kids that I spoke to that evening.

"I'm so glad you could join us tonight," Rowena said as I stopped near them.

"Thank you for inviting me," I responded with a smile.

"Of course, we both found our last meeting quite enjoyable," Lucas added with a smile that told me he wanted a rematch.

"As did I." I would have been happy to keep trading such offers with him, but I heard someone else joining us, and they had a job to do. The brother quickly found one of his friends, a lad by the name of Wright, who I was hurriedly introduced to. It gave me a good excuse to make small talk while we waited for the other guests. Wright was an interesting fellow who loved boats and sailing. While I knew next to nothing about sailing ships, I could—and did—enjoy some light conversation about steam boats, something both of us knew enough about to discuss.

In due time, a butler—probably the second of them—called us all to dinner. Each boy found the girl he was to escort and we headed in. I, of course, was to escort Rowena. The rules on who was to escort whom and sit where were frankly Byzantine. It seemed that someone had arranged the guest list so that I would sit by the girl. I nearly rolled my eyes and made a mental note to tell Mother off later.

Soon enough food was brought in. The watchers sat at a second table, keenly looking us over, and the butler did the same with the servers and maids. They, too, were on the younger side; this was their training as well. If a mistake was made here, it would be embarrassing, but not as disastrous as it might be if someone offended or misstepped around one of the adults.

"So, Percival, have you done anything interesting over the past few days?" Rowena asked as we began.

"Other than the tourney? I did go to some lectures on science and mechanics at the Royal Society. I won't bore you with the details, but there were a number of demonstrations."

"Oh, that's up near the Basker Greenhouses. They have the most wonderful collection of flowers from all over the world," the girl across from us, Lavine, said. We'd only been introduced in passing, but it appeared she wanted to talk about that, so I happily obliged.

"Can't say I've ever been," I replied. "Anything in particular you suggest seeing?"

She did indeed have several things to suggest, enough that when she mentioned the section fed heat by underground tunnels, someone else decided to speak up. It was Wright to the rescue.

"I heard there's been more sightings of the little green man around those tunnels," he said offhandedly.

"Little green man?" I asked, having not heard about that.

"There have been rumors of a small misshapen green man, or men, dwelling in the tunnels and whatnot beneath the city. Personally, I think it's just a joke to scare people," Rowena said.

"Sounds almost like a goblin," I observed, something that got me a few odd looks. "I saw a few such creatures at a circus some years back. I think they said they were from an island." I remembered them quite clearly, a species from stories in my previous world that were real here.

"Wait, they're real? The rumors say . . ." Wright began conspiratorially, only to be cut off by a distinct cough from one of the adults. It appeared he was wandering too close to a sensitive subject. "Well, there are many rumors," he amended.

While we had to drop the subject for more mundane topics, he had piqued my interest. Maybe one of the little monsters had made its way under the city. At any rate, there were adults to deal with such things, and they'd probably deal with the situation if it became a problem.

CHAPTER 20

✳

GARDENS

A few days after the dinner with my . . . friends?—they were still so young, it was honestly odd to call them that; perhaps peers would be a better word, if also a strange one—I made my way down to the botanical gardens Lavine and Wright had mentioned. I didn't have any particular interest in flowers, though I liked them as well as anything else. It was the idea that one of those creatures was loose that piqued my interest.

My family was generally accepting of my desire to see the gardens. After all, a young gentleman familiarizing himself with botany was considered appropriate. Turned out a lot of flowers had meanings to them, and a bouquet could be either a declaration of love or a fancy way to tell someone they're a jerk. The fact that so much meaning was ascribed seemed patently ridiculous to me, but it'd be good to know for the future.

Mrs. Lutte was, of course, not fooled at all, and had stared daggers at me the whole ride there. Unfortunately for her, I'd managed to catch my parents when she wasn't around to ask them to come, and they were unlikely to go back on their word just because I had ulterior motives.

"Percival," she began as we got out, "I would appreciate it if you didn't wander off today." She was still my nanny, after all, so would be escorting me.

"I have no plan to," I told her.

"Percival," she groaned.

"Today," I clarified, "I just want to look around, see what's here. Not like any monsters are going to come out in the middle of the day anyway, Mrs. Lutte."

"It's a wonder your mother doesn't beat you," she griped under her breath.

"Not really, what would she even use? I'm tough enough that most things capable of hurting me are way too dangerous." I was being a bit more flippant than usual, but it was a beautiful day and I was going to enjoy seeing the gardens.

"Perhaps I should consult with your grandma then," Mrs. Lutte replied.

I gave her a horrified look. Most of my grandparents were fairly tolerant of me, but my maternal grandmother was a harridan if ever there was one. She also had no tolerance for any nonsense and a preternatural ability to catch me at mischief. Luckily, I could keep the dragon sated with good manners and politeness, but having a servant complain that it was impossible to have discipline around me would have repercussions, I was sure.

"You know, I really do just plan to look around, right?" I asked, hoping we could step back from what might be an impending war.

"Oh, I believe you. For everything else, you do always make your intentions clear."

After a short ride we arrived, and I was quite surprised at the place. When I'd heard about the gardens, I was expecting an outdoor affair, and while there were some outdoors, most of the plant life were in massive greenhouses. Between the greenhouses was trellis after trellis of cold-tolerant plants.

As for the gardens themselves, they were magnificent. The glass houses shone in the morning sun, almost uncomfortably warm and filled to the brim with both seasonal and exotic plants. Beds of flowers in shades of red and purple, some cascading down raised sections of wall, and vines dripping with white, star-shaped blooms. There were a few fruits, too, most of which looked to be tropical. Mixed in with all of these were ferns and bushes of varieties I'd never seen in either of my lives.

There was, of course, one that was missing, though. In all honesty I'd not expected it. Out of curiosity I stopped one of the workers and asked him.

"Sir, have you ever seen a vine that makes a light purplish blue fruit, about this big?" I inquired, holding out my hands.

"Can't say I have," he answered with a thick accent. "Do ya know the name of it?"

"No, I'm afraid not." I shrugged. It wasn't that important.

"Can you say where you saw it?" he continued.

"In a cave. I suspect the plant was magical, if that helps."

"Ah, that makes sense," he said, nodding. "Don't have no magic plants here, sir. Some of them are dangerous, and some unique. All I can say is to be careful round them things; not all are friendly."

I smiled. Didn't I know it. Last time I'd seen that particular plant it'd killed me, so dangerous seemed apt as a description.

Did I really care about the plant? No, not truly, and while I missed parts of my home on Earth, I couldn't really imagine going back. I was happy here, with actual superpowers and a family that cared for me. What more could I really ask for?

I nearly bid the man goodbye, but behind him I saw something that caught my eye. "Sir, what's that?" I asked.

"Oh? Ah, them's the steam tunnels. Keep the place warm. They run steam through pipes out from the Royal Society, I'm told. No matter how cold it gets, the hothouses are always warm. A might bit better than the way we used to do it. Had to bury the tropical plants in dung and all that." That sounded profoundly awful, but my attention was on the small steaming vent.

Now, I knew the elven lands were far more tropical than our lands, and the goblins were from somewhere around there. If I were a tropical little monster that wanted to hide, where would be better than the nice warm tunnels? Perhaps . . .

As I looked up I saw Mrs. Lutte giving me the stink eye. Her hands were on her hips, stare locked on me. Before I could get in too much trouble, I thanked the nice man and turned from the tunnel's entrance. After all, why did I need to go down there today when I was planning to spend so much time at the Royal Society anyway? Certainly I'd have plenty of time to get in via that route.

While we finished up, I spent my time trying to think of the best way into the tunnels. I imagined myself slinking through, catching the lost little monster, and maybe even ending up in the paper for my bravery. Those things had been kept in by that cage when I was little, and for that reason alone, I could tell that they weren't that strong. Heck, I was probably bigger than them now.

Then again, if I did end up causing trouble, it might fall on my grandpa. Perhaps care was a better idea.

Sadly Mrs. Lutte dashed my plans as soon as we returned home, running off to tell my mother that I'd found out about tunnels under the gardens. She'd even heard the man say that they were connected to the Royal Society, a looming disaster for any searching I might do. Grandpa would be informed for sure, and while *he* might manage to get in to look for any monsters, *I* most certainly wouldn't be allowed.

CHAPTER 21

✳

IN THE TUNNELS

Mrs. Lutte was an annoyingly smart cookie and had put together the exact same things I had. She'd also alerted my family to the matter, and now they were taking action. True, they were not really high up in the local government, but they knew people who were, and being a noble meant that you could get things done if you really wanted.

Of course, none of them believed for a second that there was a goblin beneath the tunnels, but they did believe that their son would do something they viewed as incredibly stupid if it wasn't looked into. Could I even really blame them? Well yes, I was still physically a child, so it wasn't like they were wrong.

Grandpa and I were at the Royal Society, waiting. I was pretty sure that I'd been brought along just to see how useless it would've been to go down there.

"There's almost no way anything's down there, sir, but if you insist," the leader of their little expedition said.

"I do, if for no other reason than to curb my grandson's curiosity on the matter." He gave me a stern look.

"Look, lad," the man said, turning to me, "I know it sounds exciting, but all these are is blank stone tunnels full of hot air. They don't even intersect with anything, and they're only like two blocks long." He looked back to Grandfather. "You know, we could take him with us, just to show him how boring it is."

"No, I think this is a good time for a lesson in self-discipline." I wilted as Grandpa gave me a harsh look. Normally he was very fun, excitable, and generally fond of some of my antics, but he viewed this one as dangerous.

There were five men in total, with little clubs and one single-shot pistol. Even if nobody believed me, there had been several sightings of a little green man, and it did actually match the description of the missing monster I remembered from the circus.

With a shrug, the workers opened up the seldom-used maintenance hatch and went in. We expected them to be back in under ten minutes, but two minutes in things began to change. There was a noise like yelling, a high pitched screech, and then a gunshot.

Before I could act, a hand pulled me back. I was stronger than my maternal grandfather, but didn't resist as he placed himself between me and the door, lifting his cane. Runes, previously invisible, lit upon the surface of the little item I'd always thought he carried as an affectation, energy crackling and sparking as he pointed the end toward the door.

"Behind me, Percival," he commanded, his voice taking on a hard tone I'd never heard before.

There was silence for a time, then the sound of footsteps, several pairs. The maintenance crew had returned, carrying one of their own, who'd taken a nasty gash to his leg. Another carried a corpse, a small, green-skinned humanoid, clearly dead, head smashed in and a large hole in its chest.

"Got it," the leader said in a breathy voice. "We're gonna need to check how it got in, though, in case there are more."

Within an hour, a fully armed unit poured down both ends of the tunnel. There were no other goblins, and no opening that they could find. In the end, their best guess was that it had slipped in through one of the grates in the hothouses and had been hiding down there, only coming out when nobody was around.

Sasha

Sasha looked over at her sister; she didn't really understand her. Sister Greta liked little mechanisms and parts that the others brought back when they went out, always huddled over one or another.

"He's still not come back," Sasha griped. For weeks, one of their big brother's helpers had been gone, lost on some mission or other.

"It's fine," her sister said with an unconcerned sigh. "You worry too much."

The day it had happened was supposed to be a great day for Sasha, the day she was finally given a job. Her job was to watch the entrance to the nest, protect it, and make sure the dumber cousins didn't run off. After all, she could count, and she could talk like Father did. She was one of his special children, and even had power like he did to heal and harm. She also looked different from the cousins, a little more like the people Father sometimes brought in, with hair and a flatter face.

She was still fairly little, but he'd pulled her aside that day, telling her how she needed to count the parties as they left, and as they came back, make sure all were accounted for. It was a good job, a job to be proud of, a job she knew was right. Her brother making her fail on her first day was a dark black mark to her.

But big brother Sigmund's group had come back short. He was supposed to come back with nine cousins, but only eight returned. After much worrying, she'd told Father, expecting him to give her spot to another, but he hadn't. Instead, he'd been angry with her brother, dropping Sigmund to the ground and screaming at him about being careful.

"At least there haven't been any other problems," she said.

"Only because Father won't let anyone leave. I think he still has Sigmund deep, deep in. Probably making him help with cleaning." Her sister snickered at that idea. Nobody liked cleaning.

Sigmund was the oldest of Father's special children, and by far the largest. He towered over even their father, at almost six feet tall, with long arms and bulging muscles. Sadly, he was also the dumbest and was often punished for doing things he wasn't supposed to.

"I guess."

There was a click and Greta made a happy noise. "I got it; it's moving again!" she enthused, holding up the little device.

"Okay? What's it do?" Sasha asked curiously.

"Um . . ."

"It tells time," a familiar voice said from down the cave. They both turned, seeing the bubbles of Father's aura creeping forward before he appeared. "I'm quite proud of you, dear. Good job."

The other goblin girl chortled as he rubbed her hair, then turned to Sasha.

"Have you had any issues, Sasha dear?" he asked.

"No, Father. One of the cousins got close, but I made him numb like you showed me and took him back in." She smiled, hoping to get the same approval her sister had.

"Good, and has our lost one come back yet?"

Sasha wilted at the question. "No, Father."

"Don't fret, my dear little Sasha. You've done a magnificent job. That mistake is your brother's, not yours. On that note, he'll be going back out soon, with my permission. Make sure to count those he takes and comes back with properly. I want to know if we lose another." He patted her head as he spoke, smiling.

"You can count on me!" she said in a bubbly tone.

"Good, good, you both make me so proud. Just seeing the two of you proves it, you know, proves that we can become better, and when we're strong enough, we can make the whole world better." His words inspired both of them—his dream, his goal for himself and his tribe, to make the world a better place.

CHAPTER 22

REPERCUSSIONS

The revelation of my grandfather's combat abilities left a lot of questions, questions I wanted answers to. Of course with all the excitement going on in the Royal Society and the gardens, I was going to have to wait. There were a lot of people who insisted on a thorough search of both sites to root out where and how exactly the little monster had gotten in.

Small monsters, I learned, were not totally unheard of in most cities. Deep in the sewers and otherwise underground, or in some abandoned sections of towns, minor beasts could sometimes make homes. These weren't the kind of thing that generally required any high-end expert, but the creatures could be about as dangerous as a large dog. Commoners often took up the mantle of hunting them, calling themselves things like rat catcher—rats seemed to be the most likely to mutate into large sizes.

The scandal, it seemed, was not that some minor creature existed in the city, but rather where it had been found, and that it was a complete unknown. There were going to be a number of nobles, my parents included, who were none too pleased that they and their children had been in the presence of such a beast. All that would come later though.

"Is there going to be trouble with us coming back so late?" I asked Grandpa as we packed up. The day had been very long.

"No, I sent someone back to the house to let your parents know that we'd be a little late. So your mother shouldn't be too cross with me," he replied with a small smile.

"I have a question," I began.

"Before that," he said, "we need to talk about what happened. I know you feel as if you could've taken that thing, and perhaps you could have, but you need to know just how badly that could have gone. I don't want you investigating any monsters like that on your own, Percival."

"But it did turn out okay," I protested.

My grandfather frowned and began to loosen his tie, which was odd, and then he unbuttoned his shirt, which was even odder. I watched in confusion as he pulled off a pair of layers, leaving himself shirtless in the carriage, and I didn't need to ask why.

All across his chest, from one shoulder to the opposite hip were a series of scars. It looked like claws had raked him, ripping inch-wide gashes. He'd clearly survived and didn't have any noticeable disability from it, but I could only imagine the sort of pain injuries like that would have caused.

"Normally I wouldn't show such a thing to a child your age, but you should know. When I was young, my father and I went out to hunt what was supposedly a monster of only minor size. This was the result."

"That was a minor monster?" I asked, aghast. I knew there were beasts in this world, even if I'd never seen one.

"Admittedly no, the creature we met was far more formidable than we'd expected. Had I been alone, I would have surely died. You're unlikely to meet such things around here, as they stick to deeper forests and remote locations, but it isn't impossible." He leaned forward, making sure I didn't avert my gaze. "But I want you to think before going after any such thing. Think about how your parents would feel should you die in some foolish adventure."

"Yes, sir," I answered, thoroughly chastised. It was clear that I wasn't ready to tackle some of the challenges in the world just yet, and perhaps I never would be, alone.

"Now, you had a question," he said as he began to replace his clothes.

"Your cane, is that why you carry it? I didn't know it was a weapon. What does it do?"

"Oh that. Staves have come and gone in style. A walking stick that can store mana and quickly project a few simple spells is rather convenient, you see. My cane is similar, something I started carrying before moving over to Hediza," he explained. "I continue out of habit mostly."

"Hediza?" I inquired.

"Oh, perhaps a word you've never heard before, hmm? Hediza is the name of the continent where the human kingdoms are. Originally I'm from Elazia, the elven continent." This was more than Grandpa normally talked about his past.

Elves existed in this world, and I knew that my family was related to them somehow, but from what I'd heard, Grandpa wasn't really considered an elf, but some kind of mixed-race individual. Mother was, too, to a lesser extent, and I would be considered human, my ears not even coming to a real point, shaped to just a slight point, like Mother's.

"Are monsters that common there?" Details about the elven countries hadn't been covered in my education yet.

Grandpa gave me a complicated look. "There are many kinds of monsters, Percival."

"People then?" I asked.

"You're too perceptive for your own good, child," he grumbled. "Yes, people can be the worst monsters of all."

"But why?"

"When you're older, we'll speak of this, but not till then. Now, we've nearly arrived." He was tucking his shirt in as we pulled up to the house, the driver opening the door for us.

The assault that night wasn't bad. Grandpa told Mother that there had indeed been an issue with the tunnel, though he didn't go into detail, and then he made himself scarce. I had to feel that there was more to his departure than I realized.

The next morning there were a number of headlines in major papers. I didn't read them, but Father received one daily, and so did several of the servants, meaning that at the family breakfast I saw him flip it open without realizing what was on the front page: Dangerous Monster Beneath City! and a sketch of the goblin.

I had to say, their artist had taken some serious liberties. The goblin, which had been only the size of a small child was depicted as massive, muscled, and in possession of both claws and teeth. In reality the creature had been rather plain, missing the worst of these things, and nowhere near the size depicted. I idly wondered if they'd even seen the body. Certainly someone had a photo somewhere.

For a solid minute my mother looked at the headline and picture, and then she turned to me. After a stare that made me fear for my young life, she turned back to the paper where Father was rustling it around, not knowing the disaster he'd released upon us all.

"Dear," she said in that sweet voice that made you know trouble was coming, "I'd like to read the front page there."

My father appeared from behind the pages, giving her a queer look. Mother didn't ever read the paper, instead getting news from a number of gossip sources and letters from the women in town.

"Certainly, love, if you want to." He, too, did a bit of a double-take after seeing what she wanted before handing it over.

I tried to rise, to flee from the table.

"Percival, stay," my mother commanded, not even looking up.

CHAPTER 23

✳

UNHAPPY PARENT

There were no two ways about it, Mother was livid. She'd not been so sure about me being there in the first place, and my insistence that the goblin was nothing like it was depicted in the paper didn't convince her at all. It wasn't even like I'd been trying to hide what had happened; it just hadn't come up how things had gone. She had been busy, and I had, too, with lessons and the like.

Just after breakfast, Mother had pulled me from my daily activities and to her parents' house. It seemed that I was to serve as witness to her father's guilt and whatever punishment she hoped to heap upon him. Unfortunately for her, when we got there we only found my grandma, sitting prim and proper in her drawing room.

"Where is he?" Mother furiously demanded.

"You will mind your tone, Lucille, for though you may think you're too old for me to take a belt to you, you are wrong," her mother responded calmly as she took a sip of her tea. "As for your father, he felt it would be best to step back for a while until you calmed."

The two looked at each other without speaking for almost a minute solid. It was like watching a hurricane slam into a glacier and neither budging an inch. After a time, Mother sat, still staring daggers but ceasing her yelling.

"He took my son into those tunnels against monsters, Mother," my mother said through gritted teeth as a maid came to pour her tea. The staff here had retreated to the sides of the room; they knew better than to flee and irritate my grandma.

"No, he didn't," I objected firmly.

"Quiet, you," Mother snapped.

"It seems to me we should hear the boy out, being that he was the one there." Grandma said, pointing to a chair beside her. I sat, taking the cup that was poured for me. If nothing else, this world had excellent tea.

"As I was saying, Grandpa didn't take me into the tunnels at all." One woman's lips drew a thinner and thinner line, while the other woman seemed mildly interested.

"So, if you didn't go down there . . . ?" Grandma asked, leaving the question hanging.

"The men they sent to look offered to take me, but I was told no," I explained.

"Good," Mother said harshly, "but you shouldn't have been anywhere near it anyway."

I snorted at that. "Grandpa knows me, Mother, and he knows that if I didn't get at least that, I'd have been down there on my own at some point. He's right too. Had I not been there, I might have."

"Do you expect us to actually believe you won't investigate on your own?" Grandma said. She, too, was aware of some of the incidents I'd gotten into.

"I mean, I kind of want to, but is there a point? They're going to bring in people with all this scandal who would know what to look for better than I would, and even if there's something down there, all the people running around will probably scare off any remaining monsters." I was really curious, but between not being able to and not really being ready for a real fight, it seemed silly to try now.

"He still put you in danger," Mother griped.

"Those creatures were known and not a major threat. There was no indication that any had attacked anyone, or anything like that. I was kept outside the tunnel, and at the first sign of danger Grandpa pulled behind him so he could aim at anything that made a move." I sighed. "There was nothing appearing more dangerous than a standard carriage ride at first, and at the first sign of anything unexpected, he pulled me away."

"Well, that doesn't seem so bad, now does it, dear?" Grandma asked, turning to Mother.

"You know my son, Mother." All this will do is encourage him to go down into some other tunnel."

"I don't think I'm ready for that right now," I admitted. I'd been thinking about some of the things Grandpa had said and what he'd shown me yesterday. "Going after monsters I mean."

"Sincerely?" Grandma asked, stunned.

"Oh, yes, clearly I'm unprepared. I'd need a team," I began.

"Ah, there it is."

"No," Mother said harshly.

"With much better training than I have right now."

"No!"

"And weapons! We'll need magical weapons and armor for sure, and guns, the best guns!"

"NO!" Mother bellowed, rising quickly from her seat.

"Oh, calm down, Mother," I complained. "All that would take years. Practice, designing things, safe testing, finding the right people. Not like anyone is going to have me on their team right now; I'm too little."

"Now, dear, let him think. Chances are he'll find something he likes more than chasing beasts if you let him consider it a bit. You know how kids are." Grandma waved Mother back into her chair.

She wasn't totally wrong either. I was thinking about it now, about the things I would want before going on that kind of an adventure. It would take years and years of work. I was decent with a sword, but I really didn't like the firearms available in this world. That alone would be a beast of a challenge, one I wouldn't be able to tackle without my previous world's hobbies.

In my last life I'd rather liked guns. I'd even made a couple. That was perfectly legal, so long as people stayed within strict guidelines. Working out a few revolvers and semi-autos had taught me a lot about their inner workings, and seeing old military pieces taught me a ton too. Sadly, I couldn't afford any of the really cool ones.

I was pretty sure I could do gunsmithing again, and with some of this world's materials and ability to skip the worst production processes, we might be able to get things done much faster. Some of the tools used were clearly magical, and I'd never learned to work with them. That was something I needed to change. Could I even do that? I mean, I wasn't a wizard, but rather a physical magic user. These were questions I needed answers for.

That didn't even include vehicles. I wanted some cool rides, and those would be a chore to make too. A car or something was probably just not practical, but maybe with magic worked into it . . . No, I needed to know more, needed to learn more, needed to practice.

"Hmm, think I need more schooling," I finally said. Even the beginnings of my list seemed difficult.

"Well, that at least is a good path," Grandma joked.

I was also still stuck on the known unknowns—things I knew I needed to know or do. Real problems came from the unknown unknowns—the things I didn't know that I needed to know. Unforeseen problems that older people had run into already and had to solve or suffer and that I didn't know existed. Sadly, learning those was a real problem, because you'd never know if you'd succeeded or not.

CHAPTER 24

✶

FOURTEEN

I was only fourteen, and all the things I'd managed astounded me. Over and over again I thought this as I looked at my newest creation. Perhaps it was cheating, calling this my own doing. I'd certainly cribbed a lot of notes from my old world, knowledge that would prove useful in the coming years, as it already had, but it was still a lot of hard labor. Before me sat my newest and best creation, one of the first major things Grandpa Darksky and I had really built from scratch together. We'd made copies of things before, small toys and the like, but nothing like this. This was a masterpiece.

The machine was small, far too small for me or anyone else to sit in, let alone steer, but that wasn't really the point. The point was to prove the concept. Wings stretched out from the sides, and the angles and shapes probably weren't ideal, but they were close enough that they should work. The makeshift design reinforced as well as we could make it.

"I want to learn how to make that engine," I said, frowning; the enchanted engine was one of the few things I didn't understand.

"You're about the age to start forming a core, aren't you, my boy?" Grandpa asked as he rubbed his chin thoughtfully. "Have to speak to your mother about it, though, they may offer it in your school."

"Already did," I said. "She dislikes the idea. Said physicals don't normally make cores." I frowned at the mention of school; it was the one thing I knew I couldn't avoid.

In this world there were a number of different types of schooling, but real official academies didn't take people until they were a bit older. It was the equivalent of high school back on Earth, and I wasn't looking forward to it. High school had been tiresome the first time around, and I really wasn't interested in a repeat. The fact that it was going to be an all-boys school didn't help either.

"She'll come around. Ready to get it started?" he asked, trying to distract me from my thoughts.

"Ready as I've ever been," I answered with a small smile.

He nodded to me and I stepped forward, placing my hand upon the craft. Slowly, I focused on my mana, the power in my body that fed my physical abilities and all magic. Learning to do this had been a bit odd; there was a trick to it. The sensation of moving mana was difficult to describe, like a tingling sensation that could be pushed and shoved forward and into whatever it was you wanted to put it in. If I had an item on me now, it was almost natural to trigger it.

There was a small dinging sound as the tiny magical engine finished filling up, and I stepped back. The whole operation was nearly silent, an effect of using mana rather than liquid fuels and a magical item rather than propellers and jets.

Our "engine" was an incredibly simple magical item. It mostly just made a kinetic force, pushing itself, and the attached craft, forward. There were a few additional functions for this test, but the forward push was what we needed it for most. It wasn't something that could be instituted on very large scales, but for this test it would serve.

"Here it goes," Grandpa said, almost in a whisper.

The little toy plane sped up down the field we were using for the test and bounced, once, twice, thrice, and then it flew. It wasn't fast, and it wasn't particularly high, but it flew. With patience it gained altitude, achieving about fifty feet in total before the second part of the magical item kicked in. A small flap on the tail turned and the plane began a large, lazy circle, first to the right, then to the left. It finally straightened back out and the tool powered down, losing velocity and altitude slowly.

Then it plowed straight into the ground. I'd sort of expected that to happen, with nobody onboard to manually control the descent. I honestly did not know exactly how it should go; I just gave the magical program my best bet. I watched as the plane crashed, going end over end.

"Landing needs work," Grandpa observed.

"Yeah, if I had to guess I overestimated the angle it should come down at. It flew though," I answered.

"That it did my boy, that it did."

We quietly gathered up the pieces, putting them in a box. It looked a lot worse than it was, with one wing definitely needing replacement and the tail snapped off. All of this could be repaired with ease now that we knew what to make.

"I think we need to order a full-sized one," I said as we finished.

"What about getting a working model first?" he said with a laugh.

"The model works, just need to adjust the procedure. Getting a sized one made will take time though."

"Months and months if we want it done right, and we decidedly do. Ah, just about the amount of time you'd need for your yearly school break, isn't it, Percival?" Grandpa teased.

"Just a coincidence, surely," I replied, waving it off with a smile we both understood.

He was right, of course. Schools here had a weird system, with something akin to a spring break in the summer, and a large one in the winter so that none of us missed the Season. How thoughtful of them. I was hoping to time this so that I could come home, say hi to my parents, and then get a first flight in a real plane we made.

Grandpa and I slowly walked back to the house. We'd been using one of the fields near his estate that was currently fallow, something they owned but rented off to others most of the time. It was one of the ways nobles made money nowadays, buying land and then renting it to others, a tried and true strategy.

"You're back already?" Grandma said as we ended our walk across the lawn. "And here I thought you'd be out all day."

"Things went well," I informed her.

"Did they now?" she replied with a raised eyebrow, looking into the box I was carrying. "Are you quite sure?"

"It did," Grandpa said with a bit of a harrumph. "The machine flew stunningly; you should have joined us."

"Perhaps next time, dear, assuming you can get it put back together from your *successful* test. As it stands, though, I'm glad you returned early. There are a number of tools the local mayor brought by, hoping you might look at and charge for him."

Of course the other main source of income for nobles was charging magical tools and artifacts. It took magic to do it, and while there were some commoners with magic, there were never enough. Magic was the oil of this world, and there was a ceaseless hunger for more—more tools, more solutions, more spells. It filled too many niches to be anything else.

"Well, let me get this downstairs and send Percival off," Grandpa began.

"Nonsense," his wife answered. "Let the boy help you. He's old enough for that, and many hands make light work, do they not? I've already filled what I can for the moment. Now you two need to stop playing with your toys and get to work." Her piece said, she shooed us off.

"Has she always been that pushy?" I asked once we were out of earshot.

"She's only that way when you kids are involved. When it's just the two of us she's quite fun. Don't judge her for it. She really does want the best for you, Percival." I briefly wondered what he considered "kids," being that he'd lived for quite some time already.

CHAPTER 25

*

A PARTING GIFT

While my grandpa had been thrilled with our model's success, my parents didn't see the point of it. Flying with magic was possible, and if you really, really wanted, you could make a basic flying object. Well, flying magical tools tended to be terrible, and they soaked up mana like a sponge to water if you wanted them to do anything, but they were possible.

I'd even taken time to ask around as to why most of the wizards didn't bother learning to fly. The answer I received was that it was simply too difficult. There was so much going into each and every movement while flying that it was considered a mark of a really skilled magus to be able to fly.

"I'm not sure I see the big deal, son," Mother said when I informed her of our success. "You've made flying toys before."

"I've made gliding toys before, and never one like this. Except for the engine that was a full working model, it should size up perfectly into an actual craft!" It was hard to be exasperated when I was in such a good mood, but I would certainly try.

At first I didn't realize I'd slipped up, until I saw her eyes narrow. She knew me well, too well, and she clearly had gotten an inkling of what I was thinking.

"You are not building one to strap yourself into, Percival," she declared with a sharp tone.

"Of course not," I agreed. "I don't have the skills to build such a thing, and where would I even do so? It will take three or four specialists months for even the first iteration."

"Will? Not would? I see I may need to have a . . . conversation with your grandpa." Beating. She clearly meant a beating. Sorry, old man. I may have caused you more trouble than I thought.

"At any rate," I said quickly, changing the subject, "is the house in Exion ready? I'll be staying there for a few days, right? You indicated that to be so since the school's there anyway."

She frowned. "Of course, son. I received a letter from the housekeeper just today, and everything's in order. Are you sure you don't want me to join you for the trip?"

"Mother, I've made the trip a dozen times. I'll be fine," I insisted. I also had other reasons to want to go there, reasons that I knew would cause problems if others knew of them.

"Fine, now off with you. I've got to prepare for dinner, and you should too," she said as she shooed me from the room.

On my way to my room, I saw Mrs. Lutte. She'd long ago stopped being my nurse and my nanny but still worked for us as one of the many staff of the house. It was clear that I favored her, and Father insisted she both stay and be given a cushy job, even if he avoided her. There'd been no more little half-siblings after the one, and I had a feeling there never would be. It seemed someone, most likely my paternal grandparents, had given him something to think about.

She looked up when I passed by, as if she wanted to speak to me. Even though she didn't say anything, I stopped.

"Did you need something, Mrs. Lutte?" I asked.

"Ah, I have a small request, my lord, if you don't mind," she said nervously. It wasn't unheard of for staff to ask for things, but they hardly ever asked me.

"Please tell me," I answered. It was important not to agree to anything before hearing it, but I'd known her for years, been with her since

I was a babe. If there was anything within reason that I could do for her, I probably would.

"Could you send me a letter about the house in Exion, sir? How things are going there?" She looked like she wanted to say more, but I understood loud and clear.

There was no reason for me to hide the soft smile on my face, so I didn't. "Of course, Mrs. Lutte. I'll be happy to."

The next morning was, as all mornings of trips tended to be, hectic. Something somewhere had gotten screwed up, and Mother was on a rampage, leaving my father and me in the entryway while she went to solve problems and knock heads. It had been quite a while, and I really pitied whoever had erred.

My father bounced on his feet a bit before pulling out a small pocket watch to check the time. Under his other arm was a rather plain box a few feet long. He looked out of place here, waiting, awkward.

"So, your mother said you and your grandpa made a flying toy? Quite impressive magic, that," he said, sounding as if he didn't know what to talk to me about.

"Oh, it wasn't really the magic that was important father. It's a machine; it should work even without any magic."

That surprised him. "That's quite a bit more impressive then. You'll have to show me sometime."

"I'll be happy to," I agreed, smiling.

My father was distant, but it was clear that he really just didn't know how to relate to people. There were times when we ended up talking, and though he had almost nothing to do with me on a daily basis, it was clear that he cared, or at least made an attempt at it.

"Well, I was going to wait until we got to the train station, but with your mother running so late, better to now." With that said, he offered the box to me.

Curious, I opened it. Inside was a cane, not unlike the one my grandpa and so many other men carried. It was long and sleek, with a black wooden finish. The handle was simple but appeared to be inlaid with silver, leading down to a clear seam between it and the wooden shaft. I pulled it out with care. The handle felt . . . like it was meant to be gripped a different way too. Sensing the meaning, I grabbed it like one would a weapon and pulled gently. It didn't come loose, but I could feel it, almost as if it were a magical item. With a guess, I pushed a tiny amount of my mana into the handle, and it loosed, coming apart.

"A sword," I said as the blade slid out, small barely glowing runes adorning its surface.

"One not everyone will be able to use. Designed the enchantments myself—sharpness and durability. It'll never rust, get dirty, or dull. Good, basic things, foundational elements tend to be the best anyway for everyday use." He smiled, one of the few times he'd ever done so with me.

"Thank you," I said. "I'll keep it with me for protection."

"I . . . don't really do well with people, son. Stay safe though. Exion is a big place, and I would hate for something to happen to you. I know you're a good fencer, so, use it if you must, and try not to get into too much trouble."

We shared a sort of stiff hug.

"I'll try," I said, to which he only nodded. Even if he was a bit distant, there was no way he didn't know about at least some of my predilections.

Mother chose that moment to rush in, looking at both of us and the weapon in my hands.

"You already gave it to him?" she huffed. "Fine, it doesn't matter. We need to go or we'll be late. Shame there are no gates around here, or we wouldn't need to go through all this nonsense."

She rushed the two of us to the carriage, as if we were the ones who'd taken so long. School would be fun, but I sure would miss moments like these.

CHAPTER 26

*

A PROFESSOR AND A MAID

After the mad morning dash my boarding the train was peaceful. This was a trip I'd made many, many times, and even if I found it rather boring, it wasn't like it was difficult. Soon enough the train was speeding along the countryside, with fields and trees passing me by one by one.

I thought back to what Mother had said about there not being a gate. It was a sad state of affairs, but a true one. All over the country there were gates, connective portals, but I'd never had to use one, nor had I ever seen one. They connected places with instant, or very near instant, travel. Unfortunately, it wasn't something that everyone had, nor were they everywhere. There was certainly one in Exion, even if I'd never had reason to use it, but not near the summer house.

In theory, I could have traveled inland to another large city and hopped through a gate, through the nexus I was told was in the capital, and then out into the city I was going to, but there was little point. The journey would still take well over a day and it would be hideously expensive. There were, of course, rumors that there were a lot more military-only gates, but it wasn't like I could get access to one of those.

At any rate, the train was pleasant—the hum of the engine and the wheels upon the tracks, the comfortable seats and good service. It was like something of old from Earth. Here, there weren't the tiny airline seats that nobody liked, or anything even resembling the useless security theater that was put on at every major airport. No, it was lovely, almost a home away from home.

Hours into my journey I decided I wanted something to eat. Sadly, I was no longer welcome in the ladies' cars, being that I was clearly well on my way to manhood. I didn't really feel at home in the family cars either, though, alone as I was. For a moment I waffled, and then turned, keeping my head high and eyes straight as I headed to the cars reserved for men. I'd never been in them before, so why not?

As I opened the door, eyes turned toward me and there was a billowing cloud of cigar smoke. I didn't hesitate though. I stepped through like I owned the place. In my first life, I'd well figured out that if you looked like you belonged somewhere, you were far more likely to remain unquestioned about your presence, so I faked it.

Several grey-haired men sat at a table nearby, each sipping amber liquid from a tumbler. While the others here seemed to accept me, one did not, turning as I came near.

"A bit young, aren't you, lad?" he inquired.

I gave him a thorough look. His hair was white, tightly trimmed over a matching beard. The suit he wore indicated he was a member of a higher class, formal and tailored and accented with a pair of spectacles. Hands were worn but well maintained; perhaps military or something similar. He and the others had books out, and a brief scanning of titles told me they were some of the more popular treatises on economics, something I was only a tad versed in.

"With all due respect, sir, I am quite old enough." I stared him down without blinking, moving, raising my voice, or anything else. If I either backed down or showed the slightest hint of concern, it would mean I forfeit.

"Very well," he said after an extended stare-off. "Don't suppose you've any thoughts on Renou?"

"I'll admit ignorance on the majority of the subject, but from what I've seen, he focuses quite heavily on commanded production, probably too much. With proper incentive, people will make what's needed; you don't need to tell them to by law." The economist in question liked the idea of top-down structures, a little too much for my taste.

"That's . . . not a terrible point. Care to join us, young man?"

With nothing better to do, I did. The man in question introduced himself with a title meaning something like Doctor or Professor Killic, the translation wasn't exactly perfect. Speaking to him was enjoyable though. There was much I didn't know, but I'd never felt shame in not knowing something, and he and his friends were happy to have someone else to speak with. The fact that I was more well-read on the current scientific and mechanical journals than they were also surprised the gentlemen something fierce, and I found their reactions quite amusing.

Professor Killic was also heading to Exion, meaning that we had days to get to know each other. Making an acquaintance like him was an unexpected boon. While a number of people confused me for his son or grandson, over the following few days this assumption kept anyone from bothering me.

Days passed and we moved from train to ship, continuing our discussions, and gaining new conversation partners. Before I knew it, I saw the approaching city from the lounge windows. Thankfully, the city stench was blocked by a mixture of nobody being foolish enough to open the windows and the haze of cigar smoke. The latter I could have done without, but it did keep the inevitable stink of the city away.

"It looks like our time may soon be at an end, Professor. That is at least until I make it to the school," I said over my coffee. It was an excellent brew.

"You knew?" he said, chuckling.

"I suspected," I replied. "The books you loaned me look an awful lot like the reading list." Over the past few days he'd taken to sending me back to my cabin in the evenings with one or more tomes to look over some of the subjects we'd been discussing. It had been a good way to pass the twilight hours and keep up with a few topics I really didn't have much to say on.

"Ah, so they did. Yes, I suspect we will be meeting in classes."

"What do you teach?" I inquired.

"Civics, of course, a subject I daresay you should do fine in," he mused. "It's not often I meet a young man so interested in discussion as yourself. Normally it's all dueling and seeing who can be the biggest fool."

"You wound me; I love a good fencing match, and I assure you that I'm more than capable of extreme foolishness. It's just that I feel that there is a time for everything." Regardless, I did guess that his classes would be enjoyable.

"Pah, youthful nonsense."

"Nonsense is important sometimes, sir. It provides a good outlet and sometimes wisdom," I said.

"And words like that are why I've come to enjoy our discussions, Mister Shadestone," he said with a shake of his head.

"I have as well. Sadly, it looks as if I must prepare to disembark. Until next we meet." I rose and offered my hand, shaking his hand before I headed back to my cabin.

Soon I arrived at the house. It was odd, being here without my parents, without them by my side. Of course the staff had lined up as they always did when one of the family came to visit, even if I felt it was a bit unnecessary.

"Greetings, Lord Shadestone," they chorused as I entered. "Welcome home."

I let my eyes fall over them, not bothering to hide the smile on my face. I wasn't my mother and didn't feel the need to play the stern disciplinarian right now, so I gave them a smile.

"Thank you, it's good to have returned," I offered, finally letting my eyes pass over one maid in particular.

Kaylee was there in her maid outfit, all prim and proper. The smile on her face seemed genuine, posture perfect. While I was here, I could make some inquiries with Mrs. Rider and make sure my sister was doing well. If she wasn't, what would I do? I didn't really know, but woe betide any fool who caused my little sister grief, because while I might not yet know how to make her part of the family proper, I'd be showing not a speck of mercy to any threat. After all, isn't that what big brothers were for?

CHAPTER 27

*

THE WORLD'S GREATEST

On my first day at the house in Exion I'd made some inquiries, but the results were less than I'd hoped for. The housekeeper, Mrs. Rider, thought that I was just trying to get a grip on how things were run, so she'd dutifully run me through all the books. That had ended with me having a very good idea of how the finances were doing, and the expenses in general, but it hadn't told me how my half-sister was.

"Ah, Mrs. Rider," I eventually asked, "how is the staff doing, particularly the new ones? Are they settling in well?"

"I've received no complaints, my lord, and their work has been exemplary," she answered.

Did it really surprise me that she didn't think I'd care about Kaylee's personal life? No, not at all. If things were normal, I really shouldn't care too terribly much. Even if her family had been serving my family for years, so long as there wasn't anything wrong, I should wish her well and little else.

"And these numbers . . . Most of the maids are making around six silver crowns a month?" I asked, trying to conceal my tone.

"Oh, yes sir, quite the generous remuneration. Your mother has always seen to it that we're well taken care of." She smiled and nodded. She, of course, was making considerably more. "That is the money side only though. We're all provided with good room and board, and if any-one comes badly ill or is seriously injured, a priest is called. It's such a weight off the shoulders."

Six silver was nothing. I was given a gold crown a week for my expenses, or five times that. I didn't even really have any expenses other than frivolities.

"Is that normal?" I asked.

"A bit above average, if anything. Of course, there are a few talents on the staff as well, and they make a bit of money on the side selling their services," she answered, referring to those with minor spell abili-ties, like our butler and his ability to heal minor injuries.

Even with the minuscule amounts of magic talents possessed, they would easily eclipse six silver a month. Most of them could sell their services at a given time for a silver or two, though it would take much of the day to regenerate it.

That, of course, led to the question of why they would demean themselves for paltry sums. I'd asked this question years ago, and the answer was twofold. Firstly, many people didn't have the connections to sell their mana and with the small amounts that a talent might have, they may have issues against the local mage monopolies. Secondly, they were betting to win big. It was a known and proven fact that tal-ents who spent time around magic had a higher chance of their talent expanding to something greater, turning them into a full magic user and a true powerhouse of their own.

"Thank you," I replied. "Is there anything else I might need to know about this right now?"

"Not that I can think of, my lord, and it is getting a bit late." She wasn't wrong. Even before I looked at the clock, I could tell it was nearly sunset, a fact that caused my stomach to growl embarrassingly.

"I don't suppose dinner is soon?" I asked, face flushing.

"It should be nearly ready," she said with a smile.

That night I was bothered by unanswered questions. I wasn't even sure how to go about getting the answers, or if I should. I'd promised Mrs. Lutte that I'd send her a letter, but if I did so now, I wouldn't even know what to put in it. Luckily, there were a few days left before I needed to head to the school. Little did I know that with a bit of quietly moving about the house I'd find my answer the very next morning.

Long ago I'd mastered the art of remaining unseen. This had been one of my favorite things to do as a child, and it hadn't yet gotten old. There were tricks to it, and the first was locating everyone around you. With my keen ears it was easy to pick out the sound of shoes on wood or carpet, and with practice I'd learned to differentiate them. Men's and women's shoes sounded different, as did their gaits. There were even more differences depending on how fast they were walking and how stressed they were.

I used my abilities to constantly avoid being caught, and to find specific people. I could pick out most of the older staff from both houses, and each member of my family, of course. Well, so long as they didn't take off their shoes. Between that and the voices I heard, I quickly found Kaylee the next morning.

"Stoke the fire, stoke the fires," she hummed as she built her little pile of kindling in the sitting room.

When she was done, she hopped back, thrusting one open hand forward and supporting it with the other. I couldn't see her face from where I stood in the doorway, but the little 'hiya' noise she made told me she was deep in concentration.

A small flame, two or three times the size of a candle's fire, drifted forward from her palm, landing among the wood and quickly setting it ablaze. Her work done, the huffed, a bit of sweat having bloomed on her skin. She then took up something akin to a superhero pose, hands on her hips and legs wide.

"An easy job for the world's greatest maid!" she declared, though not too loudly.

It was . . . It was . . . It was the most adorable thing I'd seen in either of my lives. The outfit, the voice, the pure-hearted declaration. I had a full cuteness overload, unable to function or move. My face was even frozen, unable to come up with just the right expression.

Then she turned and saw me. In an instant her hope was gone. I'd failed to hide myself and now watched as the blood drained from her cheeks and a look of fear overtook her.

"I . . . was . . . um, please don't fire me," she whimpered, eyes lowering to the floor. Technically, she probably wasn't supposed to be using fire magic in the house.

I had to school myself, present the proper face, the proper tone. "Why in the world would I fire the world's greatest maid?" I asked with a steady, perfectly calm voice.

There was a quick reversal of the direction of the blood in her face, turning her from white to bright pink in seconds. "You're not going to go to Mrs. Rider?" she asked.

"For what? You're doing a wonderful job. Now, chin up, everything's going to be fine." I tried to sound as reassuring as possible, for while I'd tried to keep an eye on her over the years, she still didn't really know me, except for whatever stories she'd heard.

"Truly?" she said, still disbelieving.

"Truly, and if anything ever happens, if it's ever not fine, if you ever don't know what to do and are scared or hurt, come and find me. I'm not your enemy, Kaylee, and I never will be."

"Thank you, my lord," she replied after a few moments of thinking and nervously playing with the hem of her apron. "I will."

"Good, now if you'll excuse me, I have a letter to write." After all, I had my answer now. Everything was going to be perfectly well.

CHAPTER 28

SCHOOL

The little carriage rolled up to my home for the next few years, the campus pulling itself from the ever-present mist. We were just outside the city, the walls and towers of the metropolis visible from the small rise this place was set upon, still shrouded in the morning fog.

Exion Boys Knight Academy was young, modern, and considered quite a good institution for its kind. There were other academies for those with physical magic, the one in the National Capital had the best reputation, but this one was certainly rising quickly through the rankings. Some of the schools were for boys, some only for girls, and a few were mixed; though, that was getting less common these days for some reason.

Of course, there were mage academies for those using other forms of magic as well. There was really only one of note—the Royal Penumbra Academy was where any and all spell-slingers wanted to go, assuming they could get in. It differed from many of the others in a few ways, the primary being entrance. Only members of the royal family were given reserved spots; all others were by merit alone. Anyone could take their exams, and since the royal family owned and supported it, any could attend. Sadly, that particular institution didn't teach physical magic.

The gates opened on their own as the carriages approached; we were expected after all. Upon getting out, I saw one of my old friends, Lucas. He'd arrived earlier than me and had come to say hello, promising, considering how often he tried to fight me.

"Been a while," I said as he strolled up to me.

"It has, how do things fare there, Percival? Ready for all the classes? I assume you'll do fine in our dueling class." There was an undercurrent of rivalry there; he didn't just assume it, he expected it, being that I beat him in just over half of our matches.

"I think it'll go well. How about you? I heard you're going hunting a lot more."

"Been talking to Mother then?" he asked.

"She visited last month, and as you know, those two are constantly sending letters," I said, referring to our mothers, who still seemed determined to play matchmaker between me and Rowena.

"Bah to them, I like hunting. Nothing around here though. Not even sure why they have that class." He nodded to the wall.

It was subtle, but there was a shimmer to the air. Without enhanced senses I'd never have seen it, never have been able to pick it out from the background. As it was, I only noticed because he pointed to it, but I'd assumed it would be there anyway.

"Come now, everywhere of any worth is shielded. Even if there's not been a monster attack of size here on Exion in what eighty years? Still need one just in case." It was policy, as everywhere had to deal with small incursions now and then, not something anybody wanted.

"Eighty-seven, and even that was supposedly mild. Wouldn't you love something like that, one of the great battles against hordes of beasts. Good way to prove yourself a hero." There was a glint in his eye as he spoke, a hungry look.

"Not really, no. Peace may be boring, but I'd rather be bored than see innocents suffer."

"You know, you're a real killjoy, Percival. Can't you at least let me dream?" Lucas complained.

"How about this dream then, the biggest most dangerous weapons unloaded on anything that has the potential to become a threat. Cannons capable of turning hills into craters before we can lead men in to mop up the remainder with fire and steel. After all, the best way to have peace is to be ready for war, that and destroy your enemy before they can become powerful."

"Ah, there it is, my friend," he said with a sly smile. "I knew you had it in you."

He nudged me in the ribs and we headed in. There were staff to unload belongings, and my being here would both stress them and get in their way. That fact still pinged in my brain as rude or wrong a lot of the time, but I'd worked hard to ignore it over the years.

"Back on the track for our education, any teachers I should watch out for?" I asked.

"Oh, Keens is a right monster, expects you to read his mind and answer questions he frankly didn't ask. I also heard we got a new civics teacher, too, though I don't know much about him," he said, clicking his tongue.

"Killic," I said. "I met him on the way here, seems to have high expectations, but not a bad guy overall."

"Good to know. Hmm, other than that, and in case nobody's warned you, keep well and away from the female staff. Not many of them, but you don't want to get caught in any *improper* behavior with them—instant expulsion most of the time." His voice was serious and eyes hard. "Not that there are many to begin with, but that's policy here. No cavorting, frolicking, or otherwise with the girls who work here. Also doesn't matter if they're into it; the headmaster physically threw a lad out last year after he was caught with a cook. I hear they're together now though."

I almost scoffed. "There are what, five hundred here between fourteen and eighteen, and you're telling me that not a one has a mistress, or girlfriend, or something of the like?"

"What? No," he said, shaking his head. "Specifically with the girls who work here. We can go into town one day a week; lots of the lads do. A few of the seniors are even married; don't know how they work that out though."

The first hour on campus was spent with Lucas showing me around. Regardless of anything else, he seemed to have decided to take on a sort of big-brother role, letting me know about the best ways to get between classes, the tastiest items to get during meals, even some hints on some of the books I might need to look over depending on what was being taught.

I knew some of Lucas' friends, either from the many dinners I'd been to over the years, or some of the tourneys. He took the time to point out those we passed and introduce us, letting it be known that he and I were old acquaintances.

By the time that was over, I was tired, so I retired to my dorm room. Each dorm was a suite, with five rooms, four for us new students and one for an elder student around a central juncture. The senior would function as a sort of resident advisor from a college, making sure we were doing all the things we were supposed to, but he wasn't there yet. The central area had some couches and basics for preparing tea or otherwise lounging around.

My room was fairly basic, as far as these things went. There was a comfortable bed; curtains to keep in the heat; a sizable wardrobe, which was already stocked with school uniforms; and a desk, basic, but quite workable. The floors were hardwood, and polished, simple and clean.

I could work with this. I could work with this easily.

★

CHAPTER 29

MIND GAMES

Everybody up!" came the cry on our first day of actual classes. "Headmaster has called an assembly of the students in half an hour. That means get in your uniforms and be ready for full inspection in fifteen minutes."

I, of course, had no context for what "full inspection" meant, but a wild guess told me that I needed my uniform properly on and hair combed, so I began to do just that as I rubbed sleep from my eyes. The speaker had been our resident senior, Ollie, a whipish guy with small, but toned, limbs and a sharp face.

As the last of us stumbled into the common area, he looked around before heading to Kilus, the boy in the dorm room to the right side of mine and working on his buttons, which for some reason weren't quite right.

"Look, guys, I know you have no context for this, and no idea what any of this means. You haven't been taught a damn thing yet, but the headmaster won't take that as an excuse. You're supposed to get corrections and booklets on how all of this works, but that comes literally today, after he's done talking to us. Had I known we'd be doing this now, I'd have shown you some things, but such is life." Our senior, Ollie, didn't seem thrilled.

"So?" I asked, displaying my uniform for him.

"Looks good," he replied. "Good, good, it'll do," he said to each of the other boys in turn. "All right, I'm going to show you how to stand and march. Try to get it right because we don't have time to practice."

We quickly found ourselves out in the morning air, along with every other boy in the school, and headed into the main courtyard to stand at attention. The older students in charge of the dorms were allowed, to a limited extent, to move around and correct people as we all got into place—for there were proper places—and readied.

At some signal I missed we began to move, dorm by dorm, and year by year into the auditorium. There were no chairs, no seating for us, but rather assigned positions. Each group had to march into place, as we'd been shown moments ago, and stand at attention toward the front.

The teachers were gathered in the auditorium. Some, like Professor Killic, were in something akin to what one would see on a professor from Earth; others were in military-style uniforms, not unlike what we freshmen were wearing. At the center of them all, overlooking everything as if it were mildly displeasing to him, stood our headmaster, eyes sharp as we came in.

Headmaster Logan was a mountain of a man, with little hair atop his head, scars covering every bit of his face, and a mustache that would have made a kaiser proud. His face was set hard, eyes shining like diamonds in narrowed slits, his stance ramrod straight. He waited, watching, seeming to note each misstep, each infraction as we made our way to where we needed to be.

The headmaster pulled a watch from his pocket, looking down with a frown before snapping it shut and turning his attention to us.

"Acceptable timing," he said, "but one you can all do better on, will do better on. Some of you have not known discipline," he added, eyes seeming to bore into each of us. "It is my solemn duty to correct this, to turn you boys into men that will make our nation proud. Each of you will learn, or continue to learn, to grow, to become iron and steel against our enemies. We, the people of the Penumbra Kingdom, are without a doubt the greatest nation upon these lands, and I will not have any slouch destroy that legacy. None of you are ready yet, but you will be. You will grow into men to make us all proud. For now, though, welcome to another year at my esteemed academy. Exit the way you came and head to your first class."

After that short message we were all sent out, and as soon as we'd made it back outside everyone exhaled.

"That seemed pointless," one of the nearby first years said.

"Because it wasn't for your lot, you twit, not entirely," Ryan answered the boy.

"He was inspecting you, and the other older students, making sure you're not slacking off before classes?" I guessed, looking at our esteemed leader.

"Yeah, if I had to guess."

"Reckon you did all right?" asked Simon, another of our dorm's cadre.

"Better than some. I'm sure I'll know each and every mistake by dinner though," the older boy griped. "As for your lot, you heard the headmaster, off to your classes."

Simon was in my first class. Knowing nobody else and having no seating chart he elected to sit beside me.

"This morning is going to be awful," I groaned, since our professor hadn't made it in yet.

"Not get enough sleep?" he said with a laugh.

"What did you eat for breakfast?" I retorted, since I'd slept fine.

"Oh, well shit." It seemed that observation took the wind from his sails. Not a one of us had managed a morning meal, something we'd not noticed because of stress, but which would certainly be apparent before long.

I was right too. The first class at any school was always devoted to teaching the rules, and this one was no exception. While they didn't call it "home room," the first class we had was everything the Earth equivalent imbued. The professor came in slightly after we'd seated ourselves and began to run us through the expectations and obligations. None of it was too terrible. Though, apparently, the headmaster maintained strict discipline at any formal function.

By our second class, the cracks in our student body were already starting to show. Very few of us had ever missed any meals, quite spoiled by our parents. Various boys were beginning to mope or get in a slightly worse mood. When lunch finally rolled around, a full quarter of the first years could be described as hangry and ready to lash out at anyone in their way. Knowing this didn't improve my own mood in the slightest, for I hated this kind of nonsense.

It was clear to me that all of this had been planned. It would put stress on each of us, making us step out of line. The teachers could then use our misbehavior to quickly put us back in line, establishing an order and discipline, even if it was all caused by their actions. I highly doubted that they didn't know and plan this.

My suspicions were further confirmed when I saw lunch. Seldom had I seen such a pathetic plate of food. The portions were small and had a visible and distinct lack of meat. I wasn't the only one to notice either.

"Is this it?" one of the boys asked one of the women serving food.

"It is," she replied slightly nervously. "The headmaster set the menu for today, so if you've any complaints, you may direct them to him." I had no doubts that any such gripes would be seen as excuses.

"If he does this for supper, too, there'll be a riot," Kilus observed as he joined Simon and me.

"Or mass theft from the kitchens," I added.

"What's our next class anyway?" Simon asked.

"Hand-to-hand combat," I answered.

CHAPTER 30

✳

A DISH BEST SERVED

Time to strategize was minimal, and so we had to hurry. There were so many factors, so many methods by which we could move forward, and I needed to consider carefully between them before acting. Acting rashly here would only hurt us, only make things worse, or prove the annoying point that our headmaster was making.

We could probably cause a ruckus if we worked together, maybe even getting a hit or two on the teacher, but that would be counter-productive. Moreover, it was what we expected, and if I knew anything about winning a conflict, it was that you had to do the unexpected. We'd already lost the initiative, and the teachers were undoubtedly the ones with the power here, so we needed to work carefully, to subvert them. Our goal would be to win the fight without fighting. In other words, reminiscent of Sun Tzu.

Sadly, we also didn't know what the teacher had planned, meaning that any ideas we had needed to be adjustable on the fly. We needed a plan that would shift like water, flowing into any weak spot and still able to cause pain, or at the very least discomfort, to one of those responsible for the travesty we'd experienced.

"All right, everyone, line up. Most of your classes will be focusing on boring paperwork today, but not here. No, here in Hand-to-Hand

Combat we have practicals every day. First, we'll begin with you lot showing me what you know," the professor announced, not even telling us his name. "Come up and punch this target, one at a time, there you go."

The class did as it was expected and formed a line before the teacher, who held a large pillow-like shield with a target on it. This is where our games began.

The first student up to the line wasn't one in our conspiratorial group, so he just did as instructed and punched, hard, getting a word of encouragement from the teacher and going to the back to wait for the next instruction. The second in line, though, was one of ours. He sleepily approached the line and punched, missing the target by a full foot, causing the pillow to bend and slap the professor in the face.

"What was that?" the older man screamed. "Hit the target, boy! The target, right in the center!"

Taking another turn, the boy struck, this time hitting dead on, but somehow slipping and barely delivering any power at all. He had to repeat his action three more times before the professor sent him away in disgust.

When my turn came, I decided to play my role to a point.

"So I'm supposed to hit the target, sir?" I asked innocently.

"Did I not say that, boy?"

"Sorry sir, sorry, right in the center right?" I inquired.

"Today, lad, we've got more than this to do!" He roared from behind it, a smalll vein popping up on his forehead.

Our harassment campaign began thus. Simon seemed asleep on his feet the entire time, slow to react, slow to act, often a bit confused. Kilus somehow managed to look like he was five seconds from puking the entirety of class, getting concerned looks from everyone the few times he bent over. I, of course, had taken the role of the young man with the room temperature IQ. Others who'd been near us at lunch did much the same, not lashing out outwardly, but making sure everything just failed. Every command had to be repeated, clarified, repeated again. Stances that we all knew and should know weren't right, angles off just enough to make the teacher correct our positions, only to find in doing so that one foot or another had drifted out of place on either the corrected boy or one of his fellows.

By the end of it all, the instructor was red in the face, fuming at half of the class. We'd not gone out of our way to break rules, just been awful the entire time. I half expected him to retaliate, but he didn't, instead just sending us off in disgust.

Then it spread. People from our freshman class learned from us, and hushed discussions in the hall spread the tactic. Every boy was stupider, weaker, more curious about minutiae that didn't matter at all. Some stayed awake, but looked almost like zombies, others simply broke their pens every time they picked them up, making an awful mess and a distraction. Nothing was getting done at all after lunch.

I didn't make it to all of my classes that day. For example, I didn't have civics just yet, but every single one beforehand was a waste. They'd made us angry, and while we had limits on what we could do, we could still fight back. There were threats, of course, even some corporal punishment handed out. Nothing too bad. After all, most of us were rather well off, but some, not so much.

At the end of the day we finally had dinner, and the spread was actually quite nice. There was plenty of food, all of it was of the healthier variety rather than what was commonly served at dinner parties, but it tasted fine and was plentiful. So long as everything worked out well, we could end our little protest.

There were fruits and meats and roasted vegetables of all kinds. The seasoning was very light, where it existed at all, but at least there was enough. A small pile of plain loaves, made from a local wheat crop, steamed, with a small bit of butter beside it. It was enough for all of us to have full bellies, a welcome change from the rest of the day.

Near the end of the meal I was approached by Ollie, the senior in charge of my dorm.

"Come with me, please," he said, not explaining as he turned on his heel.

"Where are we going?" I asked as we made our way down the empty hall. Dinner was still in progress, and our footsteps echoed down the corridor lightly.

"Headmaster Logan wants to see you." There was no further explanation, nor did he seem to want to talk at all.

For the rest of the way we walked in silence. Whatever the headmaster wanted, it certainly wouldn't be a good thing for me. After all, I'd caused quite a lot of trouble at his school, and he didn't seem to be the type to take that sort of thing lightly. It wasn't even the second day yet, so I wondered if I'd be able to get my tuition money back; probably not. Were there other schools I could get into? Also, probably not once they'd heard what happened.

Oddly, I wasn't led to an office but rather one of the training rooms. This was another place I'd not been yet, but it was close to our afternoon classes, so I at least recognized it. The walls and floors were slightly padded, covered in some kind of hard mat. In the center stood the headmaster, eyes hard as he held a practice blade in one hand, another stuck into the floor nearby. He had no safety equipment, no strengthened clothing or armor, just his normal suit. It wasn't lost on me that there were spots of red—fresh blood—on the floor. I could even smell the metallic tang.

"Leave us," he said to Ollie.

"Yes, sir," the senior replied before practically fleeing the room.

We stared at one another for a time, taking each other's measure, and then he spoke. "Well, boy, are you going to take up the blade or not? I've already finished with your seniors, but I think it's your turn now." I reached out slowly, fingers wrapping around the practice weapon. It wasn't a foil like I was used to, but a heavier thing, shaped like the blades commonly carried as backups by soldiers. The short, leaf-shaped sword that would be taken to war.

There was a brief moment, a pang of regret that I'd eaten so much. It was feeling awfully heavy in my stomach in that moment.

CHAPTER 31

PUNISHMENT

There were times for reflection and times for action, and this was most certainly the latter. The headmaster had caught me off guard too many times today, taken the initiative too much, and losing it now would be even worse.

He'd chosen the place, the time, the weapon, and to fight. He was ready when I was not. I also had no doubts that the shortsword I was now holding was something he preferred, as opposed to my favorite, a longer, more slender blade.

Rather than let him set the tone of the fight, I launched into a series of attacks. This was nothing special, just several standard slashes and stabs, trying to catch him off guard or find any chinks in his defense. Sadly, neither was to be, as he slapped away all of my strikes with his dull blade as if they were predictable.

"Good form, but unimaginative," Headmaster Logan said, his voice like gravel. "Let me show you."

In a flash his blade was moving, and I could see what he meant. I managed to block the first, though it numbed my hand to do so. To my credit, I was even able to catch some of the other shots he made, but each came from angles just off of standard. Too unlike my series of attacks, his came in at an uneven tempo, slow, then fast, then slow again, catching me off guard. The final of this series caught on my cross-guard and lifted, throwing me several feet back.

Each of those strikes would have been an end to the fight had he made them with a real sword or with his full strength. They still hurt, but it was clear he had been holding back. Perhaps he was irritated that we'd opposed him, but this was a lesson as much as it was a punishment, and one I wouldn't forget.

I had no illusions about winning; that was likely impossible. Maybe I was good with a rapier type blade, perhaps even very good for my age, but that didn't really help much. He was easily a foot and a half taller than me and built like a brick house. In reach, physical strength, and just plain experience I fell short, and deluding myself wouldn't help.

He didn't attack as I rose and regained my practice sword. So I did, launching at him with a series of attacks, not unlike his, coming from slightly different angles and in a rhythm dissimilar from what he'd used. If I was being honest, it was a bit sub-par, but with the state I was in, it was what I could manage. The return from the headmaster was much like before, with the same result.

"Better, again."

Three exchanges in, and I was hurting. By the fifth I was sweaty and my right hand was shaking from the repeated hard shocks. That didn't matter. I just switched to my left. I wasn't as good with my left hand, but if I couldn't even hold the sword, what was the point? It also gave me a chance to try punching Headmaster Logan. That, of course, ended with him grabbing my arm and using it to hurl me halfway across the room.

"Not going to apologize for your behavior or ask for leniency?" he asked me as I once more picked myself up off the ground.

"No, sir, I don't think I will. You seemed to want misbehavior."

"Fair enough, boy, fair enough. You can't win here though. Surely you know that?"

"Perhaps, sir, but I can refuse to lose," I told him.

That got me a guffaw. Of course I took that chance to dash forward and attack, because why would I give up such a moment? Like he had so many times before, he moved to bat away my thrust, but as he did, I acted. With an additional step and change to my angle, I brought the point of my blade a few inches forward, enough so that when he pushed it away the tip grazed his chin just slightly. It didn't harm the headmaster, but if it had been a real sword, it would have cut him slightly.

His response was to add an additional flourish, one which sent my weapon flying from my grasp and well out of reach.

"Enough," he said, rubbing his chin. "Tell me, who put you up to this?"

"Nobody did, sir," I informed him.

"Do you think you'll earn my respect by being pigheaded and refusing to tell me the truth, boy?"

"Well, the truth is that nobody did. I wanted to cause trouble, to skirt the line of what we could do without getting punished."

"You failed," he said with a disappointed look.

"Clearly, sir, though I'm not sure how you knew it was me?"

"Something you should keep wondering. At any rate, I think that's enough. Go, you have classes in the morning."

"May I ask a question before I go?" I asked.

"Very well," he said, nodding.

"Why?" I asked him.

"I wanted to see who would try to take control, and how they would respond."

"How'd we do?" I inquired.

"Miserably," he declared. "Not a one of you tried to bring to my attention what you wanted. The first part of any conflict should always be diplomacy, young Percival. Now off with you."

I was sore as I walked back to my dorm room, but it could have been worse. Perhaps if I'd been an older student, or someone more used to his methods, it would have been. Perhaps if I'd done more than just be a pain, it would have been. It'd be easy to find out tomorrow, but tonight I wanted to bathe and sleep.

Headmaster Logan didn't seem randomly abusive, just almost military. Not modern military, either, but the old-school, hard-knocks kind. He wanted little soldiers, men who'd follow orders to a T and could be depended on to know what to do. That final lesson wasn't lost on me either; we were supposed to follow the chain of command before acting out.

"You okay?" Ollie asked as I made my way into our rooms.

"Fine, even learned something," I informed him. The other boys were up and listening.

"What's that?"

"Next time the headmaster does something irritating that we don't like, we should tell him. Now, if you don't mind, I need a wash and sleep."

Hot water was a wonder, and a brief soak took care of most of the soreness. I'd have a few small bruises, but I got those every time I was in a tournament. What we'd done was a lot like a tourney, but if I only fought someone better than me, back to back for several rounds. Perhaps before I graduated, I'd get a chance to duel him again, see if I could give as good as I got.

CHAPTER 32

✳

CORES

Before I knew it the first week of classes had passed. Overall, things weren't too bad. Some of the science was weird, or downright wrong, but for the most part we covered a smattering of general topics that you might expect for middle or high school students, as well as several forms of combat. There was a lot of overlap with things I'd learned in my previous life, and those subjects I breezed through. Boring as it might be, algebra didn't really change between one world and another.

There were also classes that no kid on Earth would have expected, like all the lessons on fighting and war tactics. We were learning how to fight on battlefields that were in constant evolution due to the increase in magical potency and firearms. Magic also changed how armies fought in general, with alterations in tactics, supply chains, organization, and even some of the normal rules of engagement. The last of which were very important.

In this world it was the priests who named and enforced the conventions of combat, and they were not known for their mercy to those who violated them. These priests used a different form of magic than I did, and they were almost universally inducted into one of several Orders. I didn't have a notable relationship with any personally, but as

I understood it, their power was related to living things and what they felt was "right," whatever that meant.

All that aside, I'd made it through those classes and now had only one more before I had a couple of days off, then begin it all again. That was how I found myself in one of the tucked away back corners of the school, with only a few of my fellows.

"My, my, what a promising crop of students. So many of your fellows choose not to join my class, and I'm thrilled that you have come to join me. I'm Professor Ruian, and don't worry, I'll make sure to take care of you all," the teacher told us. She was an older woman, and one of the few female instructors.

She wasn't wrong either. There were only five of us here. This class was completely optional for us, and seen as a bit of an oddball choice, even if it was one of the ones I was most excited about.

"Now, come with me, and I'll show you all about building your cores!" she declared excitedly. "Each of you will need to meditate in a specialized room, which will assist in the process of building it. While there and concentrating you'll be pulled into a sort of mental space, where you can do the construction."

"And how will we do that, Professor?" I asked.

"Excellent question, young man. It is difficult to describe, but by focusing you'll find that you can. There will be a series of lights you need to follow. Just do so and you'll have no problems. You just need to follow the color coding."

She gave a very brief description of what looked right or wrong but insisted that it really would be quite obvious.

"Now normally we'd have lectures about the basics on how to use it first, but I find that boys tend to do better if we alternate between the meditation and more practical aspects. So, follow me."

We were led into a room of dark stone, with a central plinth surrounded by circles on the ground.

"Wow," one of the lads with me said, and I had to agree. This was the most magical looking room I'd ever been in.

"Wow indeed. This pillar is the beginning, the start of what led us to the society we have today. Well, not this one, but you know." She waved her hand as if pushing away questions.

"Are they hard to make?" I asked.

"Interestingly no. You'll learn about that later though. Now let's begin, an hour first, and then we'll begin with the instruction on how to use what you'll be learning here."

We took our places and began to meditate, and we were pulled into a sort of mental illusion where we could build, just as she'd described. So build I did, slowly putting things together bit by bit, learning one very important thing—that doing this was painfully, abysmally boring, like following the simplest diagram and just putting the pieces in one by one, an endless piece of self-assembled furniture. It even felt physical, like I was taking the energy and molding it with my hands. When an hour had passed, I was pulled out of the illusion, or whatever it was, and back into the real world. There I found something far more interesting. Professor Ruian certainly knew what she was doing. She'd made a sort of game of the basics, how to make the runes work. We were each given a list of cards with numbers, letters, and the like, each of which had a basic instruction on them. The rules of how these went together were then provided, and we had to try to work out how to make a working version.

I recognized it immediately. It was coding, like in C or Python. How it went together looked exactly like coding, and some of the "runes" we were given looked an awful lot like English words if you squinted, like letters wedged together by someone making their own programming language. My eyebrows rose higher and higher as the class went on. Even if I was no expert, I dealt with this stuff enough at work on Earth to recognize the basics.

"Professor," I asked, "where exactly did this come from? The runes and all."

"Hmm? You should have covered that in your history classes, shouldn't you? Lazy tutors, I suppose, never teaching the very beginnings before going to the interesting bits. These were made by an elven ruler many years past. Most of them nowadays simply refer to him as the king or His Majesty, since he's been the only one of them to ever take that title."

"Is . . . Is he still around?" I asked hopefully. I knew elves lived a very long time.

"Oh goodness, no. That was, oh, nearly fifty-four hundred years ago, or something? Elves might live a long time, but they're not truly immortal, regardless of what some of them claim about their leaders."

My grandfather had said something similar to me, something about an old ruler who'd made flying ships, and that he was long gone. There was also the eerie similarity in some of the outfits, designs, and the like here and there, and this all but confirmed it. There had been others like me. Could I meet them? Should I meet them? Were any even still alive, or was I alone? Perhaps I needed to look into it—old history first—and see what I could find.

The next morning was supposed to be my day off, and I had to disappoint Lucas and the several lads he'd pulled along with him. I was heading to the library rather than spending the day sparring. My friend looked at me like I'd lost my mind.

"It's the first week of classes, Percival!" he objected. "There's no way you've been assigned enough work to need that."

"Just want to look a few things up, Lucas. Heard something that I want to know more about."

"You'll never get better if you don't fight more. Studying can wait." He really did seem determined.

"Look, it shouldn't take me too long," I said. "How about we meet at the arena a bit before dinner?"

"No," he finally said.

"No?"

"No, I'm coming with you. If you can't speed yourself along enough to not waste the entire day with your nose buried in papers, I'll help."

I sighed, it was sure to be a long afternoon.

CHAPTER 33

✶

THE PAST

"Boring," complained my *assistant* for about the fifth time.

"I didn't try to hide that it was going to be boring, did I?"

Lucas frowned at me. "If you could just tell me what you're looking for, then it would probably help."

"Things that stand out, things that are odd," I informed him again.

"Percival, that's all of history; well, all that's written about, at least. If something doesn't stand out, if it's not odd, people don't write about it, ergo, it doesn't end up in some dusty old tome in the library."

"That's . . ." Actually, it was a fair point, but I couldn't tell him that I was looking for things from Earth, now could I? "How about this—I'm looking for odd and large leaps in technology. Things that stand out. Like the elven king or stuff like that."

"Okay, that's actually something then, isn't it."

After poking around for a while, we found several tomes on tech, and what we found wasn't good.

"So after the creation of the core, things sort of stagnate," Lucas declared.

"Stagnate? They don't 'stagnate.' There's a millennia-long dark age. Do you know how much we lost? It's insane! Like the whole of society was pulled out from under it," I said, exasperated.

"If you believe the stories. Frankly, I think the elves are lying. They like to act all high and mighty, but honestly their stuff isn't as good as ours in a lot of places. They don't even have a proper portal network." He scoffed, seeming to think it was all lies. I, however, did not.

"Yeah, about that, I can't find it in a lot of the places I'm looking. Where did it come from?" I asked, having focused on some of the older parts mostly. Lucas seemed more willing to look at the new stuff.

"I . . . Are you screwing with me, Percival? Everyone knows where it came from."

" . . . "

"Old Auntie Penumbra." At my blank look he appeared shocked. "The Kingkiller? The Worldsinger? Top advisor for . . . well like, forever?"

"Pretend I don't know who you're talking about," I told him.

"Then you're a child or a fool. She's the headmistress at the best magic school around, and you've never heard of her? You do know who the current king is, right?"

"Of course," I protested. "He's on like half of our money."

"We've got to get you up to date on common knowledge and like, people you should know. You talk a good game, but not knowing the basics of the royal family is just sad, and embarrassing. If it were any-one but me, I'd feel terrible for you. Luckily, though, I'm here to fix this." He shut the book and shook his head. "C'mon, these aren't what we need."

He found me the proper book in moments, and it was a biography. It wasn't on the woman whom he'd spoken of, but rather the first king of our nation. King Verren hadn't reigned long, but he'd done much. It detailed his rise as a soldier in an old kingdom called Bergond, a long-lasting place that was overthrown by an empire before it died with its emperor.

Some of what I read about that emperor led me to believe he might have been a reincarnator. His ideas were . . . progressive, to say the least—nationalistic, stopping short of communism, but very insistant on having the strong protect the weak. He wasn't what I was looking for though.

"Her," Lucas said, tapping the page.

The girl he pointed to was King Verren's only daughter, a bit of a mysterious figure. She popped up a few times, causing a big stir, only to disappear once more. She introduced technologies, worked on important projects, and seemed to assiduously avoid any positions of power. Alana Penumbra. That was her name, along with half a dozen epithets, including the ones Lucas had just said.

"No biography on her though?" I asked, not seeing one in the section.

"Nope, nobody will publish one. Rumor has it that there's a royal decree to that effect, but also nobody wants to cause problems." Lucas shrugged, not having a good explanation for that.

"Problems? I mean, wait, this woman can't be alive. She'd have to be . . ."

"Over three hundred years old? Yeah, she is. That's one of the more mysterious parts of the whole thing."

I looked down at the picture of her in the book, one with her father and brother, the first and second kings, respectively. Here, at least, she looked young and blonde, with bright blue eyes and a bit of a hard cast to her eyes. Sadly, it was probably out of date, but if you could live for three hundred years, why not stay young too?

"I'll have to find a way to talk to her," I mumbled.

"Good luck with that," Lucas chortled in response. "The old, private, paranoid mage is unlikely to just waltz up to you and be like, 'Hey, we should have a chat,' isn't she?"

"Yeah, probably, but I'm sure there's a way to get a meeting."

"Questions for later. For now, we need to get to the arena."

"Right," I agreed. He'd helped me. It was time to keep up my end of the bargain.

"Then we're going to have a long, long talk about holes in your knowledge."

"Why are you so dedicated to this?" I asked.

"I . . . Man, you're stupid, aren't you? And here I thought you were bright. Well, we all have our blind spots, but don't worry. Your big brother Lucas is here to help you learn, one way or another." I got a rough pat on my shoulder as we moved, but he didn't explain why he felt the need to look after me so much.

✶

CHAPTER 34

PREPARE TO PARTY

Weeks passed, and I began to settle into my school life. There were holes in my knowledge, big ones. I knew about a lot of the philosophy, and art, and technology of the day, but about history, I was woefully unprepared. Not the things one normally finds in books, but the little bits here and there hidden in common knowledge. After all, I spent most of my time with people who didn't care or with my grandpa, who didn't know.

This meant that while I was doing well in some areas, my social life was formal. Manners had been beaten, almost literally, into me by my grandma, and I could run through them with ease. However, spending time hanging out or generally messing around with youths my own physical age was almost a non-starter. Lucas tried to do his best to help with that though.

My rival in the fencing ring treated me as something akin to a little brother. Whenever I tried to spend my day meditating or in the library with my head buried in some book, he'd come and find me, often convincing me to join in sparring with the others or generally hanging out. That was how I found myself sitting in a circle in one of the academy's unused basements tossing a small ball back and forth with him and several of his friends.

"So what are your plans for the weekend, Percival?" Lucas asked as he tossed me the ball.

"Same as every weekend, I guess—study, maybe look at some of the new journals that have come in," I replied, tossing the sphere to Simon, who'd somehow fallen in with this same group.

"Dense as always, Percival. This will be the first time we get a day to go to town," Lucas chided.

I *was* dense. The first few weeks hadn't had the normal town days, but normalcy began this week. One day a week off, a day away from the school, should I so choose it. I could go and do . . . well, without supervision, basically whatever I wanted. So long as no great trouble came of it and nobody found out, I could do much as I pleased.

"Oh, haven't even thought about it, honestly. Totally forgot with classes and all."

"Well, I'm getting some dried meats, if nothing else," Simon said. "Just in case the headmaster decides to starve us all again."

It seemed unlikely, but that incident had left a mark on the student body. I'd come out of it fairly well. Not giving up my classmates meant that I was the only one punished in our grade, something others noticed. That act alone had won me a fair amount of social capital, something I'd never bothered to use.

"There's a concert in the entertainment district I'm keen to go to," said Reese, another boy in Lucas' grade, as he tossed the ball.

"Might be good if we'd gotten tickets," I grumbled.

"Don't need them," said Reese. "This one is first come, first seated. Not sure why, but it looks like the group putting it on didn't want it to be all the richest in the city, and from what I've heard, it's magnificent."

I shrugged at Lucas, who made a face indicating that he'd be interested in going as well.

"Expensive?" I asked. I did have some petty cash, but not a lot.

"No, like I said, they want everyone to be able to go," Reese replied, waving a hand flippantly, as if there was no reason for concern.

"I'm in," Lucas said.

"Sure, why not," I agreed.

"Sounds like a blast," Simon added.

We continued our game, the little ball whizzing at speeds that would terrify normal people. That was one of the things I rather enjoyed about being at the academy. With so many of us as strong and durable as we were, we didn't really have to hold back. At home and elsewhere I had to treat everyone like they were made of paper, but here it was just . . . easier to *be*.

A few days later we all piled into a carriage and set off to the city proper, each of us thrilled to get away. I got a few looks at the cane I was carrying, but it was a common enough thing, even for guys of my age, so nobody was bothered. Carrying a proper weapon was a lot less common, but nobody needed to know what was in it until, and unless, someone was getting stabbed.

We made only a few quick stops on our way, picking up things we wanted or needed. The show was today, and from the sounds of it we needed to arrive as early as possible. Of course, had we known what we were getting into, we might have tried to get in even earlier.

The city streets were packed, carriages and carts of all kinds shoved in like fish in a barrel. Some were new, some old, and some rented or hired like ours. Lots of people were walking, not even trying, and after a time, we all looked at each other.

"So, just walk then?" I asked, getting a series of nods in return. Upon telling the driver to meet us at a restaurant halfway across the city later in the evening, we hopped out. He seemed relieved. Nobody liked traffic, particularly when there were so many horses involved.

It quickly became apparent that this wasn't just the right choice, it was the only choice. Whatever this show was, it was clogging the streets of the often packed entertainment district of the city. We got closer and closer until we were finally at the place indicated, which wasn't even a proper venue.

"They're joking," Lucas said with a laugh.

"No, I don't think they are," I replied with a shake of my head.

"This is going to be something, isn't it," Reese added with a smile.

"Oh yeah," Simon agreed.

Before us there were people in the streets. One of the larger city squares had been blocked off, a building on the far side having been altered to accommodate a massive stage. The tickets were to get into the square itself, which had some seating in the form of bleacher-like additions on the sides and a large central area right in front of the raised stage.

Apparently, they'd not been able to find a big enough arena. It wasn't odd, as such things weren't as common in this world as they'd been on Earth, at least not on this island. There were a few sport fields outside the city, and a few smaller places, like where the fencing tournaments were held, but nothing like a colosseum, and that seemed to be the type of thing they needed.

Would this disturb part of the city tonight? Certainly. Were there plenty of people who were going to get a show without paying? Well, I could already see some of the nearby businesses setting up tables on their roofs to watch. Would it be awesome? I had a feeling the answer would be a resounding yes.

CHAPTER 35

✶

ENEMY

I'd never thought I'd see another rock show in this life, and to a point, I was correct. The Starchasers weren't really a rock band, but rather a group of skilled bards. Musically, however, it was something akin to folk-rock or the pagan rock bands that had existed in my previous world. A refreshing change from much of the music my family liked, which was much more . . . staid.

However, even if I wasn't quite sure where to place their style, their show was another level entirely. Two hours of nonstop illusions to go with the songs—giant battles between monsters, and spinning planets above the skyline. They'd had enough spellcasters in their troupe to bring in scents, temperature shifts, wind and, of course, a light show that would stand up to anything.

"Excellent suggestion, Reese," I said, wiping the sweat from my brow as we trotted through the city streets. Superhuman or not, a party made a man sweat.

"Agreed," Lucas said. "We should try to find more like them."

"We could try to record their music? Maybe they even do it," Simon suggested.

"Isn't that really hard?" Lucas asked.

"Don't know. You're taking that class, right, Percival?" Reese asked.

"Magic doesn't record well," I said with a shake of my head.

Magically, it was possible to make a recording, but it wasn't simple. For anything other than simple tunes of individual notes, you needed to figure out how to tell the magical item you were using exactly what sounds to make. These tended to be fraught with difficulties, and massive wastes of power.

"What about a scientific solution? You're always wandering about the Royal Society, right?" Lucas asked.

That was probably a better idea. Both phonographs and records were likely within the realm of possibility in this society already, but I didn't know how to make either of those. There were some small things like little wire radios bouncing around in my head, but nothing significant, or really useful, for transmission. That was just outside the orbit of what I understood.

"Sorry, there's surely a way, but I don't know it." I answered, shrugging. I was unable to help with this problem.

"No way the military would let them use radios either," Simon joked, and everyone looked at him with an odd glance.

Radio. That's the word he used, not some fantasy term like "far-speaker" or "talking stones" or anything like that. No, it was *radio*. There was a bit of an accent to it, but it was comprehensible.

"Which is?" I asked hopefully.

"Oh, they're not secret or anything. The military has magic items that can send sound like halfway across the country. They won't tell anyone how they work, though, so none for us. A lot like the portals."

We were closing in on the restaurant we were to meet the driver at, but before we could continue on this extremely interesting topic, there was a scream. A high-pitched wail. It sounded like a woman in distress, and after the briefest of looks at each other, we all ran forward.

Like arrows, the four of us shot through the twilight, honing, tracking, like a pack of wolves, after whatever was causing such a disturbance. This kind of thing wasn't normal, and all of us were told constantly how we must learn to defend the people. Each of us was training to become fighters, regardless of what we wanted, and today we heard a fight. Others on the street were still headed to the alley while we slipped down it at speed.

There was the briefest hesitation as our group appeared around the screaming young woman, her eyes bulging.

"My sister," she yelled, pointing at an open sewer grate. "Something grabbed my sister!"

She wasn't much to look at, with ragged clothes and a face full of scars. No, she was no high lady, no princess in distress, but it was clear she needed help. Looker or no, we weren't going to abandon her here.

With a flash of mana, I pulled my blade from the cane it rested in. Lucas drew a pair of knives from somewhere, smiling at me as he did. It seemed I wasn't the only one who'd thought to come prepared for a fight.

"Hah, nice blades," I said. "Simon, Reese, stay with her while we go after him, just in case. Lucas—"

"Not letting you go in there alone, Percival," Lucas said, cutting me off. "Let's go." He ran, leading the charge.

Most sewer lines aren't that big, with the exception of the one we found ourselves in. We dropped into the depths, landing in the filth with a pair of splashes. The smell was foul, potent, enough to make me want to vomit. From one side of the tunnel came splashes in the water as someone fled, only for the pair of us to pursue through the darkness. There was light here and there—small shafts that drifted down from above—and it was enough because of our enhanced senses, as well as the pale blue glow of my sword.

Soon we found him, for it could only be a him. Running, but slower than us was a hulk of a man, clad in a long coat and hood. I couldn't see his head, but his gait was off, his arms . . . long, like an ape. He was also massive, easily over six feet and broad like a linebacker. I couldn't place what it was about how he walked, but it was . . . wrong, like his legs were messed up somehow, like they didn't work the way they should. Over his shoulder was a sack large enough to hold a child, and that is what it almost certainly contained.

"Bastard!" Lucas shouted as he charged forward, roaring in challenge, knives leading.

The figure moved faster than any normal man, more like us. In a single move it dropped the sack and spun, hand tearing through the air like a whip and catching Lucas straight in the face.

My friend must have been as surprised as I was when the back of the hand met his jaw, sending him against the side of the sewer with a thunderous crack, and leaving him slumped there, unmoving. I heard clinking as Lucas' knives fell, slipping into the watery gunk.

"Hmm, strong. Father will want you," the figure said as he turned to Lucas.

I was briefly stunned at the words, for the creature before me looked almost like a goblin—if you fed one of the little monsters nothing but steroids, protein, and growth hormones. It could talk too. That was a completely new development.

CHAPTER 36

RETURN TO THE SURFACE

I looked at Lucas for only a second, enough to register that he was still breathing.

"You're no normal goblin," I said, hoping to provoke something.

"You know us? Very interesting. Father will definitely want you," he replied before lunging.

That first move was enough. From that alone I could tell that he was slower than me. Stronger perhaps, but slower, and untrained. My blade shone as I ducked his attempt to grab me, slicing up and into the monster's flesh. The steel moved through it without much resistance, blade shining blue before the red blood spurted outward. We each danced backward, both wary of the other. He snarled as I took my stance, ready to fight. I could see no other way out of this. Should I try to leave this creature alive? Someone would want to see it, but it was also clearly dangerous—a smart, potent monster.

"Surrender and I'll spare your life," I said, trying to keep my voice calm.

He chuckled, low and growling. "I'll offer you the same."

Fights like this couldn't go on long. We were just too deadly. One wrong move on my part and I'd be out just as sure as Lucas was. One wrong move on his and I'd put my blade into something that he couldn't survive without. At least he didn't have a weapon. He depended solely on his physical strength. I moved in, aiming high, to ram the point of my small blade into his chest, but he ducked, his longer arms aiming for my stomach. He missed by an inch, and I managed to score a deep gash into his shoulder, slicing all the way down to bone.

"Shit! Fuck shit!" he screamed as he pulled back again.

I wouldn't let up this time, taking careful, quick strikes and scoring a few more light cuts on him as he hopped backward through the sewer nearly ten feet. This was exactly where I wanted to be. He'd retreated back past the dropped sack, past Lucas' unconscious body. There was, however, another problem.

"You speak English?" I asked, realizing what those curses had been.

"What?" he asked in the native tongue, confused at what I'd said, and quite angry at what I'd done.

"English?" I asked again.

"Screw you," he replied in the native tongue again, seeming to realize where we were now standing.

I kept both my stance and my face as firm as I could. He was odd, too odd. There were too many oddities for me, and I didn't like it. My opponent, however, kept moving back, farther and farther.

"Not coming?" he asked. "All done?"

I didn't reply, but I was. The injured were far more important to me than this creature, and he seemed to know it, to sense it. I didn't move until he was well around the nearest bend in the sewer, turning and running at the last moment with a snarl. I waited longer, making sure he was well and truly away before I carefully sliced open the bag, revealing a still breathing girl inside. She was dazed, but hopefully she'd be okay. Lucas, on the other hand, was still out cold—never a good sign.

As gently as I could, I gathered up the fallen humans and began to retreat back to the sewer grate we'd entered through, though I didn't make it all the way before I was met with others. Other men had heard the call to arms, and a few brave ones had made their way down. Most were older, with beards and fearful looks as I moved out of the shadows, bloody blade still in hand.

"Who goes?" one of them shouted, trying to bring up a lantern of some kind.

"I'm one of the ones who went after the child. She lives, as does my companion, but both need aid, and we need the authorities."

"Good, lad," said an older, balding man as he came forward to grab the girl, another helping me with Lucas so I could put away my sword.

"Eyes sharp. The monster escaped," I informed them.

"Damn," one of them cursed. "Looks like you stuck it at least."

I laughed at that.

Twenty minutes later I sat, going over the story to a pair of policemen in dark black uniforms. A healer, a local priest, in fact, had been summoned, and the sister who'd called for help was holding her sibling, who was now awake and bawling incoherently. Lucas was taking more time to come around, and both of us were covered in filth. My outfit was ruined as far as I was concerned.

"A goblin?" the officer asked me for about the fourth time. "Some kind of green manlike beast?"

"Very manlike," I nodded. "It could talk."

"You sure it wasn't just some ruffian, lad? Kidnappings may be a bit rare, but . . . well, monstrous men do sometimes take little girls . . ."

"Boy's a bit young to talk to him about that, yeah?" the other said, looking like I might not know what he meant.

"Not that young, and not a fool. That was no man, and if you're unbelieving, get the healer there to examine this." I held up my blade. "Soon as he's done with my friend, of course."

"Sure, son, we'll do just that." Somehow I doubted they were taking this nearly as seriously as I was. Or perhaps they thought I was just mistaken. A kidnapper would be easier for their reports than an intelligent monster. It would also keep the papers quiet, something police everywhere were keen on.

My thoughts were confirmed when the man took a cloth and wiped the sword clean "for evidence" and put the rag in his pocket. Would it end up getting tested? I honestly didn't know, but it didn't matter. I was going to see to it that someone at least heard the truth, even if I had to pull out all the stops to do it.

Sadly, when he was finally awake, Lucas couldn't confirm my story. He'd not gotten a good look before he was knocked out. He described what looked like a massive man in a coat and hood. That was all I could hear from a distance while he was being interviewed. I wanted to scream.

At least the locals managed to find us some clean clothes and water to rinse ourselves off before we were released. The four of us may not have been residents of this area, but the screaming woman who'd attracted us eventually calmed down enough to explain that we'd come to her aid, not as part of the kidnapping. That in conjunction with our social statuses was enough to see us released. The fact that I'd come back with the girl in hand almost certainly helped a lot too. Kidnappers weren't known to return their victims. I saw the investigator hand over the bloody cloth to the priest as we walked away. A small miracle. Maybe they could confirm my story, and we could get a proper hunt for that abomination underway.

CHAPTER 37

★

THE INQUIRER

The next couple of hours were rather hectic. I began by writing letters. Writing letters was easy and could get people who were inclined to believe me to do so. Perhaps the local police would not. Perhaps they'd insist that I'd been seeing things or that there were no monsters in the sewers. Honestly, I didn't know, and it didn't matter because there were, and I knew at the very least my grandpa wouldn't turn his back on me. He knew how serious monsters were. He'd seen a goblin, albeit a very different one, and he'd taken that seriously enough. He would help. That meant that I, of course, had to inform my parents, as well, for their peace of mind, if nothing else. Our group had met up outside a nearby restaurant and, sadly, nobody was in the mood to eat; nor were we allowed in. Half of our party was rather foul smelling and quite under-dressed for the occasion. After managing to get ahold of our carriage, we'd returned to the school early, me to my letters and the other boys to meet with their friends and regale them with the story of the incident.

While I was writing, I was interrupted several times by curious students eager to hear about the monster I'd faced. Even if it had come to naught, I'd still gone up against something most of them foolishly dreamed of, something they'd love to pit themselves against to test their mettle. I'm not sorry to say that my dry, almost clinical telling of it didn't really thrill them, but it did make them pay attention, which was what I wanted. I received a lot more attention, too, when I was pulled out of civics class, one of my favorite subjects, the very next morning. Headmaster Logan wanted to see me, in his office this time, not a dojo, and I was not alone. All four of us were marched in before the bear of a man and ushered to sit. The headmaster took a seat in a high-backed chair behind his desk.

The office was, in a word, *neat*. There was not a speck of dust to be found, not a paper out of place. Everything had its place, and each place had its thing. Stacks of documents, all with edges perfectly aligned were upon his desk, books lined up like soldiers on shelves, titles and dates shining. Only one thing seemed not to belong, a lanky man in a black suit in the corner.

"Allow me to make sure that I understand things correctly, for mis-understanding leads to misaligned results," the ruler of this school declared. "The four of you heard a screaming woman and decided to take it upon yourselves to investigate?"

"Yes, sir," we chorused.

"Upon finding a girl and learning of a kidnapping, you two"—he indicated the pair in question—"remained with her, while you"—he indicated Lucas and myself this time—"went to attempt to stop the kidnapping in question?"

"Yes, sir," we said again.

"You had no aid should something go awry, no way to get any, no idea what you were getting yourselves into. I may add that that nearly got one of you killed and the other taken. Yet you charged forward, with hardly a thought."

Our group awaited his next words, not one of us looking away. I wouldn't have done anything differently, and if I knew my friends, they felt similarly. We'd done the right thing, and his tone implied we were wrong for it. We were not wrong, and I wouldn't bow under any pressure for that.

"I'm quite proud of you," he finally announced with an almost, but not quite, smile. "Execution needs work, but we can, and will, improve that. Without the gumption to step forward, we get nowhere. I'll be arranging some extra training as a reward. Simon, Reese, you are dismissed."

After it was ascertained that he'd seen nothing, Lucas, too, was sent out, leaving only myself, the headmaster, and the unknown man.

"Let us hear what happened," the headmaster said, and once more I repeated my story, blow for blow. I had a pretty good memory, and this I'd seared into it. It was too important. When I was done the headmaster looked at the other man, who stepped forward.

"Good afternoon, young lord Percival. First, please allow me to introduce myself. My name is Ignus, an investigator in the service of His Grace, the duke."

"A pleasure to meet you, sir," I said with a nod.

"And you, young man. Now, we saw that sample of blood you brought back, and I can agree that it is certainly not human, whatever it is. It has been sent off for experts to look at, but for the moment, please stop," he said, firmly.

"Stop?" I asked.

"Yes, stop trying to convince people of what you saw, and with these, if you will." He held up a number of envelopes that I recognized. It wasn't lost on me that they were opened either.

"You read my mail," I nearly yelled, scandalized.

"As part of my duties, yes. Something I don't regret and will do again if needed. The situation is . . . delicate, and must be handled as such."

I stood, struggling to resist the urge to strike the man. "You're hiding it? The fact that there are dangerous monsters in the city? How many people will you let get kidnapped? How many will disappear and never return?" I said through gritted teeth.

"We are hiding that you suspect—and we are concerned— that there may be intelligent monsters about. If it stays a rumor, that is that, but if it becomes published, there will be a panic and that helps no one." With a placating hand he stopped me from speaking. "That does not mean, however, that we're not taking the situation seriously."

"Taking it seriously? By what, letting people get taken?" I said, accusingly.

"No, by scouring the city sewers and tunnels that we can and increasing the guard patrols significantly. This evening the papers will also have an article about an unknown kidnapper capable of using physical type magic. I will do what I must to avoid a panic, but that doesn't mean leaving people to themselves." He wasn't being completely unreasonable there.

"And if I refuse to stop telling people what I saw?" I asked.

"I will do what I must to avoid a panic." At my look he continued. "Goodness, boy, I'm not going to have you killed. How unneeded would that be? But I can see to it that you're sent back to your family's country estate, and that you remain there for a time. I can also have you restricted to the school if I feel that will work, and left unable to spread worry. In time, the truth will come out, but for now, until we know more, keep yourself reserved. I'd express concern about the other boys, but they didn't see anything themselves. You don't even need to lie, just refuse to talk about it."

I narrowed my eyes at him. "Fine, for now. However, if I don't think you're taking this seriously, or if I don't see that warning in the papers, I'll make you regret it." Nothing said panic like pamphlets released from a drone, something I could definitely manage if I wanted to burn some bridges.

He laughed and looked at the headmaster. "See why you like this one, old friend. I believe he'd actually do it."

"I would," I confirmed.

"Well then, I best go and keep my word, shouldn't I? Just see to it you do the same, and we'll have no issues at all." With that he left.

CHAPTER 38

✳

EMERGENCY MEASURES

Mr. Ignus was as good as his word, and when I got hold of a paper the next morning, I found within it that there was in fact a headline about an attempted kidnapping. Rather than saying what I knew it was, however, there was simply a confirmation that the assailant was unknown, seemingly a physical magic user, and should be regarded with extreme caution. There were also some notes about searches for the individual in question and the increased security in Exion as a whole.

This, of course, stirred up the student body something fierce. Normally one wouldn't associate high-school aged kids with reading the paper, but with no social media or video games it was, oddly, a popular thing to do. Before lunch I was inundated with requests to tell my story once more. Everyone who'd heard it already was spinning wilder and wilder tales, and each was being traced back to me.

"I'm sorry, but I'd rather not talk about that," I said for what had to be the twelfth time that day. If Mr. Ignus was going to keep his word, I could at least manage to do the same, for now.

"Aw, come on, you were telling people about it the other day," one boy complained, only to back off when I fixed him with a hard stare. "My apologies," he said, retreating.

It seemed I'd gotten a bit of a reputation as well. Lucas was known to the student body as a combat-obsessed maniac who trained almost constantly. There were those stronger than him, those faster, and a few who were no less dedicated, but he had a reputation as being very good. To hear that I, a new student with only a few fencing tourney titles under my belt, had driven off a monster that he openly admitted had thoroughly trounced him was a bit of a surprise to them.

That led people to pay a lot more attention to me than before. Between that and the incident on the first day, I was building a very serious reputation among my fellows as someone to be watched. It all seemed a bit silly to me; I didn't do anything most of them couldn't. That fight was difficult, but approached cautiously half the school should have been able to survive, and that was all I did. Had I not had the blade my father gave me, I would have been in deep trouble.

That reminded me, and I quickly rewrote the letters to my family. I told them the basics that were publicly available, and that I would give them the full story in time. I wasn't planning to hide it from them. If the duke wanted it kept quiet, they'd probably not oppose, so long as he acted, which he was. My parents would also demand a full account from me when next we met, and I had no delusions that they'd accept anything less. Mother could sniff out deception like a bloodhound when she wanted to, and hiding this would only damage her trust in me.

Sasha

Half of the warren was in a state after brother Sigmund's return. He'd arrived moments ago, sliced up like he'd been in a fight and without anything to show for his trip away other than the injury. It had been bound, poorly, but enough to at least staunch the flow while I saw to him.

"Where is Father?" he asked as I tried to patch together his wound.

"Deeper, of course," I answered, as if it wasn't obvious.

"Met someone, he got away," Sigmund said, not having led with that.

One of my younger cousins, one of the smarter ones, was nearby, and I turned to him. "Get Father and Greta now!" He scampered off at speed as I sent a wave of power down the tunnel, looking for any blood that might have spilled. Even a single drop was too much, and I used my magic to scour them, and everything about him that I could—his smell, hairs, and the like—away.

Sister arrived first, looking confused that I'd called for her in such a hurry.

"What do you need, Sasha?" she asked, looking at our injured brother.

"Seal it." She blinked at my nod toward the entrance, but she was smarter than the rest of us and soon picked up what I wanted.

As the one in charge of the entrance to the nest, I could make this decision to close the door and seal it. Long ago, Father had told us that a time may come when the humans came for us, and we'd prepared for it. At first the plans had been simple, but with her constant tinkering Greta had come up with a mechanism that worked into the opening, moving stones to place so well that it became nearly seamless with the outside tunnel. Sadly, it was very fragile, and without her I had no confidence I could make it work on my own.

Within moments she had it going. It was loud, louder than I would've liked, but with a few flicks of her fingers the noise subsided. When it was done there was a mess of gears and rods on our side, but the other side would be a blank section of wall, nothing obvious to anyone who came looking.

We were still getting people and things into place while the rest of the nest went into emergency mode. It took time to spread, but cousins and siblings were moving now, aware that something had gone wrong. As often happened, I saw the magic before Father appeared, approaching us in a hurry.

"What has happened, daughter?" he asked, knowing that I was the one who'd triggered this.

"Sigmund was seen and injured by one who got away," I said, before my brother could answer for me.

"Explain," he said to Sigmund's hulking form.

"Was taking human, like you said. Got attacked by two, fast and strong, took one down, other had blade. Retreated to let you know." That last part was tacked on in a hurry, and I wasn't the only one who recognized it.

"Don't lie to me, boy," Father hissed, causing a flinch among us all. "You ran because he sliced you up, and good thing. Someone getting hold of you would be a problem." He turned cursing. "Fuck, shit, fuck, we need to be careful."

"Father," Sigmund said, earning a glare that made him shrink back. "What is inngalish?"

Father froze, looking intensely at our brother. It was as if he'd seen something he never expected, as if he knew something big had just happened, but wasn't sure where to go with it.

"Where did you hear that word, son," he asked calmly, the most dangerous emotion coming from Father, and one we all knew well.

"The one who cut me," Sigmund explained carefully. "I spoke like you do when you're mad and he said 'Eww undastan inngalish?' to me. Then when I asked him what, he repeated it 'inngalish' again."

"Sasha, are all of our outgoing parties accounted for?" he asked, turning to me.

"Yes, Father, everyone is back," I confirmed, having always kept track of who was where.

"Good, watch the door. Sigmund, come with me. You will tell me everything." With those words, he took my brother, seeming to care not at all about anything else.

CHAPTER 39

✴

EXTRA CLASSES

With an upward twist I caught the incoming blade, trying, and failing to toss it from my opponent's hand with a turn of the wrist, but succeeding in making him hop back. The buckler strapped to my arm might have been small, but it was perfect for what I was doing—quick to move, quick to strike, and not cumbersome in the slightest.

"You think you can win?" the other boy asked with a scoff.

"Who said anything about winning? You're the last group in the area," I pointed out.

In an instant I saw his eyes widen and he turned. It was about that time that Lucas' group sent up the flare indicating that the package had been delivered. While my opponent muttered something under his breath, I stepped forward, the shortsword in my hand flashing as it struck up and into his chest, right where his heart would be. There was a brief flash of light from his armor.

"You're out," an automated voice informed him.

"Honestly? You didn't need to do that," he complained to me.

"Game's not over until everyone is back at base," I retorted as I moved to leave, something he certainly already knew.

There was a bit of cleanup afterward, but for the most part we were done. The survivors all wanted to make it back; at this juncture, deaths lost each team points. Perhaps the other team could have been spiteful and tried to take as many of us as they could, but they really didn't want to lose any of their people.

My group was composed of four older students and myself, and we flew through the mock battleground, legs pumping as we tried to make our way back home. They'd been near the building I was in and had joined up at the rendezvous right as I got there. Before we made it there, a retort sounded and something small whizzed by the leader's head.

"Did nobody kill that bleeding sniper?" he asked all of us.

"Appears not," I responded. "Want to?"

"No, half the time they trap their nests, and we've already won. Just keep the sight lines closed from him and move fast."

The sniper in question was probably just a normal soldier, non-magical. There were rules on how we had to deal with them, so we didn't accidentally injure or kill one. It was excellent real-world experience for both sides to face off against something they might see on a battlefield.

The area wasn't large or anything, only a few square blocks, with towers, houses, and the like. These buildings had been raised by magic, and were completely unsuitable for long-term living, but as a practice arena they served a lot of purposes. Mages got a chance to work on making things from the surrounding countryside, such as complex structures that could be used as rudimentary bases in wartime. The students and soldiers, however, got a free working area that nobody cared if they destroyed. Rendering these into rubble was just another chance for some wizard to learn to put buildings back together in case of disaster, natural or otherwise.

When we finally returned I was pleased to see most of us had made it. There were five or so boys running laps around the camp, indicating their "deaths," but that was a good result. They looked miserable. Superhuman or not, it was boring and tiring work running around the camp for hours; and, since they'd ostensibly already given their reports on what had happened, they'd be at it for hours more. Our headmaster didn't want us to die intentionally, so he made sure we hated it when we fell.

As soon as we made it to the command tent we were, for the most part, done, being handed a small packet of paperwork to fill out on what happened, with whom, where, why, and how. We were supposed to do all of this immediately, while our memories were still fresh, then after some rest go over it all and point out places where we succeeded or failed, and why we thought it happened the way it did. All of that was part of our grading for these exercises.

Lucas would be a while yet, but Simon and Reese flopped down beside me when they arrived.

"Remind me to never help anyone ever again," the former complained.

"I'll second that," the latter agreed.

"Don't complain, boys," came a voice I was quite familiar with, "or do you not realize what a boon this could be to you?" Professor Killic slowly approached, smiling.

"Honestly, sir, the only thing I feel like I'm gaining is soreness," Reese griped.

"There are dozens of men here—generals, captains of various industries, and exploratory companies. You know what they're doing? Scouting for talent. These extra sessions may seem harsh to you, but you're getting better at working in groups, understanding things from multiple levels. Keep at it and you're sure to get their attention."

He wasn't wrong, but we were still tired. The headmaster had promised us extra lessons, and he'd delivered. Our little group of four was now in every practical he could fit into our schedules without taking us out of any of our regular classes. I'm sure that he viewed this as a reward, but it honestly felt equally like punishment.

"We're still tired, Professor," I informed him.

"Understandably. Actually, Percival, I was hoping to have a word with you."

After sharing a confused look with my friends, I moved to join Professor Killic as he walked from the tent. He was here as one of our advisors, overseeing things like resources, plans, and the like, even if he didn't contribute anything to the students in leadership positions unless they asked.

"What's this about, sir?" I asked as we walked.

"I can't help but notice that you seem to find combat rather unenjoyable," he observed.

"Not something I mind, and I do understand the need for us to learn it. You are right, though; it's not exactly a passion of mine."

"Professor Ruian tells me that you're rather enjoying her class, though, and recently something interesting has come up. There's an opportunity for an observer on a small transport mission involving some rather specialized magical items. You'd have to make up the classes and work hard to keep out of trouble, but I thought you might enjoy it."

"They're allowing students on this too?" I asked.

"Practical education, and only for one leg of the trip. You'll mostly just be watching the real soldiers as they bring things in, but they travel close to where your family lives, and you're doing well enough to miss a couple of lectures without a problem. Are you interested?"

"Certainly!" I answered, excited to be out of class for any reason. Most of them were rather boring.

"All right then," he said, chuckling. "Our esteemed headmaster thought you would say yes."

CHAPTER 40

PREPARATION

I had a couple of weeks until my field trip, and during that time my teachers seemed driven to make sure that I was going to stay up to speed. This in conjunction with the extra lessons that the headmaster had foisted upon us meant that my nose was firmly to the grindstone. Basically, I worked all day until I fell into bed heavily at the end of the day, too tired to do anything else.

It was in the evening one night, as I lay there exhausted, that I realized this, too, was a test. Our headmaster had seen me take a leading role in some incident twice, and twice I'd succeeded. I was winning, and doing so well. Now he was giving me a chance at a special event, where I would be seen by potentially important people. If I understood his intent, he wanted to make sure that I didn't disappoint.

Well, I'd never been one to take a challenge lightly, so when I woke up the next morning, I went right back to the grind with fervor. From nearly the moment I woke up, I pulled my books in close to begin tearing my way through the homework and reading. I was fast, and my memory was sharper than it had been my first time through life. Each passage caused me to struggle, but they got me that much closer to victory.

As I went through classes that day, my teachers seemed to notice, too, that even though I had to listen to what they were saying, I was pouring over other things too. Professor Killic saw me and smiled, for he recognized the look on my face.

"How are you proceeding, Percival?" he asked after class had let out. I had a little bit of a break before my next one and didn't see any reason to move when I had plenty I could do here, right now.

"Well enough, Professor. If all goes to schedule, I'll be ready well before it is time to leave," I assured him.

"Good, good, just so long as your work doesn't suffer, I foresee no issues. Your last essay was a bit interesting, a pure voting model with everyone equal. Similar systems are used for smaller villages and the like, but postulating what a society would look like if it were universal is interesting."

"Doesn't take much sir; it would fail," I answered.

"Yes, yes, the inherent issue of the powerful refusing to allow themselves to be lowered to the same level as the weak. I cannot see a potent mage accepting something like that," he said, nodding.

"Even before that, sir, a pure democratic system fails. People are reactive, and far too much so. If everything can be voted on, then they will strip the rights from those they dislike and unbalance it quickly. There has to be a theoretical backbone, something difficult or impossible to destroy that protects everyone," I explained. The difference between a republic and a pure democracy was important.

"Even those you dislike, the disgusting and horrid?" he asked, posing an old argument.

"Especially them, sir. So long as they remain within the strictures of the law, they must be free to be wrong. Without that how will we ever truly know and dismantle their views?"

He laughed. "Percival, one day I think you'll be a man to watch. Perhaps I disagree with you on some things, but do you know how many your age actually think about what they believe? Ah, it is refreshing."

I held out a few papers for him. "Well, then I think you'll enjoy these. I've only got two more left that you've assigned me."

Working on my core, and getting it done would have been amazing, but sadly, there really wasn't enough time. There was only one way to do it, with no shortcuts for me, and that way involved hour after hour of meditation. Professor Ruian was, of course, fully in support of me trying, but understood that it wasn't feasible. She made up for this by giving me extra homework—the local form of coding.

There was no case for me being a computer scientist, but I'd worked with machines enough that I quickly made my way through it. We were still on the basics—how to do the simplest of functions and make the simplest of things. There was a lot to it, after all, but that came in time. First, one had to build the foundations. While I was unfamiliar with the particular language, the experience did at least give me a head start.

Surely there were more records of that ancient elven king who'd created the cores. Perhaps one day I'd travel to those ancestral lands and learn more about him, more about both where my family came from and someone whom I was almost certain must be another interworld traveler. The only thing tempering that was that Grandpa was from Elazia and never spoke of it. That was odd, as older people did tend to reminisce, but he didn't, not at all.

Putting those thoughts aside, I continued with my work, with the exercises, the classes on combat, math, science, and the like. All the extra war games we had to do seemed natural as I focused everything I had into getting ready, being where I needed to be. I had no illusions that if the staff didn't think I was ready, they'd deny me this chance.

Before I knew it, the day had come. It would be a short trip, and I'd packed all I would need days beforehand—uniforms and underclothes. I was in the dorm room buttoning my uniform jacket when a visitor walked in. Headmaster Logan wasn't one to wait for anyone in a place where he was permitted to be and had stepped into my room like he owned the place, looking around at how I'd set things up. At least it was clean, rather than the disaster that I normally kept. A small amount of foresight that I'd be away making me pick up the clutter and the mess.

"Acceptable," he declared, seeming to want to add "barely" onto the end, but withholding it.

"Sir," I said in greeting.

"At ease," he said. "I've merely come to give you a final once-over and issue you your weapon for this operation." At my look of confusion he held forth a sword, a proper war weapon, like the ones we used during training. "That cane of yours may be a good sidearm but you'll be acting as a guard, trainee or not, and you must carry a proper blade. This is your responsibility, and it will be returned to me in good condition, or I will have a full accounting."

I gulped as I took it, having never been actual military in my previous life, but having heard the horror stories of what happened when a man lost the weapon he'd received from friends. There was no doubt in my mind that if I returned without this sword, I might as well find another to throw myself upon.

"Understood, sir" were the words that finally made it to my lips as I gripped the hilt of the sword. I knew it was enchanted, probably with the standard issue spells. I could feel the magic flowing into it ever so slightly.

"Good, now let's go."

I picked up my bags and followed after him as he marched toward the front of the campus. It was odd, leaving this place again. For weeks, I'd been here without a break, not really having time for any more trips to the city, and soon after I got back, it would be time for our yearly break. For now, though, I was heading toward a new destination, to meet with others and show off the merits of our school. Would there be others like me there? Other youths pulled into this? Or would I be alone in this?

CHAPTER 41

✶

WORLDSINGERS

As the carriage rolled up, I noticed the docks were empty. That was odd. The docks never shut down, not for anything, not for anyone. Suddenly, I began to wonder exactly what I'd gotten into. The only people around were the guards, and while there weren't many, they all looked like they meant business.

I quickly dismounted with a few of the locals who'd been sent in as backup for the current guards on duty. They quickly made their way to the current guards and relieved them; they had clearly done this before.

"C'mere, lad," said a tall, gangly man in armor. "Yer with me for this shift," He appeared to be in charge of this little expedition.

"Yes, sir, I'm Percival, Percival Sh—" I began before being rudely cut off.

"Don't care. What I care about is you pointing out anything odd you see. Questions?"

"Are we expecting trouble, sir?" I asked.

"Not as such, but can never be too careful. I'm Grawlin, by the way, and I'll be with you till your babysitters show up." Grawlin had to be either a nickname or a surname, because nobody would name their child such.

"Understood."

It was hours, hours of boring looking around before anything happened, and then I saw it. Slowly moving out through the fog was a ship, not a transport, or a cargo ship, but a warship. On its decks were half a dozen guns, mounted on structures that clearly turned, but not as smoothly as the old battleships from Earth, the sides covered in iron. It also had no smokestack to speak of, which meant that it was running entirely on magic, or some engine that I didn't know about. Perhaps both. That kind of military technology was often kept secret, and for good reason, as we weren't the only country around.

The ship was achingly slow for its size, smaller than most of the boats used in shipping either goods or people, but who knew how fast it could go if needed. Regardless, the crew didn't seem bothered, allowing it to slowly drift up to the dock.

Lines were thrown, tied, and checked, and finally the gangplank descended. The first off were two people dressed in mage robes, eyes peeled as they came up to where Grawlin and I stood. In the lead was a man with dark blond hair and a smirk, and behind him was a girl who was slightly younger, with brown, mousey locks and large glasses.

"Ah, the big city," the leader said as he approached us, taking a deep breath. "Smells like shit."

It was a struggle not to laugh, but honestly he was right. Exion always had a potent stench, even if you got used to it, and if anything, the docks were the worst. There really was no escaping the smell so long as one was outside, and while most people learned to ignore it, you could never forget it.

"You done playing around?" asked Grawlin, grumpily.

"He's never done playing around," the woman responded. "You must be Mr. Grawlin, and you are?" Her voice was strict, like a displeased matron, as she looked at me.

"Percival Shadestone, ma'am. My school sent me to observe."

"Wonderful, another child to babysit," she replied smoothly.

I took some offense to that. This woman didn't know me, didn't know how I'd managed to handle myself up until now. No, she just assumed. Also, I was growing quite nicely and would soon be an adult man, if a young one.

"Don't let Saya get to you, kid; she got herself tied in a knot at the age of two and has never loosened up. Let your big brother Walter show you around." He didn't even wait for confirmation, instead wrapping an arm around my shoulder and pulling me back to the ship. "Let's leave them to fight over who should be in charge while we oversee the actual work, huh? Got to unload everything and have it ready quick as possible. Oh, by the way, can you sing?"

Walter, for that seemed to be his name, rambled quickly the whole way back to the warship, just enough to drown out his partner's angry retorts in the background. He even sang a bit when she started to yell. Of course, I had questions of my own.

"So . . . do I get to know who you two are?" I asked.

"Hm? Oh sure, we're Worldsingers, kid. Here to deliver some goods to some of the local cities. Can't tell you what those are, but suffice to say we need not screw it up." He led me across the deck, soldiers ignoring my presence since I was with him.

"And you're not going to question that I am who I say I am at all?" I asked. It seemed that he was being awfully trusting for someone on a secret mission.

"Hmm? How many kids your age with your aura and a few drops of elven blood are there around here, you think?" I froze. Not many people could tell the latter, but any spellcaster could see my aura. "Saya's good at her job, but don't forget I am too," he said, his voice going flat for a second. "See, I actually read all the files, all the write-ups, all the descriptions, and I remember them. Did you think that little song back there was for nothing? No, that's what I needed for a full exam on you."

"That's . . ." I hadn't even noticed the magic, didn't even feel it.

He slapped me on the back, laughing. "Don't worry, Percival, just follow my instructions and we'll get along just fine."

We watched as the crew unloaded two large crates, covered in runes and obviously magical items, into a pair of waiting carriages. He went on and on about the city, the smell, the long trip. I was more interested in the cranes, which looked to be entirely mechanical and of a design I'd not seen before. They had a weird looking ratcheting device on them, the internals hidden behind a steel plate I wanted to pry off.

It was as they were lowering it that something caught my eye. A tiny red glow from one of the pipes leading into the harbor, just a flash, a moment, there and gone again.

"See something, kid?" Walter asked, noticing my focus change.

"Thought I saw a red light in the tunnel over there," I replied, pointing.

"Thought you saw, or did see?"

"Did see," I said uncertain.

With a nod, several guards, themselves physical magic users like me, surged toward the tunnel, blades in hand and rifles on their backs. These guys weren't playing. They charged in with abandon.

"What are you doing?" Saya said, marching up to us. The work had stopped, all the men instead arming themselves and looking about.

"Something in the outlet over there," I nodded forward, hand on my own blade.

"Something? What something?"

"Not sure, but we've had some issues with the sewers lately, stuff going on that shouldn't," I replied, having been there for one of those incidents personally. The two newcomers didn't seem to have gotten that memo, though, and looked at me strangely.

"Kid's right, some band of criminals, was in the papers a bit ago," Grawlin muttered, having wandered over with Saya.

Before I could tell them that they were monsters, not men, the guards returned.

"Nothing, sir," the leader said with a shrug.

"Any sign?" Walter asked.

"In a sewer? Can't smell a thing, and the water keeps any prints from even forming."

"On alert then," Saya said, looking at him. "I'll handle the unloading while you keep watch."

"I'll let my men know too," Grawlin grumped before moving off.

Once Grawlin was out of earshot, I looked at Walter. "Monsters in the sewers, not men. City's keen to hide it though," I whispered.

"Thanks for the heads up, but monsters, men, doesn't matter. These goods are getting where they're going."

CHAPTER 42

✦

CARRIAGE ROBBERY

The carriage rocked and swayed. I wasn't allowed in the back with the goods, but I'd at least managed to get a seat inside rather than outside. Maybe because the two in charge liked me, maybe because I was young, maybe just because they expected something and didn't want me in the way.

"Should I prepare for an imminent attack?" I asked, hoping to get some information.

"Be ready, but we're not expecting one," answered Walter. "Nobody should be after a standard delivery of magic items."

I looked back at the large crates. Maybe I'd never seen what a standard one was, but that didn't look anything like standard.

"Standard?" I asked incredulously.

"You're too perceptive for your own good, kid."

There was silence for a time, just the noise of wheels on the stone cobbles and the slight shake of the vehicle as we passed through streets. Outside, people moved about, our guard before and behind keeping people at bay, but no more than someone carrying a bank's money would.

"Don't suppose you'll tell me where we're going?" I asked. I'd deliberately not been told.

"Suppose I can. The first stop will be the Ducal residence, then we're heading north. The location doesn't have an address, and isn't really near any cities, but it's between two little hamlets called Riverside, and Old Hill."

Much like in my previous world, a lot of people named towns after local formations. However, in this one, and this island in particular, since it was so newly settled, the language hadn't drifted far enough to make those names no longer common words.

"And what are we doing there?" I inquired.

"You're doing nothing but guarding and keeping an eye on things. Well, not even that; you're just watching," he answered. "We will be doing some work that you don't need to know about. I'd suggest getting used to that because if you ever become a soldier, you'll get a lot of missions that you'll only be told what you need to know about."

"Fair enough."

His partner was outside with the rest of the guards, doing . . . whatever it was she did. Many of the mages had their own spells and abilities, and while there was some attempt at standardization, most people supposedly found them difficult to reproduce time and time again. This meant that each mage had their own repertoire. While some might be similar, many of them, like the nice lady with us, did things their own way. I had taken up a spot by one of the windows, looking out. Minutes rolled by, the city bustling outside, dilapidated buildings slowly passing us by. I could have fallen asleep had I not been a "guard," but as my mind wandered, something occurred to me.

"Hey, Walter, we're going to the Ducal residence, right?" I asked.

"Yeah."

"Why is our route taking us halfway across the city?"

His eyes widened, and he began to sing without answering. Crap, that was an answer in itself. I tried to get into a fighting position as half a dozen spells flared to life around us. Walter smashed some button on the seat before him. As far as I could tell, it didn't do what it was supposed to do because of what his song became.

"Oh bugger all, oh bugger all!" he loudly proclaimed, melodic in the local tongue.

The carriage, which had until this point been moving at a rather sedate pace, lurched and sprung forward. Whoever was driving was pushing the horses hard, and I had to alter positions to grab the singing/screaming mage and keep him from being thrown about too roughly.

As we braced ourselves inside, I could hear things going on outside, shouting and multiple explosions. Those were met with a stream of gunshots and the screams of horses and humans. As we were tossed, the echoing panic seeped through the carriage walls and dampened whatever spells Walter was trying to throw up.

I was still trying to assess threats, almost blind as I was and stuck in a box, when there was a series of thumps and the carriage began to quickly slow itself.

"The horses were loosed and brakes put on. Get ready, kid!"

No argument there, I did exactly as he said, my sword slipping from the sheath with a hiss. Seconds ticked by, and I had no idea what was going on. There were people all around us. I could hear them in front and behind, but the windows were facing nothing but what looked like an alleyway. There was a lot of movement at the back, near the cargo doors, so I tensed, ready for when they opened.

They didn't open. They flew away. Some enterprising person had hooked them to a chain up and ripped them off. That shouldn't have worked. I wasn't an expert on carts like this, but I did know they were supposed to be hard nuts to crack.

Then it all clicked—the weak doors, the failed emergency button, the fact that we were where they wanted us. We'd been betrayed, by someone with quite a lot of access. This was confirmed when I saw half a dozen men in the open space wearing rudimentary gas masks.

Drugs had long been a way to disable enemy mages. For as long as anyone could remember, just about the only way to bring down a mage without killing them, and often one of the more convenient ways anyway, was some form of toxin. I had to assume that was what was in the canisters the masked men were now tossing into the carriage.

Sealing my nose and mouth, I charged. Could I have cut through some, or maybe even most of the canisters? Sure, but it would have been a waste. Instead, I went after what looked like the leader of the group.

"Damn!" I heard the familiar voice of the man I'd met earlier. What was his name? Grimclaw? Grimaw? Something like that, didn't really matter at this point.

A blast of noise came from behind me, slamming into some of the others as I flew like a rocket, blade leading. The traitor tried and failed to move some weapon before himself, but he was too predictable. Half a year ago that might have stopped me, but with a tiny adjustment to the angle, I delivered a crippling blow to his chest, cutting right through his leather armor like butter.

Turning, I saw one of the men raise and fire a shotgun-looking implement at Walter, though I didn't see the result. As I leapt for him, one of the others kicked me hard into the edge of the carriage door.

The door hinges may have been weakened, but the structure was most certainly not, and I hit it hard. That alone wasn't enough to stop me, but it did make me gasp instinctually, filling my lungs with whatever poison they'd concocted.

Kicker stepped up to the plate again. Sadly for him, even the best and strongest of drugs took time, enough time for me to slice up and into the meat of his calf and send him screaming backward. Some people had to learn to play nice the hard way.

I tried to rise, but there was a *BOOM*, and I felt myself pushed back, back and falling again. As I lay there, one man was above me with another weapon, before his fellow pushed him.

"Forget the kid; get the portals, you idiot!" he said, keeping his compatriot from finishing me off.

Pain flared in my stomach, and the world began to spin. I tried to get up, tried to raise my sword, but my muscles just wouldn't respond. As they pulled the box from the carriage, I could do nothing but watch helplessly from the pavement.

Time seemed to get a bit wonky, and I knew not if I lay there for seconds, minutes, or hours before something descended from above.

Immediately, I recognized her. Panic washed across her face, a very cute face. Her hair was everywhere, dress stained with red. How odd. I wondered if she'd gotten paint on it somehow.

"Walter!" she screamed, looking around before seeing him in the carriage then looking to me. "Kid, it's gonna be all right. I'm going to get a healer."

"You're cute," I responded drunkenly. That's the only sentence that my brain was forming at the moment.

She rose to do something, who knew what, and my head lolled to the side. There was another girl there, in a drain opening of all places. She was also cute, if kind of green looking, and wearing the silliest big red goggles with lenses all over them. They looked like part of a steam-punk outfit, like something from a movie. I wanted to ask her if she was a cosplayer or going to a convention and tried to wave, but my noodle arms wouldn't move. Sadly, it was rude to talk to girls you weren't introduced to. My mother had told me that a lot, so I just smiled for a moment before falling to sleep.

CHAPTER 43

✳

HOSPITAL VISIT

I awoke with pain radiating outward from my gut. The room was unfamiliar. The bed, the walls, and all around me there were curtains and people talking. As the fog cleared, it was apparent that I was in some kind of hospital ward, though I didn't know quite where. With a groan I tried to rise and look around more but found it rather difficult. A matronly woman quickly poked her head through the curtain, looking down at me.

"Lay back down this instant, young man," she demanded.

"I'm alive and have clearly been seen by a healer. I'm sure I'll survive. More importantly, where are my companions?" My comment drew a guffaw from a woman by the door.

From her attire, it was clear she was associated with a temple, probably the Shield, but not a main priest. Rather, she appeared to be a helper of some kind, in this case a nurse at the hospital. The temples ran all the hospitals, primarily because they monopolized the priests to an insane extent. There were laws about it and everything.

"Statements like that are why foolish young blowhards end up spending far longer in recovery."

"You didn't answer my question."

Her face softened, if only for a second. "The man who was brought in with you was alive, barely. They're still working on him, but it's nasty."

Healers could work powerful magic, save people on the brink of death, but there were limits. The body could only take so much at once, and even if it was stable, that didn't mean they were okay. My gut wound was a good example, it must have been quite bad if I'd been shot by a scatter gun that close. I would be fine in the end, but it was probable that I would need several sessions or weeks of recovery.

"All right, I'll rest for a bit then." Having at least that information I laid back down, satisfied.

I was there for hours, it seemed, the nurse bringing me some food at one point, quite a lot of it actually. When she noticed the way I was looking upon the relative feast, she told me that I needed to get more food into me so I could keep healing. Not long after that, a harried-looking priest appeared and worked on me for a few minutes before excusing himself once more.

Not long after that, a familiar face parted the curtains to my little cubby and stepped in. The lanky frame of the investigator slipped through, looking too tall and too long from this angle, almost painfully so.

"Young man, we really must stop meeting like this. Sorry for the delay, but with how wild things have been, the fact that you were here didn't make it to my desk quite as soon as I'd have liked," Ignus said and gave me a toothy smile.

"And, once again, I'm not the one at fault," I informed him.

"Oh, I know," he said. "Most people involved in crimes won't shoot themselves, and certainly not a gut wound. You may have done better than the other poor fellow, but had you not been brought in quickly, I assure you, you'd be dead."

"Did you get them? I know the one guard was involved, heard his voice through the mask."

"Did you now? Good to have that confirmation. Do you know his name by any chance?"

"Gramin or something? He wasn't particularly talkative."

"Grawlin, yes. He and several others from his unit disappeared," the investigator said, nodding. "I'll make note of your testimony. Now, if you don't mind, I'd like the full story please."

I gave him just that, though there wasn't too much to tell. We were hit hard and fast, with nowhere near the amount of response I'd have liked. For his part, Ignus was happy to sit and listen, taking notes and asking a few clarifying questions here and there. I even told him I saw a girl in the sewer, though it may have been a delusion, since I was sort of out of it by that point.

"Now, young man, I know it may be a bit of an imposition, but I'll ask that you stay put until you're released. Just in case I have any more questions." The way he said it told me that there might also be some suspicion directed my way. After all, I was involved in multiple incidents.

Before he could get up, I heard the door to the hall open and the sound of thick heels clacking angrily against the floor.

"Ma'am, my people need to do their jobs. I know that this is a serious matter but you can't just do whatever you want," a deep baritone voice said, making Ignus turn sharply.

"Oh, Your Grace, I think you'll find I can in fact do whatever I want." The reply was feminine, but . . . old, very old. That said, whoever she was, her tone didn't imply any concern. "Tell me, do you know how many of those particular devices have been wholly lost to enemies before?"

"I . . . um . . ." the man struggled.

"None," she said. "None since the founding of this kingdom, and do you know why? Because of what I do to the people who steal them. Now, two of my people are hurt, several of yours have abandoned their posts, and I am taking this matter into my personal hands. If you do not like it, feel free to complain to His Majesty."

The man, ostensibly the duke himself, had no response to that. Ignus looked toward the curtain, a visible sweat forming on his brow. I must have looked no less alarmed, because there were precious few who could afford to speak to such a high person poorly, and fewer still that could talk to them like they were a naughty child.

The heels clacking against the floor passed us, and Ignus looked back once more.

"Please excuse me, Percival. There's something I need to go look into." He didn't even wait for my response before making himself scarce.

There were people speaking down the hall, though I couldn't make it out. Soon enough, though, I had a new visitor, one I'd only seen in a photograph. Old Auntie Penumbra, the Worldsinger, the Kingkiller, split the curtains to my room, looking down at me as if to judge me. Her eyes narrowed for a few moments, like she was seeing something rather unexpected.

When she finally spoke, it was in my first native tongue. "Hey, we should have a chat."

CHAPTER 44

*

AUNTIE PENUMBRA

Well, how are you today?" asked the reigning archmage of the kingdom after setting up a few barriers.

"I . . . You speak English?" I asked.

"Oh, that's right, you're a physical. It would be obvious if you could see my aura. All of us have rather similar auras, bubbles, as it were. As soon as I saw you, I knew. It's just obvious."

I'd been told that my aura looked like metallic bubbles before, and that it was a bit odd, but nothing too surprising as almost everyone's was different. However, she was right—I couldn't see them.

"So you're also from Earth? Wait, you'd have to be from like, I don't know . . . seventeen hundred or something? You're supposed to be three hundred years old or so."

I was promptly bopped on the nose. "It's impolite to ask a lady's age, but something like that. Ah, I guess I can tell you that time doesn't exactly work the same for the transfer. I don't really understand all of it, but we were scattered all throughout time and sent to this world. There are a few others, too, but those aren't exactly my secrets to tell."

"The ancient elven king who died however long ago," I pointed out.

"Perceptive, but others too."

"You, obviously, because you created the portal network."

"Technically speaking I didn't come up with it, just figured out how to make them. All that's ancient history though. What happened to the missing one?"

"Stolen," I told her. "But you already knew that."

"I did, but it doesn't hurt to confirm," she admitted. "Did you have anything to do with it?"

"No, of course not. What would I do with a portal?"

"Lots of things, some of them rather dangerous. There's a reason we don't keep too many of them around, and that's because they're disasters if used incorrectly. If you were older and properly educated, I could run you through even the basics of the security protocols, but if you've even started making a core, I doubt you're far."

"I . . . I started at least." It was clear she was looking down on me.

"No worries then, you'll get there eventually. Please tell me everything. Leave nothing out."

I'd already had to run through this story a few times, so once more wasn't a big deal. She asked about details, all of them, and didn't even blink when I told her that I thought I saw a goblin in the sewers. She just tapped her chin thoughtfully.

"Wonder how those got off that island. They didn't seem particularly smart."

"Um . . . someone brought them to the city, and they escaped, and as for smart, some of them can at least speak. One of them spoke English." Following her lead, we were speaking in English, a good protection from those who weren't reincarnators.

That got a sharp look, a very sharp one.

"You're sure?" she asked.

"Very," I nodded.

"That is concerning, and something I'll be bringing to the attention of a friend of mine when I get the chance. We certainly don't want them spreading if they're anything like the old stories. Who knows if that's true though."

"I mean yeah, elves live for like, way longer," I pointed out.

"The pure-blooded ones never age. Fact of the matter is that most are kind of mixed now. They have reproductive problems, so ended up mixing with us a lot."

That was unexpected. I mean, I'd heard stories, but I'd thought they were just that. Nobody could really live practically forever, could they? Then again, I was talking to a centuries-old woman. Of course Archmage Penumbra was at least old, very old.

"That's . . . How do you know?"

"I've met a few over the years. Not many, mind you, but a handful. They tend to keep quiet and run things in the background. Actually, a lot of the really old beings in this world, myself included, are fairly private. Maybe at one point we weren't, but at least so long as I've been around, we've let others take the limelight."

"Don't suppose you'll share the secret of immortality with me?" I asked hopefully.

"I'm not immortal, ageless or otherwise, so I'm afraid not. I did put a lot of effort into anti-aging magic, and am almost stable, but even I'm slowly dying. Priests can keep themselves from getting that way, but only if they have no doubts about it being the right thing to do, and bards can slow the process dramatically if we put tons of effort into it. Sadly, I don't know of anything for physical magic users. If I did, many others would still be alive." There was some pain in those last words, the pain of loss, of loved ones gone.

"I'm sorry for prying," I said, regretful that I'd torn at old wounds.

"You are by no means the first person to have asked that question, Percival, and I have grown used to answering it. Some take my answer very poorly too." For some reason, I didn't doubt that in the least. An immortal telling you that you couldn't be one too was not something anyone really liked to hear.

"So, what now?" I asked.

"What now is I go after those fools who stole that gate. The danger is greater than they can imagine if they play with it too much, and I'm not willing to let them try. The first time I played with them, I nearly found something far worse than any beast that has walked this world. Keep that in mind should you ever end up in possession of one. For there are things far worse than men or monsters out there." She rose, and I quickly followed, hopping out of my hospital bed.

"Well, obviously I'm coming with you," I said as she looked at me with an odd expression, seemingly unbothered by the fact that I was half-dressed and putting on my damaged clothes as fast as I could.

"You're a child," she muttered.

"Lady, I'm like forty, well if you count both lives, and I do. I've also fought my fair share of monsters and trained with a blade. I'm coming along because you need some backup." I was having some difficulty putting the sword on my belt.

"Fine, fine, one second." She hummed a tune, and my destroyed outfit put itself back together, like it was being destroyed in reverse. Then she chuckled. "If my mother had seen that, she'd have loved it."

There was another undercurrent of pain, of loss. Perhaps it was because we were speaking English, or because I was from the same home world, but I got the feeling that this was something a lot of people didn't see. The reports of this woman's behavior were few, but all pointed to the idea that she was a towering danger to those who angered her, not the sad old woman I saw before me now.

I wondered how many people she'd lost. Not that I would ask, but it had to be countless friends, lovers, and perhaps even children. That would be such a weight, a weight I wasn't sure I'd want to bear. Were people even meant for that? I didn't know, but I did know that the fact that I'd been reborn gave me some hope in the existence of the soul, knowledge that death didn't have to be the end, and that was rather reassuring.

Steeling myself, I locked eyes with the old bard. "All right, let's go teach some thieves a lesson."

"That I can agree with."

CHAPTER 45

✶

IN-FLIGHT DISCUSSION

The hospital really did not want to let me go, but they had fairly limited choices on the matter. Fairly limited in this particular case meant none at all, and while I was sure to hear about it later, my escort just pushed us past.

"So . . . where to now?" I asked. "We could go look for clues or try to track down their movements . . ."

"Hm? Oh no, I know where they are," the grandmotherly figure answered. "I came to see you to see what we would be getting into, not to find them. I did that practically instantly."

I gave her a long, hard look . . . "So, why all the interviewing?"

"They're not trying to escape right now, and I wanted to know who, how, and what I was dealing with. I can track the things for a good long ways, so there's no real need for me to rush."

"You LoJacked them?" I asked.

She looked at me long and hard, squinting as if she were searching through her memories. "Pfft, how old were you?"

"That's a rich question coming from you, great-great-great-grandma," I retorted, not liking how she'd questioned my age. I hadn't been that old.

"Sonny boy, I've got descendants with at least five greats in there, I'll have you know. You should respect your elders."

Some of the people in the halls we were going down were looking at us weird, as we were clearly not speaking in the local dialect. Add to that I was also engaged with banter with one of the most powerful people in the kingdom and, well, we got attention. Most of them were moving quickly out of the way, but a few moved to lean in, to hear what we were saying. Neither of us cared much, since nobody here could speak English. Then again, I might end up surprised.

"Figures, so, we're going to retrieve the gate then?" I asked.

"That or destroy it. I'm honestly fine with either."

"I know for a fact that magic items take a lot of effort to make," I pointed out.

"True, but the duke has shown that he can't handle another one of these, and if I get it back, I have to figure out how to deal with it. That's going to be a headache, not much of one, but so long as our enemies don't get the gate in the end, I'm satisfied." She was just so unconcerned, like it didn't matter, like the items didn't matter.

"All right, where to?" I asked as we walked out the front door.

"Spells first, Percival. Just sit back. Have you flown before?" She started to sing before I could answer, and I felt magic flow over me.

First, I began to fade from view, my body growing instantly opaque, then completely invisible. Even with my enhanced sight, I couldn't see any part of my hand in front of my face. I didn't know too much about magic, but this seemed advanced. The shield around our school was supposed to be invisible, but we could see it. Not this though.

While I was still processing this, I felt myself get lighter and lighter, as if gravity was losing its hold on me. I tried to be careful, one jump could have sent me soaring; yet, soon enough, I began to float, hovering there in there air. Moments later we began to soar, not like a plane, but easily as fast as any bird.

"This is so cool," I whispered, loving the feeling, even if I had no control at all.

"You can speak normally. Nobody will hear us," the archmage responded as we began our way across the city.

"This is amazing," I said. "Shame I can't learn it."

"Didn't know that I ever would. My daughter taught me after she learned. Before that I never really cared about flying. Don't feel down though. You can probably still make a balloon or something."

"I've been working on planes with my grandpa," I informed her.

"Really? They're interesting, but with the portals I never felt the need. Also don't know the ins and outs of how exactly they work. Something to do with the wings right?"

"Yeah, the shape. For the best results, they need to be really specific, but even those that aren't perfectly optimized still work, just not nearly as well. We won't be building passenger jets anytime soon, but I think we'll have something akin to an old prop plane by the time I'm old."

She laughed at me. "Don't underestimate people. Once they have the basics of something, they'll advance far, far faster than you'd expect. Science here is also a lot better than it was on Earth at a similar time. Heck, trains developed in decades, not centuries. Though I may have encouraged that one a little bit. Blame me if you like, but I like leading people toward some of the more modern conveniences."

"Did you have something to do with the maid outfits too?" I inquired. It seemed odd that they were just exactly the same.

"Some of those were already here when I got here, though I do think they're quite cute, don't you?"

"How many of us have there been?" I asked.

"No idea, but certainly a few. It seems the time between arrivals is shortening, too, though I don't know why. I might be good, but the magic involved goes completely over my head. In other news, we're here."

We landed on a small rooftop in the lower-end of a residential part of the city. I'd expected them to try and get a boat or something to get their ill-gotten gains out of Exion, but it seemed not. Instead, they looked to be hiding, waiting. That was odd.

"That one . . . Oh, sorry, forgot you can't see me pointing," she said. "The larger building below us, the one that looks like it used to be an inn or something. The one with the red sign out front. They're in there."

"So what's the plan? Call for backup and level the place? We're always being told how we should use overwhelming power for missions at the school."

"We have overwhelming power—I'm here," she chided.

"If something goes wrong . . ."

There was a long silence, then a sigh.

"In the past I'd have agreed with you, I'd have brought more people. Now, though, I can't stand the idea of any of them getting hurt, and my life isn't nearly worth what it used to be." Now it was my turn to be quiet and wait. "They can find the location in case we fail—we won't, but just in case."

"What do you mean, your life isn't worth what it used to be?" I asked.

"I told you I wasn't immortal, Percival."

"You're dying, how long?"

"Depends on a number of things, but maybe a decade, two at most. My organs are shutting down, and even with my expertise in anti-aging magic, I can't quite get them to stop. Even the priests I've consulted have told me there's not much they can do. All the spells holding them together are fraying at the edges, and nobody believes that I have to live forever, so the priests can't fix it."

"So you're just throwing your life to the wind?" I asked, aghast.

"No, I'm doing all I can to keep my students safe. My affairs are mostly in order, and if I'm being honest I don't really want to have to suffer as my body shuts down bit by bit. If I die, I die, though there's one or two things I'd like to do before that."

"Well, I don't want to take the risk, so . . ."

"Percival, you're not going in. I just brought you along to keep you from pitching a fit, and to get a measure on you. I always need more people to act as advisors to my however-many greats nephew, and once I'm done training you, I think you'll fit the bill."

"I am absolutely going in. You can't do this on your own," I said with resolve.

"First lesson," she chided. "When someone you're not very sure of casts spells on you, resist them." In the second it took me to process her words, my body froze, leaving me unable to move once more. "Now stay here, I'll be right back."

CHAPTER 46

*

GOBLIN GIRL GRETA

I was frozen, on a roof, completely unable to move, and more than a little pissed about it. This kind of thing irked. It didn't hurt physically, but honestly, I couldn't believe she'd do something like that; it was just . . . rude.

It was unclear just how many minutes passed as I stood there, stuck and seething, but eventually there was a sound nearby, feet stepping toward me. They sounded small, as if belonging to a child, and as I listened, still a statue, they came very near.

"What's this, what's this?" a high, feminine voice chirped curiously. "However did you get here? And frozen? Ah, I see the spell. That's very interesting."

As she spoke, the figure moved before me, a tiny goblin girl, the one with the large goggles. The lenses were flipping back and forth like the eye tester from an optometrist office as she leaned in.

I tried to yell, tried to call out, to strike her, anything, but the archmage's spell held me fast, only letting a breathy noise escape my mouth.

"Oh, where are my manners? I'm Greta," she said. "You already met my brother Sigmund, yes? He's a bit dull, though, so I can't imagine he was a good conversationalist; nor does he really bother with manners at all." The more I listened, the more she sounded like a curious young woman, out to learn all she could.

No matter what I did I couldn't move much other than my eyes, and they darted around, looking for some escape, something I could do.

"And why am I here? I can see you want to know. You see, Father really wants to see you, to meet you. Oh, don't worry, I'm sure he'll be nice. He seemed so excited. When Sigmund failed so poorly, he sent me out, and you know, you're very hard to find. Even searching for similar mana signatures to Father's, I couldn't locate you for weeks and weeks, and as soon as I did, they ran off and hurt you. Just in case something else happens, have this. It was the backup plan for getting in contact anyway."

She placed what looked like a letter in my jacket's inner pocket, patting it gently as she continued to ramble.

"Well, I was going to get that item, since it looked like you might be dead and I wanted to salvage something from this fiasco. Can you even imagine how thrilling it was to see you show up so close? Ah, well anyway, since you're here now, let's go. Father is waiting!" I sensed the magic wrap around me as she picked me up with it and began to turn me, moving me back toward the edge of the roof.

I was panicking, internally swearing up a storm and promising myself that as soon as that old bag rescued me, assuming she could, I was going to give her a piece of my mind.

Then the world shook as the old inn exploded.

Several things happened at once. I flew away, tumbling across the roof as the goblin's magic failed. The spell holding me in place failed too. Not the best sign. And, finally, the little mage who'd been trying to kidnap me was surrounded by a blue sphere, obscuring her from view as some automatic, or near automatic, defense activated.

Being sent airborne was one of the great fears of any physical magic user, and so we'd trained for it. With a kick of my legs I spun in the air, righting myself and tumbling down the roof, fingers and feet skidding across the shingles and catching whatever I could to slow my momentum. As I came to a stop I drew my blade, ready for anything.

"Well, that was unexpected," Greta said as her little bubble faded.

"Expect this," I answered, charging her.

She *eeped* as my sword sliced into her defensive shield, the sphere reappearing briefly as I cut downward and partially through it. With a quick move, my opponent threw forth her hands, pushing us both back again and gaining some space.

"Can't you just come nicely? I really didn't want to fight you," she complained.

I didn't bother responding to my would-be kidnapper, instead surging forward. She released several bolts of energy at me, each of which I cut with my blade. The enchantments on my sword may not have been anything special, but they were at least enough to dissipate minor spells and attacks.

Over the next thirty seconds the two of us circled around the flaming crater that had been a building moments before, her trying to gain space, me trying to close it. There were shouts and screams, other people coming and doing things, and down below I saw several figures in darkened armor appear out of the corner of my eye.

It seemed Greta wasn't the only one with defenses. The archmage strode toward the newcomers, seeming displeased. The goblin froze, turning toward them in alarm.

"Another? And that much aura! Crap, I need to go!" she shouted, apparently having seen something that alarmed her.

If she was going to turn away from her opponent, I was going to punish her for it. After all those lessons with the headmaster, I certainly knew better. I was atop her before she could move, my stab piercing deeply into her protective magic and scoring a slice across her cheek, even if a small one.

"You're not going anywhere," I growled.

"Good grief, you're angry. It's not like I was trying to hurt you or anything!" she shouted, bouncing back again. This time I followed in close pursuit, not letting her get even an inch away.

"Don't worry, I'm taking you alive." Another strike from me, and a small line cut across the sleeve of her shirt, which now had blood on it. I was battering down her defenses bit by bit.

There was a *brzzt* sound behind me, and a bright flash as blue-white light rose, a curl of lighting ripping upward around the angry archmage, going above the buildings and leaving an afterimage in my sight. It was followed seconds later by a deafening roar of thunder that shook the surrounding city. I didn't have time to look though. I had not a moment to spare before continuing my fight.

"Sorry, but no," Greta said. "Read the letter, all right?" I noticed her goggles had shifted to black lenses just a second too late. With a wave of her hands there was another brilliant flash, this one right in my face.

I cursed, swinging where I thought she was but finding nothing. I couldn't see properly, so I moved to my other senses. Sound? I could hear lots of things, shouts and screams, and another nearby peal of thunder, but not my opponent. Smell? The only thing I could smell was ozone. That was bad, and I began blinking, trying to clear my sight, which was returning painfully slowly.

When my vision finally returned enough that I could make out my surroundings, I noticed that Greta, the goblin girl, had indeed decided that Shakespeare was right when he noted that discretion was the better part of valor, and fled. That was annoying, and judging by the fact that I couldn't hear much going on below, I might be needed there.

Jumping down, I found a true battlefield. It seems old lady Penumbra had been rather displeased with someone trying to blow her up and had elected to bring out the big guns against them. Several of the would-be assassins were dead on the ground, glowing lines around them, where the electricity had melted the cobblestones. The last of the men was try-ing to flee, crawling away from her as she casually walked forward.

"Are you nearly done?" she asked. "You're not the first to try and blow me up, you know."

He yelled something in a language I couldn't understand, but as I got closer I realized who it was. Grawlin, looking much the worse for wear.

"Atali? Goodness, why are you using that language? Eh, we can find out later," the old woman said, continuing her stroll.

The man wouldn't have it though. I saw him pull something from his belt. He brought it to his throat and only a second later there was another explosion, though this one was nowhere near as large.

"He killed himself," I said as I rushed over. The man's head was a ruin. She didn't stop him? Certainly someone like her could have.

"Yes, they do that sometimes. We need to head to the duke's palace, let the investigators take it from here."

Soon enough people began arriving, police and emergency services. I tried to talk to Alana a few times while we waited, but she held up a hand, silencing me. As I looked at her, I saw things that worried me. Her skin was paler, sweat forming on her brow, no matter how much she tried to hide it. She also wasn't casting anything, instead waiting for others, and once they'd arrived, commandeering a carriage for us to travel in.

As soon as we were inside and the door closed, I saw the strongest mage in the kingdom slump, breathing hard.

"Are you—" I began.

"Tired," she replied. "Haven't had to fight like that in a while. Just need to rest a bit; that's why we're going to the palace. We'll stay there tonight, and you can tell me all about it in the morning."

Shortly we arrived and headed through the front door, where we were met by the duke himself and a pair of servants.

"Archmage Alana, we need a report on what happened. There's panic in the city," the duke said, trying to sound firm as he approached.

"Yes, yes, first just let me . . ."

She never finished, body going slack instead. Though it sent a shock through us as she began to fall forward, both myself and the duke rushed to catch the ancient magus, keeping her from slamming into the stone floors of the estate. As I held her there, she didn't feel like some hero, some epic leader, or some unbeatable archmage. She felt . . . so very frail.

✳

END OF AN ERA

I was seated in a plush waiting room. Perhaps I could have left if I'd asked, but the pacing city lord before me seemed busy. The duke had instantly called for a priest when Archmage Penumbra had collapsed, and the healer was currently working on her in another room. She had managed to do something to a ring she'd been wearing in a few moments of clarity, and we were currently just . . . waiting.

After a time the priest returned, his look solemn.

"How is she?" the high noble quickly asked.

"Dying. I'm sorry, there's nothing I can do."

"What do you mean *dying*? She cannot die here. Go and save her!"

"There are limits, Your Grace, and she's well past them. Even if I could figure out what she's cast on herself to keep her body working, which I can't, there's nothing left to heal her with. There is nothing I can do except keep her comfortable. She has perhaps until sundown, if there's anyone you want to contact."

Before the priest could be yelled at again, a maid hurried in through the opposite door. She looked panicked.

"Girl, you'd best have good reason for interrupting," her employer almost growled at her.

"Sir, my apologies for the rush. I needed to warn you that we have arrivals from . . ."

She, too, was interrupted by the door opening once more, this time disgorging two men who were clearly bodyguards, followed closely by a figure everyone in this country would recognize. The king himself had arrived, with several of his own people in tow.

I made to kneel, only to be fixed with a harsh glare and a harsh word. "Don't be foolish, boy." Apparently now was not the time for niceties.

"Your Majesty, I wasn't expecting you," the formerly most important person in the room said.

"My aunt called," said the king. "A message that I needed to come and quickly. What exactly is going on, Noct?"

"Archmage Penumbra has been injured, and the priest here is unable to heal her. I was just preparing for a more experienced healer to see to her." The priest in question looked taken aback, as if questioning his credentials was just out of the question.

"Oh, don't bother," came a weak voice.

While everyone was pointing fingers and bursting into the room, it seemed the patient had gotten herself up and made her way to the doorway of the room we all occupied. She stood there, leaning on a staff. Over the next few seconds she made her way slowly into the room.

"Auntie, you should be in bed," the king said, almost gently, as if telling off an elder relative. Though, being that they shared the same last name, that shouldn't have been surprising.

"I quite agree," the priest protested. "Your organs!"

"Are failing, and there's nothing to be done about it." She made her way up to the king and pinched his face. "Sorry, my boy, but it looks like I may have overestimated how much time I had. Well, that and over-pulled on my mana a bit. Been too long since I was in a real fight."

The ruler looked stunned, like he'd been told the sky was falling. "Auntie, sit, we'll find another healer and sort this out."

"Afraid not. There's only two I know of that could fix this, and I know for a fact that neither will. Already tried speaking to them about it. Did you bring the gate I gave you?" Behind him one of the aides raised his hand, his other holding a large box. "Good, good, don't have time to play with the network."

She waved at the assistant and he began to move, assembling what must have been the king's personal exit strategy. The box unfolded and pieces came out, slipping quickly into place to form a large ring.

"What are you doing?" the king asked as the archmage winced, using him to steady herself as some wave of pain overtook her. Her knuckles were white where she gripped and teeth clenched for just a moment.

"I've got one or two things I need to do before the end, child. There are a few notes that need to be sent, and one last little adventure I need to go on. Do me a favor and look after the lad, would you? He's a decent sort, and I didn't quite have the time to train him up." She nodded to me, getting several eyes to look in surprise. "Think he's got some potential."

"I will, but you're not going anywhere alone. My guards and I will accompany you."

"No," she told him, her voice hard with finality. "You cannot go where I am going."

"You can't just leave," her nephew, the king, said, "You have a duty."

"And it is done! I buried my husband, my children, my grandchildren, and more than you can count. Do not try me, boy, for I don't have the time. You're ready, ready to stand on your own. It is time."

The portal had been put together, and though the servant hadn't started it yet, he didn't seem to need to. With a few notes sung, the old woman pointed at it, and it roared to life. She stepped past the distraught royal and toward the glowing opening in space.

"Archmage," I said, standing off to the side.

"No worries, child," she said to me. "I've got an old friend I'll tell about you before I die. Interesting fellow; maybe you'll meet some time. Good luck, and joy be with you all." With those words she stepped through, the gate closing behind her, never to return again.

CHAPTER 48

✳

BACK TO SCHOOL

The king seemed distraught, though I wasn't sure what to do about that. All things said, he only spent a few minutes moping before he had slapped himself in the face repeatedly and risen.

"Where are my senses?" he said to himself. "This is no time for moping. There's much to do and no time at all to do it. Nobody in this room is to speak a word of what transpired here to anyone until the news is released. That is a royal decree! Am I understood?"

There was quick assent. I didn't like it, didn't like all the secrecy, but I understood. Someone had tried to kill one of the pillars of our kingdom, and if they found out they'd succeeded, there'd be problems. Perhaps they intended to hide it for a time, perhaps try and figure out who and why, but when the investigations were over, I had no doubts that if the guilty party were located, there'd be hell to pay.

"Boy," the king said, turning to me, "I promised I'd see to you being trained, so we'll see about giving you some extra."

"In the name of all that is decent, Your Majesty, please do not mention that within earshot of Headmaster Logan," I half-pleaded/half-joked. If that maniac heard that the freaking *king* thought I needed more training, I'd be lucky to ever get a wink of sleep.

The guards bristled until the formerly moping monarch loosed a small chuckle. "Lad, I needed that. Logan, eh? Well, he knows his business, but I'll send someone to look things over. I did make a promise, after all. Can't have you lacking in your sword skills."

He pulled the duke aside and they left me then, their business not really meant for my ears. That night I spent in the duke's palace, since it was getting on in the day and everyone was exhausted. My host didn't see me afterward, but some of the staff did, and I could hear them gossiping about the royal visit. None of what they had to say was true, though, because everyone who'd been within earshot had gotten news of that royal decree, and nobody was fool enough to violate it. I didn't live here, but even I knew the walls had ears.

As morning found us, I was taken to a carriage. I had a school to get back to. A man joined me, one of the guards the king had brought with him when he'd first arrived. He sat across from me in the confined space and basically just bristled.

"So, I'm Percival. A pleasure to meet you."

He didn't speak, just glared. This went on for several minutes. I didn't break eye contact. Sure, this guy could probably beat me to death if he felt like it, but one didn't end up serving the royal family personally if they didn't have control.

"I am Sir Kendrick. Well met." He didn't sound like he meant it, rather like he wanted to strike me. "Allow me to make this clear—I am here because His Majesty has ordered that your training be exemplary, and nothing else."

"The only thing I think my training is missing is access to a machine shop," I said with a shrug.

"I highly doubt that, but why?" He was still gruff, but I'd piqued his interest.

"Because while I'm a passable swordsman, I'm much better at making things than fighting, and I would really like to upgrade my arms. With access to proper tools and a bit of time . . ." I had to think, what all could I do?

There were realms of possibilities—guns, vehicles, and perhaps one day I could even build something like power armor; though, I wasn't sure the latter would be worthwhile. Transports that were better armed and armored were clearly needed, as the armored carriage we'd been ambushed in had been far too easy to crack. I also wanted firearms, several for differing purposes, and ones of high caliber. With my strength, it was possible to have things closer to anti-material rounds in handguns without detriment to me, and they'd be needed to fight against magical opponents.

"Lots of things," I said. "I think I could do lots of things."

For the first time Sir Kendrick smiled, rubbing his beard. It wasn't a pleasant thing. "So that's what she saw in you? Not your physical capabilities but your mind. I see. That tracks with the archmage . . ."

"You know her well?" I inquired, being careful not to imply that she wasn't around.

"No, nobody can claim that, though she's always favored the royals. Archmage Penumbra has a lengthy history of . . . shall we say eccentricism. Yes, that is a good word."

The man didn't seem to be inclined to speak further on the matter, and I was happy to let him stew. If he took what I had said as valuable, that might catapult my timetable on getting some real weapons. I'd need them, too, if what I was seeing was correct. Those goblins weren't likely to give up anytime soon, and I'd need something to take them on.

That thought brought my mind back to the letter, still sealed and tucked in my jacket pocket. Nobody had searched me, and in all the excitement I'd nearly forgotten about it. What did it say? I didn't know yet, and I certainly wasn't going to open it right here and now. I knew they wanted to meet, something I'd not be going to without at least . . . I didn't know, a satchel full of explosives or something.

Soon enough we pulled up to the school, and I was released to go to my dorm, where I was tackled by half a dozen of my friends, Lucas in the lead.

"Percival, I thought you were dead," he said, wrapping an arm around me and almost in tears. "We heard you were hurt and managed to sneak out to see you, and what do I find? Bloody bandages and neither you nor your things in the bed. Even the nurses weren't sure where you'd gone."

"He cried," Simon offered, earning himself a half-hearted punch from the other boy.

"Ah, things got a bit weird," I answered.

"Is that so? Well next time bring more backup."

"My backup was the problem," I told him.

"Very well, then better backup."

"Sure thing, the next time I need to ride to war, I'll let you know."

"If you don't, you'd better write some notes explaining to people why you're dead, so I don't have to," Lucas said with a shake of his head.

Eventually, the guys let me go, and I made my way to my room. There were so many things to do, and I really didn't have time to do them if whatever was going on came to a head. Once there, I took out the note and opened it.

The writer was clearly from Earth, as the whole thing was in English, and fucking cursive. Who did that? Did he not want me to be able to translate it? If I'd been even slightly less educated than I was, it would have been completely illegible, and as it was, it took me the better part of the evening to decipher the damn thing. The only reason I could was because of my improved memory and the fact that my elementary school teachers had been so determined that I learn a skill that was almost literally useless. It also didn't help that the writer had horrid handwriting, just another reason to punch this "father" in the face.

The gist of it was that he wanted to meet me, something I already knew, and directions on how to set that up. There was no given date. Rather, I was to put a light atop one of the buildings near a museum and meet him inside the next day. Bring nobody else, blah, blah, blah, don't tell anyone, and a few veiled threats that if he had to keep tracking me down, he'd be most displeased. Yeah, I really did need to kill this guy, whoever he was.

✴

CHAPTER 49

ARMS

I had time, maybe not infinite time, but at least some. The goblins couldn't well go check records, and with the government determined to keep things secret, they were unlikely to be able to figure out exactly who I was. That wasn't a guarantee, but it was a pretty good guess. Even if they did, I was still at the school, and they'd have to have a death wish to attack here.

Time was good. Time meant that I could prepare. Some of what I needed to do would be a bit ad-libbed, but with my improved memory and previous training there were options. After all, I'd been enough of a redneck to know how to improvise at least a few things.

First things first, I needed something ranged, and heavy hitting. Luckily, I had the skill set for just such a thing. My memories may have been good, but they weren't perfect. Sadly, I was also devoid of some of the drawings I'd made over the years. Tested or not, those were important for planning. I'd have to go with the simplest version of what I needed, that I could make.

It still took days before I was ready for even the first attempt at what I was doing; that was fine though, since I needed to go shopping beforehand. I spent night after night utilizing all of my precious free time to prepare schematics and plans, then reexamine them and fix things I should have seen the first time around.

When I was ready I went looking for one of my teachers.

"Professor Ruian, I have some questions," I said as I made my way to her office.

"Oh, Percival, lovely to see you, and as you know I'm always happy to give instruction. Having trouble with your homework, dear?" she asked.

"No, ma'am," I replied. "Actually, I am interested in the creation of magic items, specifically the outer shells."

"A personal project? I know you're rather taken with the engines and the like that they use in the trains, but I'm afraid you'll need to complete your core before you can work on something like that."

"I know, Professor, but would it be possible for me to make something non-magical using the same tools? We don't have a machining shop here in the school, and there are a few designs I'd like to try. You see, I've spent years going over some things with my grandpa, and I'd like to make progress on the personal project before seeing him again." I gave her my most innocent smile.

"No reason you couldn't. Most people don't with anything other than the larger engines and the like because of the mana cost, but if you're willing to pay, then I can show you how to do it." She thought for a second. "You'll also need to procure your own materials, of course." I produced a sizable billet of steel from my bag. It was, as far as I could determine, the best on the market for my purposes and had been one of several purchases I'd managed to make the last time we'd had a weekend in town.

"I see you're ready to start now," she said, a little surprised. "Well, no need to wait then."

She led me down the hall to one of the workrooms. I'd never had cause to be in here, but it was clean, well organized, and full of something that looked like desks. They were odd, due to the clear circle indications on parts of them and a glass inset. There were also markings that looked a little like a keyboard layout and a pad on each.

"These are . . ." They looked almost like computers if you squinted.

"Not the newest models, but still serviceable. Your project isn't too big, is it? These have a bit of a maximum size constraint. If the pieces you need don't fit in that box, there's nothing to be done about it." She pointed to a square as she spoke about each of the items, easily large enough for what I needed.

"Should be fine, ma'am," I answered.

"Good, otherwise you'd be out of luck. Now, come here and I'll show you how to use these."

As she began to work, I recognized exactly what I was looking at. It was a 3D modeler. I'd played with tons of these for work or pleasure. That wasn't to say that they were good. Heavens no! They lacked a lot of basic features and functions that would have made this child's play, but they were good enough for me to do what I would need to. Briefly, I wondered if this was one of the advancements given by Archmage Penumbra, and I felt a pang of sadness that I'd never gotten to spend the time with her.

"I think I've got the hang of it," I said as I got the first piece ready.

"Look at that," she said. "It's like you're a natural. Are you sure you've never used one of these before?"

"Quite so, ma'am."

"Well, if you're making an engine, remember to leave gaps for the movement and whatnot, and be very careful not to stand near it during the first test. Some years back a man nearly killed himself during a demonstration at the Royal Society. I had a friend who was there, and she said it was only the quick intervention of a nearby spellcaster that kept anyone from getting injured."

I didn't stop myself from laughing. "That spellcaster was my grandpa, and my, was he cross."

"Well, then promise you'll not do anything foolish, and I can leave you to it."

"Of course, Professor," I said with another smile.

"Right then, if you need anything else, let me know."

She left me, and I reflected on just how trusting the people of this world were. Well, perhaps not trusting, but not the hovering guardians of my previous life. There, no child, even a teenager, would have been left alone in a room full of tools to their own devices. Of course, they didn't have the same culture as this world either, so here it seemed reasonable. Probably didn't hurt that I'd proven myself capable many times before either.

I mused on this as I diligently made part after part. Some were simple, some were a bit more difficult to put into the tool, but all would work. I measured each with a pair of calipers just to make sure they were as perfect as I could get them. There was a snag when I had to remake one, but putting the formed piece into the section for materials worked just fine, so it wasn't a real loss. It did use a ton of mana, though, and by the time I finished I was quite drained.

That evening when I got back to my room I began the assembly. Parts were held while pins were tapped gently where they needed to be, fitting just right and just tight enough to hold things together. Grease was applied liberally to parts, kept away from others, allowing movement and seals where they needed to be. Bit by bit, it all came together into a metal work of art.

My revolver was based on old black powder guns from Earth, and as far as I knew, nobody had made one like it before in this world. It shone, the steel fresh and unblemished, missing the little imperfections most roughly machined parts ended up with. The whole contraption was also massive, overbuilt to account for my own lack of ability and of a caliber no non-magical person could hope to wield reasonably, with a bore nearly an inch wide.

CHAPTER 50

✶

PREPARATION

It was a few more weeks of work, and then came our next weekend off, the last one before the holidays, and I had been white-knuckled the whole way through. I needed to be ready before the Season, where I would certainly be found by those damn goblins again, and I needed to be ready.

I'd considered letting the headmaster and the powers that be know right now about the planned meeting, but there were demerits to that idea. The biggest of which was that I could kiss goodbye any freedom I had while they came up with a plan. I knew I'd need help before things went too far, but we weren't ready yet. As I left the dorm in the early morning, a large suitcase at my side, I was practically tackled. Lucas looked peeved as he grabbed me by the shirt and pulled me eye-to-eye.

"I thought you were going to inform me when you were planning to go do something stupid again?" he asked, smiling but clearly angry.

"I am."

"And yet here we are, Percival. It's clear you're up to something. You're miserable at hiding it, and it's something you've been planning for days. Do you think your friends didn't notice all your odd behavior?" He seemed to think for a minute. "Odder than usual at least. So, what's happening?"

"I'm not even going to the city, just have some things I need to test before things go up in flames again." I began to pull myself, and Lucas, toward the small carriage I'd arranged to take me to a local woodland.

"Great, what are we testing?"

"*I* am testing. Shouldn't you go find the others and spar or something?"

"No, I tried to get them to join us, but you wouldn't believe how they whined. Furthermore, I'm not letting you alone outside of this school. If something happens to you, my sister will kill me."

"What's Rowena got to do with this?" I asked.

Lucas looked at me for a solid minute. "Man, you are dense."

I filed that away for later. Lucas' sister, Rowena, was a bit younger than me, and I'd accompanied her to several events but never felt that she was more than an acquaintance. For one, she was far too young for me to view her as anything other than a child, not something I wanted anything to do with; and two, it just never really popped into my head how she might feel about me. Sure, she was nice and all, but I really didn't feel that way about anyone in this world.

With a sigh I shook my head. "This is not a good time for that, you know? Monsters, attacks, and all that. I don't want her getting mixed up in it."

"Me neither, so let's see what we can do about solving it."

Since he insisted, I didn't fight too much when Lucas joined me. It wasn't the worst idea anyway, as playing with explosives was dangerous, and what I was doing was wholly untested. If something went wrong, it would be good to have someone around just in case, and a willing volunteer would be better than an unwilling one.

Less than an hour later, the two of us strode through the forest like it was a high street, leaves crunching and twigs snapping underfoot as we trod. I had my gun and sword, and judging by his gait, Lucas had his knives should something go wrong. That was an odd skill I'd picked up through the last few months of training—the ability to almost see where people had weapons hidden on themselves. Just one of the many results of the headmaster pushing us so hard.

"So, what are we testing anyway?" Lucas asked as we moved into a small meadow.

"This," I said, pulling out the pistol I'd made. "I lacked ranged options in the last couple of fights, and I'm solving that little problem."

"Goodness, think it's big enough?"

"No, I think it'll only be slightly useful against a proper mage's shield, if I'm being honest; though it should certainly pack a punch."

"Well, load it up then and let's give it a shot," he said, nearly bouncing on his feet.

"In a vice first, just in case," I informed him as I handed him my spare pair of earplugs.

He watched me load the revolver in silence after I'd set up the holder that I'd be taking the first couple of shots from. It was basically just a vice with a string attached, but it would serve perfectly well. When I was finished putting one round in, all I'd be using for the initial shot, he spoke up.

"Odd looking, isn't it? Is that one of those that shoots several rounds at once? I've seen a few, but they always have a bunch of barrels to them."

"Just watch," I told him.

We stood behind trees as I pulled the string for the first time, the earsplitting *BOOM* and smell of gunpowder reaching us quickly. Everything went well, and the rest of the day we took turns trying out my new weapon. It was manageable, but brutal, the shockwave from each round ruffling hair and clothes, and even with the earplugs, it was still incredibly loud.

"That was grand fun," Lucas declared as we made our way back to the meeting point with our carriage. "Wherever did you get that? Some new gunsmith? Or perhaps a new design from the older ones?"

"I made it," I said, not caring to lie to one of my few friends.

"Sincerely?"

"Sincerely."

"Well, it's quite lovely. If I ever decide to take up shooting, I know who I'll come to for a proper firearm."

"I'm surprised you didn't just ask me for one now," I admitted.

"Oh no, I'm terrible with guns, and they require far too much upkeep for my liking. I'll take a blade any day. Plus, the smell and sound of explosions would irk me if I had to deal with it all the time. I'll leave all that to you, my friend."

"I'll take that as a vote of confidence, something I will always welcome."

"Mind telling me what all this is for though? I mean a man doesn't arm himself like that unless he's going to war."

I just laughed. "Well, we might well be going to war soon enough. I hope you want another chance at that monster that dropped you."

"Oh, I'd love one, and this time, I won't go down." His smile told me he was ready.

"We'll talk during the Season then. Be ready."

CHAPTER 51

✳

RECRUITING

Three days before returning home, I strode to the headmaster's office and knocked, slightly afraid because there was no way the adults in my life were going to let me off scot-free after hiding the whole goblin threats thing.

I knocked on the headmaster's door, heart beating fast.

"Enter," I heard after a few moments.

"Good afternoon, sir."

"Ah, Percival, I wasn't expecting you today. What brings you here?" He was gruff but not angry. After all, I'd been keeping up with his insane training regimen without any complaints from my teachers.

"Right, sir, I was hoping to speak to either Sir Kendrick or Mr. Ignus, preferably both, but I find I have no way to contact them."

He fixed me with a long stare, narrowing his eyes.

"Why?"

"I received a letter I think they should know about."

"Would you care to share it with me then? I can easily relay the contents."

"I really do think I should speak with them first, sir. It is a matter of some importance."

As our eyes met across his desk, I felt the pressure of this mountain of a man and his displeasure at my refusal, like an ocean pressing upon me, urging me to surrender. I knew better, though, for while my business was important, and he'd probably find out since he seemed to be connected in ways I didn't quite understand, surrendering here was the wrong move. This information wasn't for him; it was for the government at large.

After a few moments, his facade broke and he chuckled low.

"Better, much better than the first time we met. Going to the right people, insisting on the proper channels, yes Percival, you've improved well. We'll make a proper soldier of you yet. Return to my office after dinner."

While that was like being told the time of your execution, it was also rather expected. Sure, the headmaster seemed to have connections, but that didn't mean he had important people sitting around his office or able to be called at a moment's notice. It also gave me a bit of time to reflect, make sure that I had things ready.

The time seemed to fly by almost as if I were in a daze, and soon, once more I found myself standing before the same door, knocking.

This time there was no call to enter, rather the door was simply opened, and inside I saw four men instead of three. The final addition surprised me, making me stop and blink in the doorway.

"Grandfather?" I asked, looking at my father's father sitting there.

"Ah, Percival m'boy, glad you're here," he said smiling. "Come, sit with me."

My paternal grandfather and I had few interactions overall, with him mostly staying in Exion throughout the year. Because of this, I hardly saw him, causing me to wince internally. I really should have taken some time over the school year to visit during one of my weekends in town, but I'd neglected to.

"Certainly, I just wasn't expecting you here," I answered as I joined him.

"Since you seem to attract attention," said the headmaster, "I sought to have your parents join us. Sadly, it looks like they're still on their way to the city. However, your grandfather was more than willing to attend this little conference. I've been telling him all about your studies and adventures this year." As he spoke I felt sweat roll down my back. If he'd succeeded in telling my mother everything that had happened, I had no doubt I would die.

"How thoughtful," I remarked, trying to smile and failing. "At any rate, this is a translation of a letter I received," I said, handing it over to Sir Kendrick.

The knight frowned as he read over the letter, eyes darkening bit by bit as he went through it all before handing it to the investigator.

"Translation, from what?" asked Mr. Ignus.

"A variant of a code used by a kindly old woman I met only the once." That answer got me a few quirked eyebrows, and a small scoff from the knight. I assumed he'd met the former archmage.

"Could we have the original?"

"Impossible I'm afraid. It burned after I read it." I didn't bother to add that this was because I had set fire to it, but hopefully they wouldn't ask.

"The old auntie was known to do that from time to time, though I doubt this was from her," Sir Kendrick said.

"No, I believe it was from an oppositional group." The message itself only relayed that it was from 'Father' rather than a proper name.

The investigator didn't seem pleased when my grandfather held his hand out, silently demanding the letter. I'd not passed it to him, but he didn't seem to care if they wanted him to see it or not. He also had a proper title. He wasn't a lord, or a sir; he was Baron Shadestone, and while I didn't know what all he did to support that title, I did know it came with at least a bit of power.

"He's not going to engage in this foolishness," he said as he finished, practically tossing it at Headmaster Logan.

"I think I must," I answered.

"What you think is irrelevant, now that the authorities know where these people—whoever this 'Father' is—are going to be, and they can set a proper trap. You are my grandson, and not bait in some half-planned scheme."

"It would be difficult," Sir Kendrick said. "People watching a location are sometimes hard to find, but I agree..." Sir Kendrick answered.

"More like impossible to find," I said. "We know there is an enemy, and this is potentially the best way for us to get intelligence on them. I'm not suggesting I go in alone, or without aid, but I must go."

"Where did this letter come from?" Ignus asked, curious about the origin.

"It was slipped into my jacket pocket while I was in the city."

"*That* is concerning," answered Ignus, eyeing me while rubbing his chin.

"Allow me to reiterate—my grandson will *not* be functioning as bait."

"Grandfather, I really must. If there is an enemy in our midst, then we need to catch them now."

"Oh, and that requires you? Your teacher here told me that you interacted with Archmage Penumbra, and that she requested you to get proper training, and I can assure you she is more than capable of impersonating you. If this is such an issue, have her called and see to it that she protects the lad she was so interested in." Nobody met his eyes as he spoke. "What?" he asked after a few moments.

"It is considered a state secret, but I'm afraid she's gone, presumed dead," Sir Kendrick answered. I didn't know if he had that authority, but he probably knew his business.

"Oh." For the first time in this conversation he seemed genuinely worried.

"I don't know how much of a hand, if any, this enemy had in that, but as you can see, a wound such as this cannot be allowed to fester. I will be going, this meeting is just to ensure that I'm not facing them alone."

"Heavens above, boy, how were you planning on explaining this to your parents?" he asked.

"After the fact," I responded, as if it were obvious.

There were a few scoffing laughs at that, but agreement that something had to be done. So heads came together to discuss what was possible, and what plan should be sent upward for approval.

CHAPTER 52

*

DECEPTIONS

I didn't manage to get off free from my little ploy. Basically, everyone was furious at me, and my grandfather was promising to tell my parents, immediately after I'd lured our enemy out. Convincing him to keep quiet even that long had required a whole slew of concessions from pretty much everyone involved, and lots of extra guards for the whole endeavor.

There were even a few familiar faces joining us. The two Worldsingers who'd been tasked with delivering the gate, which had been stolen, were among the guards, and both looked like they wanted blood. That was easy to understand. They'd been betrayed, their leader and organization hurt. Walter had also been severely injured, though with magic even that could be recovered in time.

"So we're all ready?" Mr. Ignus asked, looking around at the assembled crowd.

"The plan is sound, though I still dislike it," my grandfather replied. We were meeting in one of his estates, just outside of Exion.

"Nobody likes it," the investigator said.

"I do," Lucas added in.

"You are only here because Percival insists upon it, and he needs someone to go with him. I still think we should have one of my men go with you instead," Ignus said, turning to me.

"No, Lucas is a known friend of mine; your men aren't. Our enemy demanded I come alone, which is obviously stupid, so we're not doing that, but if there's an unknown, they might not show. This is a good compromise."

"I can't believe your parents agreed," Grandfather grumbled to Lucas.

"Me neither," the smiling young man answered.

"Pay attention, people. We have two days, and we all want our pound of flesh. If any of you can't manage, we'll replace you, because we are not failing at this." Ignus slammed his fist on the table as he spoke.

Ignus wasn't the highest ranked person here, not by a long shot, but he was the leader of this operation. The reason for that was simple—he knew the city better than anyone, he had more connections than anybody else involved, and if something was happening here, he'd be best set up to deal with the consequences. He was also highly motivated. After all, people were causing trouble in his city, and this was his issue to solve.

"Understood? Good, now, once more from the top."

Two days later Lucas and I walked side by side down the road to the meeting point. From the outside we looked like two young noblemen, fancily dressed, every button perfectly done. We each had a cane, and each of them was, of course, a weapon. Below my jacket was my revolver, below Lucas' a small stubby blunderbuss, one shot only, but packing a heck of a punch. Though our outfits looked like formal wear, that, too, was a disguise. We each had on layers of armor, enchanted to the best standards we could manage with the notice we'd had.

As we neared the location I'd been given, a work crew ushered us to the side. Two days ago they'd begun repaving the street. Of course, this was one of our teams. Men acting as simple laborers when in fact each was a fully trained warrior, ready to leap upon whoever came to meet us. Surprisingly, I couldn't even tell they weren't just normal workers. The street they'd been paving was pristine.

Across the street a young couple kissed lightly, the woman blushing and pushing her partner away playfully. They'd just moved in, freshly married by all appearances and new to the neighborhood. While I couldn't see it, I'd been told that the Worldsingers had impeccable aura control, able to pass by even skilled detectors without setting them off.

Everywhere our teams lay in wait, ready to spring, each member subtly keeping an eye out. None of them acknowledged the others more than they would any other passing individual, and we'd been told in no uncertain terms that half of the men here would be unknown to one another. There was some concern with the number of people involved, but apparently they'd increased the vetting process exponentially.

The building we finally made our way to was four stories tall, and completely abandoned. There'd been some discussion about trying to get people in to check it out, but the access was limited. Someone had done so, but having others inside wasn't viable for this mission. There were no residences, no businesses in here, only an old factory that was between owners. That was probably why "Father" had chosen this particular place.

Shortly after arriving, we made our way to the roof and lit a small lantern. It was left out, and it wasn't large, or even that out of place, just a small candle-containing lamp. Then we turned to leave, knowing that tomorrow was the meeting day.

"Well, here I was expecting some excitement," Lucas said as we headed for the door.

"Could you not—"

Before I could even tell him off for raising flags, all the sound around us died in the air. I recognized it as magic instantly but didn't have time to yell before the floor gave way. I was impressed, very impressed, pissed, too, that they'd managed to catch us so off guard. I tried to jump, tried to grab something, but with nothing solid around me, I had nothing to push against as I fell.

The slide we fell into, for it could only be described as such, was metal, shaped by magic into a perfectly smooth, oiled surface. We tried to yell, tried to grab onto something for leverage, but there was nothing, no purchase or sound as we slipped beneath the stones of the city street.

Would our allies realize what had happened? Probably, but would it be soon enough to intervene? I doubted it.

Less than ten seconds after we fell, we were spit out into a tunnel, one of the many that crisscrossed the city. Our undercity might not be as extensive as some other older settlements, but that didn't mean it didn't exist. As the two of us flew from the tube, we spun, drawing our weapons and looking around for enemies.

Before us were a pair of figures, two female goblins. One I recognized, and one I didn't. Both looked more human than the caged ones I'd seen, almost like smaller people, just with green skin and slightly pointed features. They looked at us as we landed, eyeing the weapons.

"Hi, again," Greta chirped, smiling. "I'm glad you decided to take Father's invitation."

"I believe you were asked to come alone though," the other added, looking unenthused.

"You're not alone, and I highly doubt you're this 'Father' I keep hearing about," I retorted.

"That is fair enough. If it is only the one, we can proceed then. Father wants you to come with us, and offers his word that should you do so, you won't be harmed."

"And I should trust him?" I asked, not having to mention that the instructions were not really accurate.

"Father has been known to use trickery, but his word is good. If he says he'll do something, he will. If he tells you he won't, he won't. I believe that if you meet with him honestly, he won't try to harm you at all."

"Honestly, Greeny, we don't even know you," Lucas said, seeming quite displeased.

"Fair enough, though there's no need to be rude, human. I'm Sasha, the guardian of our people, and I give you my word that if you come to this meeting, I will do what I can to see you are released safely afterward."

"And if we refuse?" I asked.

"Then I will take you there by force if needed. Will you though? You've already come this far."

She had a point.

CHAPTER 53

*

PLANS

So, is it far?" I asked the people taking me to a second location. I knew that you should never let them take you to a second location; fight to the death if you had to. Though, it was a poor idea. I really did want to talk to these people.

"Not too far, just enough to keep others from intruding," Sasha said, looking back at me.

"Do you mind if I ask a few questions while we walk then? Get to know each other?"

She didn't seem particularly excited, but nodded. "Very well."

"Why?"

"Why what?"

"Why are you all doing this, chasing me down, kidnapping people? I'd assume also killing them since nobody has reported it before, but all of it."

Odd. She looked uncomfortable when I mentioned the killing. Maybe she didn't know, or didn't have a part in it? Yes, she certainly knew.

"It's . . . unfortunate, but necessary."

"For what?" I continued pressing. I really did want to know why they were going through all of this for seemingly no reason.

"Father's goals. It's true that some people have died, but it's not without purpose. He . . . He wants to make a better world. Didn't you know? Maybe that's why we're fighting then; I'm sure once he explains it, everything will be clearer."

"Better how?"

"Like us . . . Before him, before he began to improve us, all of our people but him were savages—unable to speak, barely able to think. Many still are, but we're changing, all thanks to Father and his designs. Because of him we're able to be so much more than we were, and when he's done, your people will be so much more too. He knows how to live far longer. Did you know that? Like, immortality, for everyone. Isn't that worth a few lives?"

I could tell that, if nothing else, Sasha believed that what he was doing was right. That was important because people seldom followed those they thought were evil. They always had a reason, a sense to their actions. If we could find that out, maybe we could find out how to stop all this. Because I knew for a fact that anyone kidnapping people to be test subjects was up to no good. Perhaps there would be some benefit for the world, but this new world that "Father" sought to make would undoubtedly have him at the top.

"Killing innocents is wrong," Lucas said from the side. "We should let them be."

"Without a few of those deaths, I wouldn't be able to think or speak. I rather like both of those things," Greta pointed out to him, frowning.

"I rather like them, too, Greta, but there are better ways to go about this than taking little girls off the street. How would you feel if someone came into your home and snatched up one of your siblings, carting them off to kill them?"

They both got quiet for a while, thinking. Good, thinking was good. Thinking might get them to turn on their leader and stop this madness. Sure, I was opposed to them, but I wasn't genocidal. They could reason, and if they could reason, they could be made to *see* reason, and stop. That would keep any more people from dying, an altogether better solution than any other.

"We actually lost one of ours a while ago. We presume he was killed by your people."

That I actually knew about, for I'd been there when he'd been killed.

"Is that so? What was he doing when he was lost?"

That answer took them a while to respond to as well. Eventually, though, Sasha spoke up. "He was part of one of the gathering groups." It was painfully clear to all of us what they were "gathering."

"Well, you can't well fault people for defending themselves, can you? Things might have been different if someone had actually tried talking to us."

"Like you would," griped Greta.

"I'm doing so now. In the future I'm willing to, as well, but I do want you to stop kidnapping people." We finally reached some kind of intersection. These weren't the steam tunnels used in only a few places. Rather, they seemed to be some old maintenance tunnels, but I didn't know from where they hailed. Before us was a door made of steel and slightly rusted. With a calm hand I reached out and pulled on it, opening to a larger room behind.

"Ladies first," I offered with a wave.

Inside was some kind of storage area, larger than I'd have expected for something underground, used at one point for carts, if the ruts in the stone and the little stall-looking structures were any indication. It was clear, though, that it had been long abandoned, left to fall apart where it was. That was odd, since it could've been refurbished, and I wondered briefly if this kind of thing had been common on Earth as well.

"Well, well, our guest finally arrives. Welcome, welcome. I'm so very excited to speak with you," said a goblin in the center of the room. He looked slightly older—not aged, but mature—standing taller than either of the girls. He wore a long white coat, miraculously clean, and an approximation of a shirt and vest. It would have been quite stylish on anyone but a goblin.

"I'll admit I'm quite interested in speaking to you too," I replied.

"Oh? Wonderful to hear, though, I believe I requested you to come alone?" he said questioningly, looking at Lucas who was standing quietly at my side.

"Are you alone?" I asked, looking to the two girls who'd brought us here.

"Haha, well, you do have me there. I was hoping you might introduce me to the lady my dear Greta told me about. That's why I said to allow an addition, but it is of no consequence." He put his hands in a perfect scholar's cradle, looking up at me.

"I hope you don't mind if we switch to English?" he said in English. "There are some things I'd rather keep slightly more private, if you don't mind."

"Same."

"I guessed, but didn't want to assume; it would be a truly awkward conversation with one's parents. Where are my manners though? I am Doctor Anton Parkov. A pleasure to meet you."

Anton Parkov. I knew that name. I'd heard it somewhere, but I just couldn't place it.

"Please, just call me Percival. I've had another name, but after not using it for years . . ."

"Naturally, naturally. I'm sure you'd like to know what I want, but first I must ask, English? And an American, too, if I'm not mistaken. Would you mind confirming your former location and the date you found yourself here?"

I rattled off the name of my former hometown and date I'd wandered into that field while I thought about his name. It was so familiar. I could see his eyes light up when I told him, blinking in seeming confusion.

"Also, cursive? Who even uses that anymore?"

"Oh . . . bit of an oversight on my part. My apologies, it's just what I use in my day-to-day." So he was a weirdo too. Good to know, well, confirm. "Most odd though. I was taken on roughly the same day, and from the south as well, during an earthquake no less, but I came here some centuries ago."

"Some kind of time distortion, or we're landing periodically. I met another of us, and she seemed to be here for a long time too."

"Is that so? Do you think she might be willing to speak with me as well?"

Parkov . . .

"I'm afraid she's indisposed."

"Oh well, a shame. Now, for the meat of the matter. I'd like you to join with us. I assure you I can make it worth your while, and with two people from a far more advanced world, we can do so much. Even with just myself, I've achieved great things."

Anton Parkov . . . was he . . .

"Wait, your name, you were on the news."

"Ah . . . was hoping you wouldn't remember that, but have no fear my lad, the things they said about me were hardly true."

"You killed dozens, and dozens more here, at least. They were going to execute you."

"One does have to break a few eggs to make an omelet, my friend. I was hoping you'd come to understand that." As he spoke, I heard footsteps running hard in the distance, coming our way at speed, still far, but they'd be here soon.

"Yeah, no, but if you surrender now, I'll do all I can to see your people are treated well," I replied, switching back to the local tongue.

"Oh, is that so? And if I refuse?"

"Well, then, we'll have no deals, will we?"

"How about this, I'll learn what I can from you and your friend here before I move on to the rest of my research. Subjects with actual power are so rare for me." As he spoke he separated his hands, a wisp of yellow magic stretching between them.

"So much for letting us leave unharmed," I quipped, not for him, but for the girls. I had to hold out some hope, and I could see Sasha's face waver at the words.

"Father?" she said, confused.

"Plans change," he said, releasing his spell.

Lucas and I both had to leap to the side, dodging a yellow arc of energy. I didn't know what would happen if it landed, or even grazed me, and I was in no mood to find out. As we rolled, I heard Lucas draw his blade, and I reached for my weapon.

"They sure do," I replied, pulling the trigger.

CHAPTER 54

*

CONTACT WITH THE ENEMY

The first shot landed squarely in the middle of the goblin's chest, tossing him back like a ragdoll. It was refreshing, so very refreshing, to have something I made work perfectly. The smell of powder burning, the kick back as the recoil hurt. The sound. Actually, the sound hurt like being stabbed in the ear. Super hearing, firearms, and confined spaces really shouldn't mix.

There was yelling, though I couldn't tell what, and the fighting began. My hope was to disable, not kill the two goblin girls, since they seemed reasonable and there might still be some place for negotiation, but it was hard. Neither of them was likely to surrender, and I didn't want to lose.

My next shot went to Sasha's thigh, ripping through like it was barely there, though even as I watched, arcing energy raced down her body, and the wound began to heal. That was rough, because we really didn't have much in the way of disabling weaponry against a priest. My only recourse was to shoot her again in the shoulder to keep her busy until the cavalry arrived.

I looked over to see Lucas and Greta locked in battle. The little green girl had her shield up quickly, blocking the flurry of blows he was landing one after another. Just as I was bringing my weapon around, I saw the lenses on her goggles flip to black and I hurriedly closed my eyes, remembering the last time.

Lucas wasn't fast enough, or didn't realize what was coming, and by the time I came up to look he was jumping back. It wouldn't completely take him out of the fight, but it would decidedly hurt his ability to do much. We didn't need to win, though, only to hold them until backup arrived.

Two quick shots to Greta's shield sent a series of cracks spiderwebbing across it like glass breaking, but it seemed to hold. Only a few more moments. I only needed her to hold still a little while longer. Then the others should be here, and we could clean this mess up.

In the second that I considered where to place the final bullet, I saw Parkov begin to rise, his chest reforming and remolding as bubbling flesh filled the spot where I'd shot him. That was absolutely no good, and this guy did have to die. No ifs, ands, or buts about it. I turned, lining the sights once more upon him. If a body shot hadn't been enough to put him down, let's see him regenerate his brain.

Sasha must have seen where I was aiming and jumped between us, the round impacting her pelvis. Time seemed to slow as the wave of the impact moved outward, making her clothes and flesh ripple like water after a stone was thrown into it. I felt bad for her on some level. She was only trying to do what was right.

That was enough for little Greta, who wrapped the other two in her shield and sent their group bouncing back. I leapt forward as they retreated through the far opening, just in time to see a pair of flaming spears arc out, not toward me, but toward the edges of the tunnel. In the shadows, I saw them, two barrels that looked, perhaps not new, but decidedly newer. I would be between them when the flames hit.

Or I would have been had a hand like iron not locked around my ankle. I was airborne, unable to change my direction of flight, but I also wasn't alone. Lucas hauled on my leg hard, hard enough that I felt the bones crack, but it was enough, enough to stop my forward momentum and send us both tumbling very slightly back.

Greta's spell struck the barrels and the bombs exploded, a powerful shockwave tossing both parties away from one another. Before the smoke cleared, I could feel the cracking and breaking of the structure, debris and rocks falling like rain into the opening she'd made. It must have been one of their contingencies, one final act to forestall us should everything go awry, as it had.

Before the smoke cleared, our backup finally arrived, blasting into the room where we lay sprawled on the ground, coughing and hurt. They seemed displeased as a few of the mages began to clear the way, determined to at least try and follow.

Ignus was there, and he pulled me up. Not very helpful with a broken leg, and he began yelling. Man, it would have been nice to know what he was saying.

Ignus

Percival, the idiot, looked to be okay, though, as soon as I saw him pull one leg up, that was clearly not that case. He was, at the very least, alive, and had we been seconds earlier, this mission might have been a success.

"What happened, boy?" I screamed. "What can you tell me!"

"WHAT?" The lad said, pointing to his ears. "I CAN'T HEAR YOU. ONLY THING I CAN HEAR IS RINGING."

I wanted to smack myself, and him, and the other boy too. Maybe the grandfather as well. Really a lot of people responsible for this absolute farce needed a good beating, and if we got nothing from it, they might get one too. Just as I was starting to give up hope that we'd managed anything, one of the men shouted.

"Bloodstains, sir. At least one of them is hurt, and hurt bad, judging by the size."

"Good, get us through, and get these two to a healer, before the baron gets here preferably."

Anton Parkov

I'd been injured a few times, but seldom this badly, and not in quite a while. Getting shot was also a first, for either of my lives, and quite unexpected. Sure, I'd thought they might resist, but with guns? Who used guns when you had magic? That was just insane. Luckily, I'd live, having more than enough time to fix the vital things before it got out of hand.

As I got back to my senses, I looked around. Greta looked well and had us in one of her better spells. It was a pair of shield balls, perfectly smooth and with almost zero friction that she could speed along at quite the rate. We were fleeing. Injured as we were, it was a sad necessity at the moment.

Sasha, my dear Sasha, was whimpering nearby. She'd saved me, the darling girl, though, she'd gotten quite hurt in the process. I wrapped her gently in my magic, healing the wounds. They weren't as life-threatening as my own, and she was already healing them herself, but her pelvis looked to be shattered like a pretzel and that would hurt terribly. It wasn't much of an issue to numb the pain as we worked, and I patted her on the head.

"Thank you, my child. I knew bringing you was the right choice."

"Father, are you both going to be okay?" her sister asked.

"Yes, Greta dear. Did the blockage work?"

"It did."

"Good, good."

"We can get the others and go after him when we return. Sigmund will be sure to want to lead the assault himself," Greta said, almost angrily.

"No."

"No? What do you mean, Father? They hurt you, and Sasha too."

"There is no rush, and if we act now, we'll lose many. Anyway, we both will be fine. Taking the time to prepare will ensure we don't fail again. Remember, daughter, that haste from anger has caused the fall of more than one."

She nodded, properly chastised. "Yes, Father, I understand."

CHAPTER 55

★

UNHAPPY PARENTS

So, mind not telling Mom about this?" I asked my grandfather after I'd been healed.

"Oh, I'm telling her some things," he affirmed.

"She'll skin both of us. You know that, right?"

"I'm telling her, but we're leaving out a few key facts, like the broken ankle, or the fact that you were ever in real danger. I cannot believe how irresponsible you were, Percival. As soon as you fell through that floor, you should have done everything in your power to get away. Things didn't go to plan at all. What were you even thinking?"

"That the risk was worth the reward," I answered without thought.

"Your *life* is worth far more than what we gained, or even could have gained."

"Sorry." Honestly, I'd thought the risk was minimal. The man wanted to talk to me according to his letter, not kill me. Though I'd known he was insane, I'd given myself fairly good odds, particularly with all the backup nearby.

"If I didn't know it was a waste of time, I'd put you over my knee. You need to think, Percival, think about what will happen if you die. Your friends, your family. Do you think they won't miss you? Can you not imagine your mother's tears if we were to come home with the corpse of her only son? Your father as well. He may not show it, but he cares for you, boy. We all do."

"I know, Grandfather, but I needed to do this . . ."

"What you need is to complete your studies. Too many of you children are too excited to grow up. It's not all it's cracked up to be, boy. I'll tell you that from experience."

"Yes, Grandfather." There was no real point in arguing with him; he was, to an extent, right. That didn't change the fact that I'd done what I needed to.

"And you," he said pointing at Lucas. "Good job keeping my idiot grandson from getting blown up in that bomb, but if you breathe a word of what happened here to the wrong ears, I'll make sure you regret it."

"Yes, sir," the other boy said, having tried to avoid the ire of the clearly angry old man.

Before we could leave, Ignus approached me. "I understand you used a rather unique weapon. Would you mind if I looked it over?"

"I . . . Not at this time, Mr. Ignus," I said, shaking my head. I wasn't sure if I wanted to let that loose into the world yet.

"It really is—"

"I believe my grandson told you no. I suggest you accept that answer," Grandfather said before he could continue.

After that, I was taken back to my home to await the arrival of my parents. Neither of them had made it to the city yet due to a delay in their travels, so I had to wait. It would have been worse if I'd been in the house alone, or with only Grandfather, or maybe not. He'd demanded to see my new pistol and spent the better part of the afternoon taking it apart and putting it back together on a small table with hardly a word spoken to me.

The servants seemed to know something was up, even if they didn't know what. Grandfather's displeasure hung heavy in the air, and other than some of the senior staff, everyone strove to get things ready and out of the way. He snapped at them several times as we waited, all but Kaylee. He, of course, knew of her situation, and though there was little he could do for her without causing trouble, he still maintained his cool when she was around.

Eventually, though, all waiting must come to an end, and that evening one of the butlers from the country estate arrived from the port. He quickly informed the staff of my family's arrival. He then came to greet me, and my grandfather, looking worried when he felt the tension hanging in the room.

After Mother's arrival, and her yearly examination/terrifying of the household staff, my parents joined us in the sitting room.

"We need to have a meeting," Grandfather told them as they walked in. "A private one."

"Very well, would you dear?" Mother asked Father.

"Certainly," he answered and he erected a small glowing barrier around the room.

"Before we begin, why is that in my house?" Mother asked with saccharine poison in her tone, pointing to the revolver.

"It's your son's. I believe he made it himself." That's when the yelling began.

My grandfather may have thought it a waste of time to spank me, but my mother, with her physical magic, did not. She was still the strongest person in the room, regardless of the fact that I was catching up, and would be for a bit longer. Perhaps I could have resisted her, but doing so just didn't feel right.

When she learned of the situation we'd been in and how much her father-in-law had been involved, I did have to step in, though, wrapping her in a hug to keep her back as much as I physically could. She'd advanced upon him like an angry bear, and while she didn't strike him, both Father and I were quite worried she would. Unlike me, Grandfather was some form of caster, and he couldn't take that kind of a beating without serious problems.

"Love, you need to calm down!" Father eventually shouted. It's the only time I'd ever heard him raise his voice. "Before you do something unwarranted."

"You will not use my son as bait again," she finally growled before turning on her heel and stalking off. I felt bad for anyone who encountered her in the next few hours, something we'd have to warn the staff about.

"Thank you, son," Grandfather said. "I'd not quite expected her to be that angry."

"Her fire is one of her most endearing traits. Part of why I married her," Father mused. "Though I much prefer it be pointed at someone else. You should probably stay away from the house for a while."

"That seems . . . well advised, but I was explaining all of this to tell you why I was requesting some extra security for your home. Whoever those men were, we didn't catch them." He'd kept the fact that we were after goblins from them, and since nobody else had seen them, he was right to.

"Understood, and thank you."

Grandfather left shortly thereafter, explaining when we'd see the men he was sending, and how to identify them. Once he'd left, my father turned to me.

"Percival . . . why did you do this?"

"I felt the need. There is some kind of conflict coming, and I need to be ready, and to do my part."

He sighed. "I . . . am not a perfect man, son; I have made many mistakes over the course of my life, many regretful actions that I wish I could take back, but I cannot. That isn't something I want for you, and I think you know better than to get involved in this foolishness."

"I doubt I'll have much a choice," I admitted.

"Why?"

"It's complicated."

"Believe it or not, I'm quite clever. Why?"

"My mana is similar to several others, one of which is the leader of this group. I'm not completely sure on the reason or mechanism, but it is relevant to him. It has put us at odds, and is unlikely that this will end peacefully."

"It looks fairly normal to me, though that isn't my area of study. If he's after you, perhaps we should consider moving—"

"No, running won't solve problems, and we cannot simply surrender because there is an enemy."

"Then what do you think we need?" he asked.

"Weapons."

". . ."

"I'm not a fool, Father."

"Recent actions contradict that statement."

"I will get them one way or another, because I don't think this enemy is going away."

"Your mother's going to kill me, but I'll allow it, with proper supervision. Tell me what you need."

CHAPTER 56

*

NEW WORKSHOP

My father, who spent so little time around me or dealing with me at all, came through quite well. He ordered a number of mana-powered machines that I could use. The ones from the school that were so convenient were very expensive, and useful for some purposes, but not for all of them. Sure, if you put in all the math and directions perfectly, they worked exactly as advertised, but for more complicated mechanisms that required small changes here and there they were hardly helpful. If you needed even the most minor change, you'd have to put everything in again, for each iteration.

A few days after Mother had been so angry, the housekeeper took me down to the basement, where boxes and crates were being unloaded.

"Your father got these for you, said you'd left him a list and he did what he could," she told me.

"Is he occupied?" I asked, having hoped he would be the one to show me his acquisitions.

"I'm unsure, my lord," she replied. "Should I inquire?"

"No, it's fine." Honestly, this was more than I'd expected, and as things were being unloaded I began to look around.

There were a number of lathes, drills, presses, and hand tools, some from a list of supplies I'd given him, some that seemed to have been added by Father. Much of it was useful, but much was very specialist, parts someone had sold him, likely secondhand, which would be of no real use to me. Still, though, it showed that he was at least trying, and trying was really the first and most important step.

With almost everyone I knew mad at me, and telling me so frequently, it would be good to have somewhere to retreat to and let the heat cool down. I was in trouble still, and even Lucas wasn't fully free of repercussions, as he'd gone beyond what he was supposed to be doing. We were still communicating through letters now and then. Letters were an important thing in our culture, with post being a several times a day thing if you were in the city.

As soon as the porters had unloaded everything, I began to unpack it. There really was no way for someone else to set up your shop, and with my strength, moving even heavy machinery wasn't much of a chore. Sure, some of it was a bit awkward, but that was a minor inconvenience as I pulled the pieces to where I felt they belonged.

Standard-sized plates and rods were placed into proper stacks, racks lined with tools, and machines put in the proper section. It took the better part of the day, and as I finished up I looked over my work and realized something. Without thinking, I'd set this room up almost exactly like my shop back home on Earth. Sure, there was no radio, no garage door to open out to the sky, and the 3D printers were missing, but the layout, the way things were placed, it was all the same.

For the first time in a long time, I felt a wave of nostalgia, of friends and family lost, and I felt tears blooming and quickly wiped them away. Though I accepted this life, my old one was never gone from mind, the people I'd known, either in person or online, the grandmother I'd wanted to go and see before my transference; I supposed she was probably dead now, though with how time here seemed to be a bit weird, perhaps not.

Did I miss my previous life? Some days, but I didn't regret this one. I'd been given a chance so few could dream of, a second chance to live, to grow up, to love, to care for people close to me. I'd been given a magnificent family, one both privileged and who cared for my well-being, something not all could say. How could I be anything but grateful? No, I didn't regret my coming to this world, even if the memories of my previous one still ached from time to time.

As I sat and thought on things, Kaylee bounced down into the basement workroom from the stairs, hair bobbing under the little hairpiece all maids wore around here.

"Lord Percival, dinner will be ready soon."

"Thank you, Kaylee. I'll be on my way shortly."

There was also my little half-sister, who needed my help. Was she happy as she was? Would she prefer to be accepted for the sibling she most certainly was? I didn't know. I didn't know her nearly well enough, and sadly, learning would be difficult. Inside, I knew my family wanted me to keep away from her, since we'd been close as children; and on the outside, it was hardly appropriate for a young man to have a female personal servant so close to his own age. The world wouldn't know of our relation, at least not for now, but one day I'd find a way, some way, to see that she got everything she deserved.

When I made it upstairs, I found that I was the last to arrive in the dining room. My parents and maternal grandparents were here. Grandma looked peeved, as always, and even Grandpa still frowned at me. They'd both already read me the riot act when Mother had told them of my escapades, perhaps thinking that her father, one of my closest confidantes, would have better luck disciplining me than she had. I was still quite unrepentant though. Even if I'd done things I knew displeased her, there were more important things than keeping my mother happy.

"I'm glad you finally deigned to join us, Percival," Grandma said coolly.

"And I'm quite glad to see you as well, Grandma. How are things?"

"Well. Have you checked your mail recently?"

"Not since this morning," I said. "I was setting up my workroom." Grandpa perked up a bit only to sit back when she sent him a glare.

She'd made it clear that for the time being he wasn't to speak about "our toys" with me.

"I'll save you some time here, son. Why has His Grace, the duke, sent you what appears to be an invitation?" Mother asked. "How does he even know your name?"

"We met recently, and he must want me to come to some event. Did seem like a fine fellow to me."

Food was brought out as glares intensified. Everyone, even the staff, knew that I was in the doghouse, but arguing in front of them was uncouth. When they finally left us, my kin leaned forward.

"When was this?" Mother spat, "and why didn't you tell me? Did he approve of your nonsense personally? That hardly seems right."

"No, before that. You really should have listened to Grandfather better, rather than trying to throttle him. I met him, though, I've been forbidden from going into the details of it."

"Forbidden? By whom exactly?" Grandmother interjected.

"Royal decree." That bombshell stopped all of them dead in their tracks, for there were precious few that could issue one of those, and none were known to be near us.

"Go and get that letter right now," Grandmother snapped.

"Leaving the table, in the middle of dinner?" I asked innocently.

"Now," several voices chimed.

I did as I was bid and popped the seal as I walked, skimming over the contents. I rather liked the letter writing culture, but at times it was quite tiring, particularly when dealing with individuals of particularly high status. It seemed the thing to do was simply to write as flowery and long as a message as possible, rather than getting to the bleeding point.

"I've been invited to a dinner," I told them when I returned. "Myself and a companion are invited to—"

"Well, you're going," my mother told me with a sigh. This was too big an event for me to skip.

✳

CHAPTER 57

INVITATION

Responding to the duke was quick, finding a date even quicker. Mother had several potential candidates in mind, but honestly, there'd only really been one. After all, they'd been insisting that I have the same companion for almost every formal dinner for most of my young life, so having someone I knew for this event would be the best idea.

"This is so exciting, I can't believe you managed to get an invitation to the duke's residence? I've never met him, of course, was waiting until my official introduction to society, but to meet him even earlier is such a treat!" Young Lady Starshine enthused as our carriage rattled down the road.

"I'm glad you're willing to join me on such short notice; thank you for that." I replied, having only had a few days from the arrival of the letter to tonight.

It wasn't a hollow apology, either, for I knew I'd caused her no small amount of trouble. An invitation to one of our houses, not even the direct holder of a noble title was one thing, but to a duke's manor? That was a whole different story. The clothing required wasn't something either of us had lying around, nor would we have a use for later. It also meant that we'd have to apply a whole new level of manners, with parents stringently going over those again.

"There's no need for an apology, Percival. This is the chance of a lifetime." Then again, she didn't seem at all displeased.

"Perhaps, but it was unexpected."

"Mmm, true. However did you get such an invitation anyway? Not to offend, but we're both hardly the sort of people who get that sort of letter. Are you perhaps related to him?"

"Oh, no nothing like that, we just met a while back through a mutual acquaintance. I really wasn't expecting to hear from him again, particularly not so soon."

She gave me an appraising look, but since it was clear I didn't want to elaborate, she didn't push. I appreciated that. There were already enough people in my life that were digging into my business at all hours and making things quite a pain. One person willing to give me my peace and privacy was more than welcome.

"How is your brother doing, by the way?" I asked. "I haven't had the chance to see him in a couple of weeks, all things considered."

She giggled. "Oh, it's been quite the event. When our parents found out some of the details, they spent the better part of a week punishing him. They've even threatened to keep him from participating in some of the sword tourneys, though I doubt they'll follow through with that one." Then her eyes narrowed. "Of course, you were there for the foolishness too."

"Please don't, I've already had enough people in my life berate me, and I'm honestly not at all sorry."

"Maybe if you were more sorry, they'd stop berating you," she said with a huff.

"A man must do what he must do." I looked out of the window for a few moments in silence before speaking again. "At any rate, we're here."

The manor we were going to was massive, larger even than our off-season mansion back home and decked out with statues, fountains, and lights galore. The drive was smooth as we pulled in, the horses stopping just before the main entry.

Immediately I realized just how few people there were in attendance. Surely the ducal house had mountains of friends or family they could invite, but for tonight there were very few carriages about. That was odd, and it meant that this was to be a far more private affair than I'd expected.

As I helped Rowena down from the carriage her eyes were alight. She maintained her composure, as was expected, but it was plain to see that if she were allowed she'd be bouncing with joy. In this world of magic, some places were far more magical, with decorations and power that would have stood up to anything my previous world had. I was told that in the past they were even more extreme, with displays of magic and power to wow all involved, but tradition locally dictated that such ostentatious things be limited.

We were announced moments later as we entered the house, with our host and hostess smiling and greeting us. The dinner, for all that it was, was much the same as any other. Sure, there were seating changes, more and better food items, and the room as a whole was far beyond what we were used to, but since there was a procedure to it all we knew exactly what to do. There was something to that, the fact that people could depend on manners to remain mostly the same, the rules to be stable.

Our conversation was light, kept so by the strictures of etiquette, but it was clear to me that this was no simple social call. The duke wanted something from me, and as he was keen to do so, had called me to his home. Sure, he might have just asked me to come at a normal time, but that would have led to questions. Inviting a young man of noble blood who'd saved some innocent girl earlier in the year could be written off as mere curiosity about me. He even made sure to ask about the incident briefly though seemed not to care too much when I relayed the story of our first encounter with one of the odd goblins.

Once dinner was over, we all sat and chatted for a few moments before our host looked to me.

"Come, young man," he said. "We'll retire to my smoking room and let the ladies to themselves for a bit. Wouldn't want to bother them with the smell. I've even managed to acquire a bit of liquor from the mainland I think you'll enjoy."

Rowena looked at me with a raised eyebrow and almost moved to speak. She knew I didn't smoke and found it to be a rather disgusting habit.

"Don't worry, dear," the duchess said. "I'm sure my husband will bring him back safe and sound. Do you like pastries? Our chef has the most magnificent recipe that I'm sure you'll love." She took Rowena by the arm before she could interject. I had to appreciate their skill at tag-teaming us. The duke led me down one hallway after another, not far from where we'd been, but far enough, and certainly not to the normal smoking room. The room we entered looked more like a sitting room, well stocked with chairs and a faint tinge of runes around the walls. My guess was something for privacy, but I wasn't a hundred percent sure.

He did actually pour me a small glass of some alcohol, and he was right, it was lovely—fruity and light without being overpoweringly sweet, floral almost. We each took a few sips as we found a pair of chairs.

"Apologies for all the cloak and dagger, lad, but I didn't want to draw any more attention to you than we already have. Things are moving."

"How so?" I asked.

"Well, I'm not sure it's related to our local woes, but we found out who came to assassinate our archmage."

"Who?"

"Elves."

CHAPTER 58

✳

BUSINESS

Don't we have enough problems?" I said.

"Probably, but as I said, I don't believe it is related to our local problems."

I leaned back, blowing out a sigh. First goblins and now elves. If we got dwarves next, I was starting a riot. I didn't even think dwarves were a thing, but with us exploring all of the small areas of the world now, we might well find some one day. I mean, there were tiny people back on Earth in little pockets, but were those more like dwarves, or would I have called them halflings or something?

"Why?" I asked after a few seconds of thinking.

"An interesting question. How much do you understand of Elazian politics?" he asked, referring to the eastern continent where the elven people lived.

"Practically nothing."

"Then the long and short answer is that some of them are stirring against us, and by us I mean humans in general. Their nations haven't been fully united for most of history, and so they vary on their approach to humanity drastically."

"Great."

"Quite the opposite," he said. "Do you happen to speak any of their languages? We could add that to your training . . ." I paled right before he smiled, chuckling under his breath. "Sorry, needed something to lighten the mood. I've been informed that they're working all the students at the school to the bone already. That's good; we may need you before too long . . ."

"So you called me here to tell me this?"

"No, I called you here to let you know to keep watching out, and ask you for a favor; furthermore, to see how you are."

I raised an eyebrow. "If the favor is within reason."

"Good, not agreeing immediately. I believe it is, but I'm unsure how you'll feel. One of my men told me you came up with a new design for a firearm, one he's keen to get hold of."

He wanted a revolver design. It wasn't like I couldn't give it to him. In fact, it would probably be good for us all if I did. That didn't mean that I didn't want something for it. It would be a massively important weapon for him, after all.

"I don't mind selling you the design."

"Truly? I suspected you might play it close to your chest like so many mages tend to with their best spells."

"No, that would just encourage someone to steal it from me, and I don't fancy being robbed. Let them come for you and your manufacturers instead." That got me a laugh.

Over the next twenty minutes or so we worked out a fairly simple deal. I would be getting some money and access to a few chemists and the like that would be difficult for me to arrange. I wanted nitrocellulose, and I wanted it in the right-sized pellets, and those would be hard to get without help. Also, primers. The duke looked at me like he suspected I was up to making more goodies, which I was, but didn't push.

When it was all worked out to both of our satisfaction, we departed, heading back to the others. This manor was something. Where I lived in the country could've compared to it in size, if not in opulence, but here in the city, this amount of space for one family and their servants was on the far end of senseless. It took minutes for us to walk across it once more, both because none of the hallways were straight and due to the distance.

The women were deep in conversation about one of the local events, and from what I heard as I was coming along, it sounded like they were all simply going on about their favorite parts. It was what one expected to hear, particularly when the participants were of differing social classes. Nobody was being negative, even if they'd not liked something, lest they offend, and all of them were focusing on something that was so innocuous there couldn't possibly be an insult.

That didn't mean there wasn't more going on. Much of the nuance of the conversation was lost on me, being couched in the manners and practiced ease of the ladies involved, but even now I could pick up a few bits and pieces. The duchess clearly thought that things should be fancier and more involved, whereas the others involved disagreed, without actually disagreeing at all. This was one of the ways higher born women interacted—the seemingly simple things with far deeper meanings that took effort and experience to decipher.

"Your Grace makes an excellent point," I heard my date say. "Perhaps I should look at things that way," meaning "I'm really sorry for disagreeing with you on this, please don't take offense."

"Of course, with experience we all see things more clearly," came the response from the duchess. Translation: "It's fine, you've straightened yourself out and you're still young."

"Ah, ladies, how go things?" the duke asked as we returned.

"Oh, you know. And your discussions?" his wife asked.

"Well, well, we're all done."

We had a brief back and forth about how it was getting late, and how we really did need to go, along with a promise to exchange letters in the future. That was a given, since someone would need to pick up designs for the revolver. I already had those done, and with the fact that I was moving on to bigger and better things, it was of no concern. It did occur to me that my parents might disapprove, but what they didn't know couldn't hurt me, or something like that.

"You don't smell like smoke," my companion pointed out as we rode home.

"I don't smoke."

"But I'd wager His Grace does."

"Probably, but mostly he wanted a private conversation."

"I understood as much."

"Did you enjoy yourself at least?" I asked her. "I heard some of your conversation with the duchess."

"Oh, so much! It was a better time than I'd hoped, and knowing them will only help me in the future. I think our hostess liked me better than I could've hoped, and even asked me about joining her for tea at some point." That was a surprise, and good for her. Connections like that couldn't be bought. "On another subject, should I consider this the beginning of our courtship?"

That was a landmine that I hadn't expected, but I'd stepped right on it.

"I . . . hadn't thought of it, but we should, shouldn't we?" It was awkward to me. She was still so young, and even if my body was, too, my mind wasn't. Would it matter though? It wasn't an actual proposal, just a statement that we were connected at our age. It would be an official declaration of potential in the future, and would mean little more now than her accompanying me to other dinners and the like.

Pleased, she reached forward and squeezed my hand, and that was the maximum of any significant contact for now. Even holding hands in public would be seen as scandalous. I sighed, still unsure of what the future held.

CHAPTER 59

GROWING UP

There were few things in this world that I really truly loved. My family, some of my friends, and my new workshop were among them. During the days of the Season I might have expected to have an actual break, but I would have been wrong. I needed to get things done in my shop, keep up with social events in the evenings, and my mother was insistent on me keeping up with my sword practice. There had been a change in the latter.

"Yours again," Mother said as I planted the point of the practice weapon into her belly.

"Good fight."

"Not really," I said. "I'm completely out of practice."

It turned out that my continued growth, added with the absolutely insane amount of practice that I was doing, meant that I was now beating her consistently. It felt odd, winning against the person who'd managed to defeat me so soundly all of my life, but it was bound to happen at some point. My magic was no weaker than hers, and with my size and simple practice, something she seldom did when I wasn't around, I'd gained much of what I needed to win.

I thought back to the first tourney I'd been in and how I'd thought of the adults as amazing, impossible for me surpass. Now I could do many of the moves I'd seen then. That didn't mean I was the best by any means, as there were still a lot of my fellow students that could keep up with me with ease.

Lucas, for example, was a better swordsman than I. He defeated me in the majority of our fights, though I'd like to think I gave him a run for his money. My goal wasn't to be the best at cutting people apart, though, but rather to have more of a mixed style. A blade and a firearm together seemed a better combination for me, since distance fighting was something many of our contemporaries lacked.

"I suppose you're growing up." Mother sounded almost sad as she spoke.

"Oh, I like to think I've always been a bit older than I looked."

She laughed at that. "Maybe, but you were a right little menace as a child. Always wandering off and disappearing, only to show up in the oddest of places. Why, once our cook found you in the servants' passages here in the house."

"I remember," I told her. Sinea was such a scared girl.

"You were what, two? How do you remember that?" At my shrug she shook her head. "That memory. Like your grandpa, huh?"

"Suppose so."

It was a point of fact that elves had a much better memory than humans, to the point that even I had noticed when I was young. Parts of my memory were so clear—not all of it, not even the majority, but sections that I knew were important were almost like a slightly blurry photograph.

"Son, promise me you won't do foolish things and get yourself killed."

"I'll try."

"That isn't what I asked."

"Perhaps not, but it is what I can give you."

She looked like she wanted to argue, to fight me over it, but she didn't. She'd done so before, berated me, told me off, but now? Now she seemed afraid and sad, afraid that I would leave her, sad knowing that I would soon no longer be the child she'd seen for so long. Below it all, though, I could see more, just the barest hint of pride that I was growing well.

We split soon after, both going to deal with the other tasks we had for the day. As I returned to my room I passed my sister in the hall, working hard while I was hardly working. She was cleaning all over, under the watchful eyes of the older maids. She was good, very good, and improving steadily, so far as I could tell. Of course, there really was only so much I could tell, separated in status as we were. If I paid too much attention to her, or seemed too interested, it could cause all kinds of problems, particularly with us both now hitting the cusp of adulthood. Others wouldn't understand my reasons, and I couldn't tell them without causing all sorts of trouble, but still I wanted to look out for her.

Back in my bedroom I got to my letters for the day. My plane project with Grandpa was currently grounded, the craftsmen busy with a lot of other orders and being very careful about this odd one. It would take time, as many things did. The first prototype probably wouldn't be ready for a while yet. That was frustrating, but I wouldn't forget about it. It wasn't like it was something new to me, or impossible.

The duke's people had sent a letter confirming they'd begun work on their first prototype revolvers and would be getting back to me with supplies and questions soon. Both sets of grandparents had events they wanted me to attend, nothing much, but things I needed to be there for. Lucas had sent me a threatening letter about what would happen if I misbehaved with his sister, couched in friendly, flowery nonsense. Said sister had also sent me a letter, an almost daily occurrence. I responded to all of them as needed, managing not to laugh too hard at how much Lucas and I were alike.

Sighing, I sat back. There was so much to do, and so little time to do it all in. There'd been no more attacks from the goblins, at least, and I knew that the authorities were taking that quite a bit more seriously now. Time would tell, but surely we weren't done with them yet. As for the report that elves had been after the archmage, I didn't even know what to do about that. Perhaps I'd ask Grandpa for some lessons in the language, shore things up. Yeah right, if I ever found any free time at all.

For now though? I think it was enough for me to get things in order and go back to school. There was much more to learn, much more to make, much more to prepare for, and there, at least I'd be pretty safe. Headmaster Logan may have been the most demanding man I'd ever met, but he knew his business, and I was sure that if any enemy showed up in *his* school, they'd be regretting it sorely. Heck, I'd pay good money to see him fight any of the people who'd been giving me trouble of late, for I still remembered the beating I'd taken early on.

CHAPTER 60

✳

A GREATER FUTURE

Sasha

I looked at my sister. I'd felt off for the past several days. I leaned up against the door to the warren, tapping my fingers in thought. Beside me my sister tinkered, playing with some mechanism or other.

"Do you think father was . . . wrong?" I asked her.

"How do you mean?"

"He told the humans they'd be let go unharmed if they didn't attack, but . . ."

"No, they were clearly trying to betray him," Greta answered. "Look how quickly the others showed up."

"Maybe, but how would he have known that?"

"He's Father," Greta replied. "Of course he knows."

"Still, I can't help but think that we might have been able to talk it out. Father even seemed angry at them."

"I'd be angry, too, if you betrayed me."

Greta understood, but she just didn't seem to be as worried, at least not on the outside. We spent too much time together for us not to know each other's mannerisms. I could tell that she was bothered by this line of thought. Not wanting to push, I changed the subject.

"What have you got there?" I asked, nodding to the small item Greta was working on.

"Oh this, the cleverest thing," she said. "It's an engine of some kind, works on a heat differential of all things." At my blank look, my more intellectually inclined sister sighed and explained, "One side is hot, the other cold, and it spins."

"That's . . . neat, but does it do anything else?"

Greta didn't like that response at all. "Spinning is enough; it's the very foundation of work! If you can make something spin, you can run a wheel, or another mechanism. You could even pump water with it if you wanted!"

"Fine, fine, sorry I asked. You know I've never much cared for that kind of thing." I waved my hands in an attempt to calm her down.

"You and everyone else, well, almost everyone else," she grumbled.

"Almost?"

"Well, our esteemed Father knows it's worthwhile, of course, and there are one or two others who are showing some promise."

"Our siblings?" I asked, not having seen any that would be inclined to this sort of thing.

"No . . . some of the other altered ones. There's one in particular who's more clever than most, though he's still young and learning." I could hear the hope in her voice.

"You like him," I said, only to have her scowl at me. She and I stood at an odd place in the tribe. We were special, powerful in ways that few others were—smarter, different, better, but also alone. We were too different, to the point that few of the others, particularly the males, were of any interest at all. My sister and I were of one mind in this, that taking one of the unaltered ones as a mate would be . . . wrong, something that had led to Father going out of his way to start altering some that weren't our siblings, in hope we might find someone.

Sadly, our brother Sigmund had no such compunctions and was fathering children at a steady rate. This wasn't great, because though they were slower to grow than our siblings, they were also . . . stupid.

Yes, stupid was the word, and large. They were still young, but even now some of them were getting to be real pains in the ass. The unaltered ones knew to obey, but his offspring were stronger, more aggressive, and while none had fully manifested their progenitor's strength yet, there were some signs they could in the future.

"Perhaps," my sister replied. "Have any caught your eye yet?" That drew me out of my thoughts and back to the present.

"No," I admitted with a sigh.

"Did you know the humans take only one mate?"

I blinked at that. "Really?"

"Yes, odd isn't it? They also get really connected it seems."

I had to think on that for a few moments. The idea of having only one other with you wouldn't work for most of our kind, I didn't think. It also wasn't expected, though some of that might have been what Father had told us about the place before. On the island we'd apparently died in droves, so having only one wouldn't really work, but here . . .

"Would that be so bad?"

"You know, that's why I like you, Sasha."

"Huh?"

"You actually think about things. Most of our siblings would hear something like that and they'd just write it off as humans being humans, but not you. You took the time to think about what it would be like, and if that was something you'd like, and I love that."

"Without thinking, how can we improve?"

"Hehe, exactly."

"You didn't answer my question though," I said. "Would it be so bad?" She stopped tinkering and tapped her chin.

"I don't know, I'll think about it."

That made me chuckle, because what better response could she have had?

A few moments later she finished with whatever she was doing and held up the device before making a small flame under it. It spun faster and faster, the little wheel chugging along. Honestly, it looked more like a toy than anything else to me, but if she said it was worthwhile, it would be. Greta knew what she was doing.

"One more step toward a greater future, for all of us," she said, watching it spin.

"Yeah, for all of us."

CHAPTER 61

★

TIME OFF

With the holidays ending, I found myself back at school, which was a mixed bag. I liked my school and my friends, and being around them. On the other hand, there was my schedule. At the end of every day I was exhausted, broken, and ready to fall into my bed, only to have to wake up and do it all again the next day.

Professor Killic, who I'd met on my first trip here, met me after class one day.

"How are you finding your second year, Percival?" he asked kindly. Sometimes we still talked like this when we had free moments.

"Busy, but at least I'm now only in exercises for three years instead of four." I answered with a smile.

"Ha! The advantages of getting to your second year, my young friend, though you do seem to have a knack for finding all kinds of things to work on. How are you liking your new class, metalworking was it?" Sir Kendrick, the knight sent to make sure I was being well trained, had pulled through, getting me somewhere I could work, if I ever found the time.

"Yes, I must say that I'm quite excited for it, though Professor Turner has only covered safety so far."

"An important subject before we start any large undertaking."

"Perhaps, but when almost every lesson boils down to keeping your limbs and clothes well clear of the sharp spinning and or hot bits, it does get a bit repetitive."

"Many spinning things in Professor Turner's class then?" he said with a joking smile.

I groaned. The joke had been done absolutely to death, mostly by the professor himself, who thought it was absolutely hilarious. "More than a few, though that's to be expected."

"Ah well, though I didn't pull you aside to talk about other classes so much as my own," he said with a pointed look. I wasn't doing nearly as well as I should in his class. Every day I struggled to find moments to do this or that, never truly able to give as much attention to any one subject as I should. That was hardly an excuse, though, was it?

"I'm guessing you didn't like my last essay?"

"Like it? I liked where you were going with it, but the delivery was far below what I know you're capable of, and while I'd have found it acceptable for another student, you know better."

"I, uh," I could make excuses, dissemble, but I didn't want to. "Sorry, sir, I should've put more effort into it."

He gave me a complicated look. "Percival, I'm not sure if it's my place to say it, but you may be spreading yourself too thin."

I had to wait to respond until after I'd finished laughing. "Oh, I agree, but I'm not sure how that's possible, Professor. I somehow doubt Headmaster Logan will allow me to attend fewer combat classes."

"You could drop either your new course or stop working on creating magical items," he said, looking at me hopefully. "I hate to say, but neither of those are really that important to men of your stature."

"No," I bristled. "Well, I may stop the one after learning the basics, but I'm still working on the first level of my core, and that I won't compromise. As for the metalworking, I enjoy that more than almost anything else, and I'm good at it."

"Well, will you at least take a bit of time to rest? We've a weekend off coming up, and you clearly need a bit of rest. In fact, I know of a lovely little town a short ride away called Bamblebrook, perfect place for a weekend off."

"Sir," I said with a sigh, "I was planning on doing your next essay that day."

Normally I'd have shoved that into an evening, but I was avoiding going to Exion proper since I knew the local goblin population almost certainly had someone watching for me. Until I was ready to get armed up again and prepped for a battle, I was staying away. Sure, I could've asked my grandfather to loan me a couple of guards, and he would've, but I wanted to be even more ready than I had been last time.

"Come by my office the day before and give it to me verbally," he said. "We'll discuss your thoughts and counterarguments. It'll take less time and show me you know what I'm trying to teach."

"That . . . Certainly, sir! Thank you." I wasn't going to turn that down. I could come up with the major points in minutes rather than hours, and I'd always enjoyed talking things over more than writing them down.

He wrote down a few notes about the little village he'd suggested, along with what I'd be speaking on. We weren't supposed to get the latter for another few days, but having the extra time to run through my thoughts would be a massive help. Extending the papers to me, he fixed me with a hard glare.

"Take my suggestion and rest. Even if you decide to go somewhere else, you need to take the day off. I'm giving you a chance here, Percival, and if I should find you've wasted it, I'll be quite unhappy."

"Have no worries on that account, Professor," I assured him. As if I'd shoot myself in the foot by ignoring his kindness. I knew full well that if I did, I wouldn't be getting another opportunity like this.

That evening I tried to invite my friends, but none of them were up for it. Each and every one had something else they wanted to do rather than join me on our one day off for a relaxing afternoon in a local village. That was disappointing, particularly with Lucas, who wanted to go to a bloody sword tournament of all things, but there was nothing to do about it.

Bamblebrook village was only an hour away by carriage. Even if one took their time, they could leave in the morning, spend the day wandering about, and be back before it got too late. Hiring a carriage for the day was no great issue either, so I had my plan in hand.

Even Professor Killic's assignment went swimmingly. Since he was asking for nothing more complex than a discussion on supply and demand in a wartime economy, and the ways one might meet their needs. It wasn't my favorite thing, but I pointed out a few of the more successful things that had been done during the world wars, with victory gardens to supplement food rather than lawns or the like and using rationing schedules. I surely hoped that we'd never need to do such things, but one never knew where the world would go. The professor seemed pleased with my suggestions, though pointed out that some of them would really only help with morale.

When the day arrived, I woke up as early as I possibly could, took my cane and good clothes, and hopped into my ride. Streets passed at speed, missing the small amount of traffic around the school on such days and hardly seeing another on the road as we passed through the pre-dawn darkness.

Bit by bit the sky lightened, showing hedges and little stone walls around fields of grain, some hardy crop that grew through the cold winter. Tiny cozy cottages sprung up here and there, well back from the road and on hillocks that dotted the countryside, homes for those who lived here, worked here.

As the sun rose, the carriage crested a hill, crossing into a little valley with the village spread out beneath. A small ribbon of water wound down and through the town, which must have at some point been much larger. The walls were small, but sufficient, and I could see where there'd once been houses but now were open lots, instead planted with vibrant flower gardens and little fountains. It looked idyllic and homey, somewhere one could curl up with an old book and a cup of tea and just while the day away. I smiled as we rolled toward the little settlement, sure that Professor Killic had given me just what I needed.

CHAPTER 62

MEETING IN BAMBLEBROOK

The carriage dropped me off just outside the gate to Bamblebrook. This choice was made because the streets inside were painfully small, and while they could be taken, I didn't have anywhere in particular I wanted to go. Since it was easier on everyone involved, I'd opted for this measure, and as an added bonus, I got to see the little town from the point of view of any other visitor.

The walls were aged, and well built, if a bit antiquated. It always surprised me how many places here had walls, but the reasoning was clear. This world had monsters of all varieties, and even a moderately sized one could prove quite dangerous to a town. Small monsters popped up here and there and were dispatched with ease, but mid-sized to larger ones could be a real problem, so every settlement of note had some form of wall, even if it was a smaller one people could flee back to during emergencies.

The main street was beautifully cobbled, and so thin it was clearly built for pedestrian traffic in anything other than emergencies. Surely the carriage that had deposited me hadn't been the only one to make that decision, something likely encouraged by the local population at large. My feet clacked against the smooth, rounded stones as my eyes drifted all around me.

Each side of the street had a number of small restaurants, with coffee and tea served along with light pastries to the early morning guests. I watched as a girl in a pink apron put out the sign that her little institution was open. I liked the look of that one in particular, with an awning to keep the sun away, covered in little flowering vines. So, I decided to be her first morning customer.

"What can I get for you this morning, sir?" the waitress asked as she seated me.

"Something light, I think, and some tea. What would you recommend?" I asked, curious as to what she'd offer.

"The house special is the best," she assured me.

"That then."

As it turned out the house special was two eggs and a bun served with a gently whipped cream and orange marmalade. The flavors balanced perfectly, with the cream unsweetened, as well as the milk bread roll, which was perfectly light and fluffy, and the eggs providing a much-needed infusion of protein without too much fat. Even the tea paired well, giving credence to the idea that this might be one of the better cafes in town.

I, of course, ate alone, with few others yet choosing to be at any of the little shops this early. Schools like mine had a military schedule, and as such, food was served early in the morning, but for most of the upper classes, this wasn't the case. Well-off people often ate their morning meal late, very late, because of course they did—the servants needed time to prepare such things in the mornings. Your staff really only could wake up so early if they were going to be working all through the day, so there was a sort of hard limit on how early breakfast could be had. For example, at the summer house we seldom ate a meal before about ten in the morning.

After I finished my breakfast, I bid the nice girl good day and continued on my way. The town's little brook, for which it was almost certainly named, fed right through the local park, so I decided to head there next. It seemed a good place to relax and enjoy the morning, if nothing else.

There were lovely little paths through the park, one leading me on a quick little walkabout for much of the morning. I strolled, taking time to enjoy the flowers and little statues, in no rush since I didn't have anything else planned for the morning. Eventually, this led me to a little stone bridge that crossed the stream and gave a near-perfect view of the entire park.

"It's a lovely view, isn't it?" a voice asked beside me.

I turned to find a man smiling beside me. He was slightly taller than me, with pale white hair pulled back in a ponytail and porcelain skin that women I knew would kill for. He also had deep shadows under his eyes, as if he hadn't slept for days.

"Yes, sir, it is." I didn't know the man, and while I didn't want to be rude, it seemed off to talk to such a stranger.

"If you don't mind my saying, you seem troubled. Whatever could there be that would cause such a young lad to look so stressed?"

"Is that not the pot calling the kettle black? You're not much older than I am." It was true too. He looked to be perhaps in his twenties, and quite sickly.

He laughed. "I assure you, I've aged gracefully, though it's true that I've not been myself for a while. Haven't been out in some time, you see. In fact, my daughter forbade me from coming here. Can you believe that? Ah, she'll live though."

"She probably just wants the best for you," I assured him. At his age, his daughter had to be at most about ten.

"Perhaps, but you still haven't answered my question."

"Many things," I replied. "It just feels like I don't have the time I need to get as strong as I need to."

"Ah, I'm afraid I can't really understand that one, but a bit of advice from an expert—don't go seeking power. That road leads only to pain and heartbreak."

"Pfft, I don't want power for the sake of power. I want to keep the ones I love safe." I already knew not to seek something like that to the exclusion of other things.

"A noble desire, but my statement stands."

"What about you? What has such bags under your eyes?" I snapped, quite tired of this man's unsolicited advice.

"A friend of mine died recently, one of many over the years."

"Oh, my condolences," I said, biting my lip. I was sorry now for losing my temper with a man in mourning.

"Murdered, too, and I haven't the slightest idea why. It's quite frustrating. Though, I don't suppose a youngling like you has ever seen such a thing."

"I have, actually. A while back I met an old lady who was betrayed by someone who should have been on her side. I couldn't do anything to help either. It . . . was so wrong." I didn't go into specifics, but there was nothing wrong with telling him such a general story.

I could see his jaw clench out of the corner of my eye. Perhaps the story reminded him of his friend. "And the killer?"

"She got him back, old spitfire that she was. Might've missed some of his friends though."

"I see."

We sat in silence for a few minutes, neither looking at the other until he spoke again, pointing.

"Do you see that?"

He pointed at a large descending bird, easily the size of a horse with a wingspan wider than some storefronts. Without thinking I jumped the rail, drawing my sword from my cane as I did, for it looked to be going toward a pair of children playing in the park.

On a hillside overlooking Bamblebrook a few seconds later . . .

"Should we have done something about that?" my companion asked. Even with his hair cropped short we could pass for brothers.

"No, the boy has it well in hand." Sometimes it was good to let the young take care of problems; it built character.

"So was it him?"

"I don't think so, no. He did, however, give me an interesting tidbit. Let's go back to that city, do a bit more digging around, maybe break into their morgue."

He laughed heartily. "Ah, just like the old days, traveling around, doing things we're not really supposed to. Damn, I've missed it."

"You never did grow up, did you?"

"Of course not. Why would I?"

It was my turn to chuckle. "Come on, let's get moving while it's still early. Let's find our culprit, so I can teach them why I was feared."

"Sure thing, boss," he said, and then whispered under his breath, perhaps thinking I couldn't hear, "it's good to have you back."

CHAPTER 63

★

CLEANUP

My conflict with the oversized avian was disappointingly short. Sure, it was big, and fast, but as most people who studied such things could tell you, when a mammalian predator gets hold of an avian on the ground, it's pretty much over for the bird. There was still a fair bit of blood, though, and two very scared children, who'd somehow come out unscathed.

There was screaming for a short while, as a hysterical woman—my guess was that she was the mother of the kids—ran over and embraced them. The beast hadn't gotten too close to them, as it was rather weak for its size, but they looked to be in shock, as were most of the people running around, eyes like dinner plates as they looked on. Reactions like that were, of course, understandable. While we were okay, there was a rather massive amount of blood flowing from the dead beast's neck.

"Is everyone quite all right?" I asked as I sheathed my blade and moved toward them. It was a faux pas to speak to women you didn't know, but in situations like this, nobody would be bothered. After all, it wasn't like I was doing anything uncouth.

In times like this it was best to keep yourself calm and collected, at least on the outside. I wasn't so used to things like this that my blood wasn't pounding through my veins, but it looked like the danger was over, and causing panic wouldn't do, so I kept my voice soft and even.

"You . . . That thing attacked my . . ." The poor mother was having a hard time forming coherent words at this point, but she'd stopped screaming, which was a plus.

"Worry not, the beast is dead, and it got nowhere near your children. Why don't we go find somewhere to sit down for a bit?"

Her reaction was understandable. The vast majority of people weren't used to violence like I was. This lady had probably never been in any sort of life or death situation, and certainly not one as unexpected as this had been. She'd gone from a pleasant day in the park to her kids almost dying, so she was likely flooded head to toe with all the nice stress hormones that someone's body could make. Oddly, her kids were handling it much better than she was.

"I . . . Yes, thank you."

She let me lead them over to a nearby restaurant, one with a large covered seating area, and fell into one of the chairs. A few quick words got the waitress to bring them some tea and biscuits, for which she refused payment, and I left them to it. After all, the authorities showed up and looked around, and I could already see several fingers being pointed in my direction.

The victims settled, I walked back to the scene, and I was impressed. The local police had managed to get there in record time. Only a few minutes had passed since the incident, and there were already three on the scene, quickly getting interviews while occasionally scanning the sky.

One of the officers was interviewing a woman who looked stressed, but under it all, it seemed she was having a grand time. Gossip was present in every world, and it was clear that this would be the highlight of her week.

"Oh, yes sir, I saw it all! I was just sitting in the park, as one does, and out of nowhere there was this shadow. That thing over there swooped down right out of the air at a pair of children—children for goodness sake! Like a blur, it was, seemed to just appear." The officer, who had an amazing mustache, was writing on a small pad with hmms and yeses spread through. "And this man showed up, tall as a lamp post and broad like a barn, with a flaming sword in hand. He appeared like some sort of specter and tackled the beast to the ground before cutting its head fully from its body, he did! I've never seen something so amazing!" I had hit the thing from the side. Tackling it to the ground? This lady had a bit of an imagination, and my sword most certainly didn't flame.

"Good morning," I said by way of interruption.

"Can you not see I'm talking to the . . ." Her speech tapered off as she turned to tell me off.

"My apologies, ma'am, but would you mind if I had a short word with the officer?"

She sputtered a few confirmations before walking off with a red face.

"Tall as a lamp post and broad as a barn? You look like my nephew, and we could barely call him a man." We shared a small chuckle.

"Where are my manners?" the officer said, extending his hand. "Officer Larly."

"Percival Shadestone," I replied. "And yes, I'm the one who slew that."

"Well Mr., ah, Lord Shadestone, thank you for that. If you hadn't seen it coming, we may well have had deaths," the officer said with a grateful nod.

"I'm owed no thanks on that account, sir. The man I was speaking with saw it, not I." I looked around for the gentleman in question but didn't see him. "Odd, he must have left."

"Have to thank him, too, then. Don't suppose you caught his name?"

"No, though he's a local, I think. Younger man with pale white hair and wearing a blue . . ." A robe? No, that seemed odd.

You'd think that after living in this world for years some things would pop out to me, but it wasn't always so. Coming from a modern country, and used to odd clothes, unless I was looking for them, I seldom noticed. That man, though, he'd been wearing a robe. That I was certain of, not something one saw around here very often, not at all.

"A robe, I think. How strange."

"Afraid I don't know him, but I'll ask some of the other lads."

"Thank you for that. Don't suppose you know where I could acquire a change of clothes?" I asked, looking down. It wasn't too bad, but there was blood all over my clothing.

"We've a bard on staff that can clean it up. Useful for cleaning up scenes sometimes."

Their spellcaster pulled through, unruining my outfit before I was sent on my way. Sure, it was going to be a mess of paperwork for someone, and of course, there'd be cleanup, but I was hardly needed anymore. I did get a bit of attention from some of the locals and visitors, but nothing more than expected.

While the park was now closed, for obvious reasons, I did end up enjoying the rest of my day. There were a number of bookstores with absolutely silly fiction about places with metal and glass skyscrapers and something akin to digital assistants. I mean, who thought of that nonsense? There was also a bathhouse, which didn't really fit in with the pseudo-Victorian world I'd been reborn into, but it was magnificent.

For my next two meals, I even splurged on some wonderful restaurants. Perhaps not quite as perfect as breakfast had been, but good nonetheless. While eating, I listened to the stories being bandied, relating to my actions that morning. Some of them were truly off the wall, but most were close enough to the truth.

I filed a brief report with the school when I returned and expected someone would speak to me about it at one point or another. Then again, the incident had been fairly minor overall, so perhaps not. What I wasn't expecting was to be woken even earlier than our normal time to find two teachers and a knight in the office I was promptly led to.

Professor Killic threw a newspaper forcefully on the headmaster's desk. "One day, boy! One day! I send you to one of the most peaceful, relaxed hamlets in the whole country, and somehow you find the only beast for thirty miles! What happened to relaxing?"

"It," I said, yawning, "wasn't that major of an incident, sir," and then I looked down.

"You made it to the front page," Headmaster Logan answered, nodding downward.

"So I did . . ." I answered as my eyes fell on the article.

"They even have an illustration."

"I see, sir." Admittedly, the picture used looked more like something from a novel cover than what actually happened. Some epic battle over a pair of cowering youths.

"There's even talk in the article of giving you an award. Saving children in the middle of town like that, turns out they were some editor's kids. He's making quite a big deal of it."

"Sir, it really wasn't a major thing. The beast was pathetically weak, and it wasn't like I was looking for it."

"Oh, I believe you, but you do have a knack for finding trouble. For anyone else I'd suggest a chaperone, but based on previous adventures of yours, I fail to see how that would help." The other two men in the room scoffed at that one, and admittedly, it was a pretty good joke.

"Please don't take away my days off, sir," I pleaded. I really needed to get out sometimes.

"I'm not, but I will ask that you try to keep away from populated areas during your outings in the future, if only to reduce needless panic."

CHAPTER 64

INVESTIGATIONS

Ignus

I shifted through the city's offices, eyes peeled for whoever and whatever might be a threat. The city was always under threat of some kind, be it bandits, organized crime, corruption, or something like the monsters now growing in our underbelly. Though, none of those compared to the fact that otherwise well-known men had betrayed the city.

"Report," I said as I entered a meeting room.

"The undercity is still quiet. We know they're down there somewhere, or at least we expect it, but we can't find hide nor hair of them," one of my men answered.

"Unacceptable, those beasts have done more than enough damage. I want them found, and I want them destroyed completely."

"I don't know if that's the optimal path, sir," said one of our investigators.

"Explain."

"From what we've seen they're intelligent, and from what those boys said, they can at least be talked to. This 'Father' is decidedly a problem, but if we can remove him, we might be able to negotiate with the rest." She didn't seem bothered by my sharp tone, knowing that I valued her opinions.

"We'll consider it if we can find them, but they need to be fixed, and now. As for our other issues?" I turned to the other side of the room.

"The traitors have all been confirmed by the priests we brought in to have been elves. We're having them quietly examine all of our people now, saying that we're worried about something from the underground problem. Seemed prudent since they don't look connected, and we don't want to scare any more traitors. We found one the last night . . . but this morning he was found dead in his cell. It was . . . extreme."

I'd seen the report of the capture on my desk this morning, but not the death.

"Extreme how?"

"The body, what's left of it at least, is still being examined. Someone went in there and tortured him—looked like they were skinning the man before he was killed."

Wow, that was extreme. My people would sometimes torture, quietly, and well away from any priests, but none of ours would have done that in this situation. We needed answers, but the killing told me this was personal. I'd have to see that this, too, was investigated, but one of my other officers was looking alarmed too.

"Speak up," I told him.

"One of the coroners was complaining this morning that someone messed around in the morgue—had files out, left bodies where they shouldn't have been. He thought it was one of his coworkers, but with that . . ."

"With that, we have another party involved," I said. "Potentially more of these infiltrators found out about our captive and decided to remove him."

"But why the torture? It doesn't make sense," said the same girl from before, and this was why I valued her opinion. She would point out when I made such foolish mistakes.

"You're right, a third party? Maybe they thought he'd betrayed them? We just don't know, but we need to find out."

Each of these people had been chosen because they excelled at something. That was why I loved it when they disagreed with me. Too many times I had gone through life with folks thinking that they needed to suck up; that was wrong. The thing I needed most was to win. It was the only thing that mattered in my line of work. There were people out there that thought they were the best, and everyone should sit down and do exactly as told without argument, and those people were fools. Everyone made mistakes, everyone missed obvious problems. It was only by surrounding ourselves with those whose skills exceeded our own that we could overcome our failings.

The duke employed me for similar reasons. That was part of why I liked him so much. Sure, he had to maintain appearances, but when it came down to it, he needed things to get done. So, he found me, a man who would get the job done, who would protect his city from enemies. He gave me what I needed and listened when I counseled him, basically an ideal boss.

"Have someone sent to the morgue. Doubtful that we'll find anything of use, but we could. Other than that, make sure any more infiltrators who get caught don't mysteriously die. We'll be sending out word to other areas of the issue, so they can look for more once we're done here." I'd already informed the royals so they could purge the capital, but nobody here needed to know that.

There were a few other minor details to cover—the results of the sewer searches (nothing), distribution of men, other possibly related crimes—but none of those were surprising in the least. We had one, perhaps two or more enemies in the city, so figuring out what went where and with whom was a chore. When the meeting was over, I moved off to one of the workshops nearby to check on another project. Honestly, it seemed like more and more of my day was being taken up by meetings, even though I much preferred working in the field. The cost of leadership, I supposed.

"How are things going?" I asked the man there, a foreman of sorts.

"Not well."

"Go into detail, please." Really he should have without me asking.

"These new weapons work, but resizing them into something usable isn't. Nobody other than a magic user could hope to wield one without breaking his wrist to shards. As for downsizing it, that's presented its own plethora of problems."

"You can't just shrink the parts by a given amount?" I asked.

"Absolutely not," he replied, aghast. "There's an explosion in there, and the mechanics of it aren't simple. Sure, we've got plenty of machines with tighter tolerances and comparable pressures, but this is a very different field. Getting it all correct is taking time, sir. We need men who are experts in both making guns and making small machines, something we just don't have on staff."

"I'd like this done quickly."

"Then could you put us into contact with the creator? Get a consult from him and maybe even have him run us through his design philosophy? I feel like there's a system to it, because this isn't something that you could just make this well out of nowhere." Interesting, very interesting.

"I'll consider it," I said. "We want this project kept fairly quiet for now. What about the other thing I asked about?"

"That I can answer," the foreman said with a slight smile. "That chemical he asked for in pellet form is done, and I know what he wants it for."

"Don't keep me in suspense then."

"It's another form of gunpowder, and an amazingly good one too."

The boy had asked for nitrocellulose, something I'd never heard of, but a chemist had managed to figure it out. He also wanted it in specific particle sizes, something doable, but odd. So I'd decided to hand the information over to our technical men, see what they made of it, at least after the chemist just gave me a shrug.

"Is that so? How interesting. See what you can learn from it, and how it works in these new firearms. If things go well, we can arm all of our men with them by next year. That might be the edge we need against the lowlifes in this city."

CHAPTER 65

✳

THE UNKNOWN ENEMY

Southern Elazia
Nicon: Palace of the People
High Leader Scoran

I laid back as the girl dyed my hair, one strand at a time, careful, painfully so. There could be no room for any mistakes, it had to be perfect, look perfect. It was well known how fast an ancient's hair changed from the normal color to white, not that one of those had been born in centuries, but it was important people at least thought I was perfectly pure.

It was nearly true that I had no human blood, but only almost. Generations could be counted back, generations where no human had marred my line with their filth, where only the best had been added to the family. Still, though, age crept upon us, slow, like the rocks approaching, but it came. Now only a handful of true pure elves lived, and Atal had more than half. My poor nation had none, hadn't for so long, the foolishness of our ancestors ruining our chances at real power.

"How go the breeding programs?" I asked one of my aides as he entered the salon.

"Well, Leader, we're keeping the taint of mortality pushed back bit by bit."

"And the research on the solution?"

He sighed. "Less well, I'm afraid. Though our greatest minds and strongest healers try, they're just not able to push out all of the humanity from a person. They claim there's something missing, some part of the puzzle they don't yet understand."

"No progress at all?" I asked, slightly disgusted at their failures.

"Some," he replied. "In the poorest subjects, we've managed to increase their purity by around five percent. The doctors tell me that they've even managed to purify one enough that she could, in theory, reenter society."

He handed the papers to me. The girl had been only a tenth elf when they picked her up, but after her alterations she was now fifteen percent. Pathetic, but enough for her to have a place. However, her health had deteriorated dramatically, and though the tests were now showing her blood to be cleaner, it seemed she might die in a year or less. Poor thin-blooded thing had no chance.

"Hmm, no I don't think she can. Look here, she wasn't one of the volunteers, but rather some rebel. Tell them to keep working, though, see if this one can be of some use to society. How about the other part of our work?"

"Going well, Leader."

If only the results had worked on the actual volunteers, then perhaps it would be enough. I myself was sitting at ninety-five percent. So close, as close as they'd improved her, but I knew it would be fruitless. Most of the better subjects died. Though they'd known they might, it was simply the chance at true immortality that had spurred them to try. A few of the volunteers did manage a percent or two, even if it seemed to cause horrible side effects. I had hundreds of years until my age showed, though, so there was no rush.

"Good, once our nation is restored, once we are ourselves again, then we'll have the time to grow our power. We'll rise and show the world what our kind once were, what we could be again. The mistakes of the past will be wiped away as we achieve our destiny, my friends."

The dye was done, so I rose, smiling at them. It felt almost like one of my speeches. The stylist beamed, my aide nodded. Then the man saw me looking at the other file in his hand and frowned.

"What news?" I asked after sending the stylist out.

"We anticipate failure, with some of our operatives still held prisoner. I recommend we pull the rest out."

"She hasn't been seen in months though. Are we sure she's alive?"

"No, Leader, though this wouldn't be the first time she's disappeared on us."

I spat. The gall of that human, stealing the secret of gate travel from elvenkind and hoarding it. How much of our heritage had she absconded with? Even her life was too long for one of her kind, stretching years and years longer than any of the mortals had any right to. At first I'd thought she might be one of ours, as it was known her kin had elven blood, but no, it was some magic. Some of the fools in the western lands had even taken to calling her the "immortal archmage," a blatant insult to the true immortals of this world.

"Failures, all of them. Shame we couldn't stir one of the ancient ones to our cause. They could have put the fool in her place."

"Indeed, sir. Even those who don't like the humans are loath to move though. You know as I that they sadly move slower and slower as they gain in years."

"Perspective, my friend. When you've been around for so long, things must seem to be able to wait. That is the one thing the Great Ancestor never failed at. We should be more like him, always working, always improving, for all of our people."

"There's one more thing, Leader," he said, interrupting my thoughts.

"Hmm?"

"Some creatures were found. The reports are sparse, but it looks like they're mixing with the humans."

One more file, with barely a page to describe these green creatures. It even had their name and the island they'd come from. As I read down the page I saw more and more about them, and the memories in my mind tickled, showing me pages.

"With me, at once!" My memory was almost perfect, but for something like this I had to be sure.

We moved down the halls of the palace and into the room of records. I sped through the aisles, knowing exactly where I was going. Here, deep down in the archives there was a book, ancient stories from the Great Ancestor, stories I'd long thought spoke of lost beasts or tales of creatures he'd heard of.

"Yes, yes, I knew it was here. Look, the words here tell of these monstrosities, warn of them. Goblins, small green creatures, much like men, known for their fast breeding and plundering ways. An enemy of all decent creatures that should be destroyed. Even a reference in the margin here, of a hero known for slaying them." The little drawing showed a warrior who it appeared had once had decorations on the side of his helm that had been broken off, but oddly didn't show his face at all. Instead, his helmet remained on his head.

"And they've made it into the human lands? Should we do something?"

"Yes, send a fleet to purge that island with fire and death. We'll also not be retracting our assets in their lands, but reassigning them. They're to find and destroy these beasts wherever they might be."

"Yes, sir."

ABOUT THE AUTHOR

Wandering Agent is the North Carolina–based author of the Melody of Mana series as well as other fantasy and isekai stories.

JOIN THE FELLOWSHIP

follow us on our socials

 podiumentertainment.com

 @podiumentertainment

 /podiumentertainment

 @podium_ent

 @podiumentertainment

www.ingramcontent.com/pod-product-compliance
Lightning Source LLC
Chambersburg PA
CBHW032357310726
48973CB00007B/2057